Cruel Obligation

Lori Laidlaw

Published by Lynda French, 2024.

CRUEL OBLIGATION

First edition. March 1, 2024.

Copyright © 2024 Lori Laidlaw.

ISBN: 978-1998074242

Written by Lori Laidlaw.

In appreciation of all the good guys who slay the dragon and rescue the damsel in distress, *sort of...*

About Cruel Obligation:
A Depraved Mafia Villain, a Naive Girl, and a Hot Hero

Serafina Liriani: This morning I lost my home, my job, and the people who are the closest thing I have to family - all because somebody told a lie.

I know I'm stupid for thinking life should be fair, but I'm only twenty so I can't just give up. I've got to figure out a way to look after myself and it seems like working for the Cirelli Family is how I'm going to do it. *"Not mafia, not really,"* my new boss explains, *"but... connected."*

Remo Cirelli: I want her. She's freshly pretty, sweetly shy, and as curvy as a good cook should be. Too bad she has a boyfriend. Too bad so many of my family members are poisonous. Too bad everyone wants something from her, but not me... I want everything.

Dominic Ferragamo: They all want her but I'm the one who'll get her in the end and it will be the end, for her. She may be *"pure as the driven snow"* now, but I'll turn her into slush. I'm hungry for miserable, icy, and dirty, and I'll make a banquet out of Serafina.

This standalone has a hopefully-maybe-probably ending with no cliffhanger.

Warnings:

There are worse villains than Dominic Ferragamo in the dark romance genre but be warned that he is a violent, deranged, sadistic psychopath and some of the characters are his victims of:

acts of extreme violence

1

bondage

coercion

depraved brutality

fighting

MF and MM degradation, physical assault, sexual assault

punishment/discipline/impact play with implements

The rest have enjoyable sex lives.

Playlist:

Here are a dozen of the songs I listened to repeatedly while writing, These, plus the playlists for "Girlie" and "Lockdown + 3 Alphas = Heat", work as inspiration for sexy love stories:

"Bad Things" by Jace Everett

"Bust Your Kneecaps" by Pomplamoose

"Cold Shot" by Stevie Ray Vaughan

"Hey Ya!" by Outkast

"Johnny Appleseed" by Joe Strummer

"Never Quit Loving You" by Jill Barber

"Out of Sight" by James Brown

"Rock and Roll" by Led Zeppelin

"This Guy's in Love With You" by Herb Alpert & The Tijuana Brass

"Try" by Blue Rodeo

"Viva Las Vegas" by ZZ Top

"You'll Lose a Good Thing" by Barbara Lynn

One

Serafina

I brought oversized cupcakes to share in the office today, but then I got fired from my job and shunned by my co-workers, so I grabbed back the box of treats. I definitely need a sugar fix to get me through the worst day of my life. Especially since it's not even noon yet.

Gigi sneaked out the back of the factory like one of the smokers and was waiting for me when I came through the door. I quickly swiped at my tears determined not to give her the satisfaction of seeing me cry, but she didn't comment. Instead she stuffed a folded wad of bills in my pocket saying *don't worry, it will all blow over.*

I guess she's feeling guilty as she should since it's all entirely her fault. She lied. I don't trust myself to speak so I just shrug my shoulders and keep walking.

Losing my job also means losing my home so I have no place to go and nowhere to sleep tonight.

Two

Serafina

Dietrich Strutt my boss, ex-boss now, told me my stuff would be packed up and left in the carport until garbage day when he'd throw it out. *It's probably just junk anyway*, he said with a sneer.

I've always been a little afraid of him, but now I'm angry at him, too. He wouldn't listen, he didn't give me a chance to say anything to prove my innocence. You'd think he'd know me by now, I grew up in his house and my only job has been working at his company. His and my Dad's company.

I think about that, and about how different things could have – should have – been if my parents hadn't died when I was a little kid.

I need a job, I need a home, and I need a latte so I head to our local coffee shop where I can definitely get the latter and, using its Wi-Fi to search, hopefully get the first two items as well.

Sherry's behind the counter and after taking one look at me offers an extra-large latte on the house. Her kindness is too much, I can feel my chin quiver as I struggle to hold back the tears, but luckily her surface gruffness saves us both from the embarrassment of me sobbing.

"Geez you're a sight to make eyes sore! Go clean yourself up Fina, and when you come out I'll have your drink on the table. After you have it you can tell me what's going on."

She's turns her back to me and starts fiddling with the coffee maker so I take her advice. I shudder when I look in the mirror. My eyes are red, my hair has gone haywire, and I've got remnants of my earlier tears streaking down my cheeks. I fish my comb and a wet wipe out of my bag to do a hasty repair. Part of me feels I can't be bothered, but if I'm going out for job interviews I have to make an effort. I've never been on a job interview before.

True to her word Sherry is waiting for me with my super-sized cup of comfort and ready to hear my tale of woe.

As usual her platinum blonde hair is piled high with improbable curls cascading down at the back in a too-youthful hairstyle for her face. She's a good-looking woman but at fifty-five she needs to stop pretending to be twenty-five. Her voice is raspy from her pack-a-day smoking habit but she's sensible and kind and I always listen to what she has to say.

"That's better," says Sherry when I come back out again. "You've got a real pretty face, Fina, although it could do with make-up. Now, tell me what the heck is going on?"

We both sit down and I manage to tell my story even though I'm still bewildered and unsure about what went on.

"Okay so this is what happened: my boss accused me of altering a petty cash check, payable to me, by adding a one and increasing the total by a thousand dollars. The forgery was so obvious I laughed when he showed it to me. I could have proven that I never cashed it and that it never went through our bank but he just fired me and wouldn't even let me talk. And he threw me out of the house, too."

"You and your boss were living together?"

"No! well, yes but not the way.. not like how that just sounded, oh eeewww. Dietrich Strutt and my father were in business together. When my parents were killed in a car accident Dietrich and Marta, his wonderful wife, took me in and raised me with their son, Peter who was ten at the time. I've lived in that house since I was seven years old. It's my home, but not anymore."

"So you need a place to stay and a job to pay for it."

"Exactly. I'm almost twenty-one years old and a high-school dropout but I'm darn good on a computer. I'll search the employment agencies first."

"What skills do you have? I know you worked in an office..."

"I worked in the accounting department so I can do spreadsheets and stuff like that, but I don't have any official training or certifications. I'm a really good baker, in fact do you want a cupcake? I know we're not allowed to bring outside food in here but since there's no one around try one of these. I made them last night."

Sherry admires the look of the big cupcake and when she takes a bite her eyes widen in surprised delight. She takes another - bigger - bite and mumbling through the crumbs tells me it's utterly delicious. Her praise lifts my spirits even more than getting a free latte.

"Forget accounting, Fina. Look up domestic employment agencies and see if you can get a position cooking and baking and stuff. Maybe you can even get something with accommodation, maybe at a resort or something?"

"Sherry you're brilliant!" My fingers fly over the keyboard since I type 120 words a minute. My search proves fruitful and an hour later I'm on my way to the Home Sweet Home Agency. Sherry and I discussed it and decided I should just show up instead of phoning for an appointment. I'm desperate and I don't care if it shows.

There's nothing *sweet* about the offices of Home Sweet Home. It's all shiny chrome with a gray color scheme and really bright lighting. The office is open-plan with low dividers between desks. I can see several people working on desktops. Deeper back in the room there are two offices, glassed-in, which I guess belong to the bosses.

The receptionist gets snooty when I confess I don't have an appointment but I have no time for her attitude. I simply brush past her and make a beeline for those offices at the end. Along the way people stop to stare at me barreling along with the skinny girl struggling to keep up in her high-heels. We make enough commotion that an older woman has come to the door of one of the offices.

"What's going on, Amanda?"

"I tried to stop her Mrs. Antonacci, she doesn't have an appointment and–"

"And I'm sorry, Mrs Antonacci is it? My name is Serafina Liriani. *Paisana*. I've landed in a bad situation, not my fault, and I need a job as a live-in employee. I can cook and clean and bake. Here, try one of these that I made."

I thrust a cupcake at her but one look at that svelte figure tells me it's unlikely she's got a sweet tooth. Fortunately the next-door office is inhabited by a man who homes in on the treat like a sugar-seeking missile. He takes a big bite and is loud in his approval.

"This is fantastic, unbelievably good! Probably costs too much to make to be profitably marketable but my God it's the best cake I've ever tasted. Here Aggie, have a bite." He breaks off a sizable chunk then pushes it at Mrs Antonacci insisting she eat. I'm surprised when she does and delighted by her smile.

"It's heavenly and I congratulate you Ms Liriani but... as I'm sure you can appreciate any positions with accommodation provided require rigorous background checks and..."

"And nothing, we can fit her up right away. Antony Cirelli, he's a sucker for desserts and living out in the country means all his employees are live-in."

"Cirelli? No way, Jack, she's just a girl."

"Exactly, she'll be fine. No offence Miss Whoever but you'll be perfectly safe with the Cirellis. They're a family of handsome, stinking rich men who can have any woman they want. Frankly, they're not going to date the hired help."

"But what about her qualifications? references? criminal check? and Antony Cirelli will have to interview her–"

"Antony can't keep staff. The location is impractical and that couple who run the place aren't hospitable. Nobody lasts long but who knows? maybe this young lady will like it and decide to stay."

"My life-story is simple. I've worked at a family business, in the Accounting department, for the past three years. Prior to that I dropped out of high-school to nurse my adopted mother. She had terminal cancer and wanted to end her days at home. She taught me how to cook and bake.

Her husband, my boss, recently remarried. I left in a hurry and I.. I really am desperate, I have no where to go. This Cirelli home, no matter where it is, sure sounds better than the homeless shelter."

"I'll call Mr Cirelli and see what he says."

"No, I'll call Antony from the car, I'll drive Miss Whoever there myself."

Jack

We're almost at the Cirelli home when I suffer an attack of conscience and start having second thoughts.

The feisty, determined young woman in the office has turned into an insecure child hunched into the car door looking out the window. She's nibbling on her fingers and hasn't spoken for several miles now. If she starts to cry I'm going to have to turn back. But dammit I called and now Antony's expecting us.

He's okay and she'll be fine with him. Actually, Antony is the definition of *upstanding citizen* living his blameless life and providing shelter for an extended family. And they truly are family rather than *famiglia*.

That's also part of the problem though because it's a house full of males and here's this young girl with a gorgeous face, an abundance of long curly hair and an over-abundance of curves. She looks positively edible. Am I delivering her to some hungry wolves?

No, I'm looking for trouble where it doesn't exist. These are good men, good people.

Aggie dealt with the previous placements who complained but I got a look at them and they were definitely opportunists. Greedy, grasping girls trying to cash in. Antony showed his steely, uncompromising backbone and a $1,000 bonus for their trouble kept them sweet.

At least it's the Cirellis and not their cousins, the Ferragamos. That Dominic is just pure poison, I would never put a young girl under *his* roof.

Aggie tried to stop me but I wouldn't listen and now... Except that I *know* Antony Cirelli is a good man. Serafina Liriani won't come to any harm in his home, he'll see to that.

The homes on the acreages out here are mostly hidden by mature trees, but what glimpses you can get are impressive. Serafina is sitting up straight and looking out the window with interest and that's a good sign, right?

Serafina

I thought seeing a half-naked Gigi, the boss's wife, in the arms of Andre, our super-hot new salesman, was the worst day of my life. Not that I had a chance with Andre or anything but because Dietrich Strutt, my boss, is the scariest man I know. He'll kill me if he finds out I knew about those two.

Gigi is really playing with fire and now that I know she's put me in a compromising position as well.

Do I pretend I didn't see? no, that's impossible.

Pretend I don't realize what they're up to? no, that's silly.

I was lugging a heavy banker's box full of files, with a plastic bag of canceled checks balanced on top, down to the old store-room. I struggled to open the door handle and was too busy trying to keep the bag from slipping away to pay attention to the scene in front of me. Once I noticed them I couldn't believe my eyes.

Gigi is lying on the beat-up old couch with her head hanging down over the arm, and she's naked from the waist up. The implants keep her boobs sticking straight up instead of falling down her side.

Andre is standing over her with his pants around his ankles pumping his dick halfway down Gigi's throat while massaging her breasts. Even through my shock I notice that his bare ass is exceptional.

Gigi is writhing and moaning with her puffed-up lips working on his dick and he's got his eyes squeezed shut. I had about thirty seconds to escape unseen but instead of backing out of the room and running I just stand there in shock. I'm such an idiot.

When they notice me Gigi pushes Andre away with a scream and he shoots his load all over her face. That shakes me out of my stupor and I literally drop what I'm carrying and hightail it out of there. Too late.

Can I just say her secret is safe with me because I'm way too frightened of Dietrich to ever tell and risk him getting him pissed off at me? Ugh, I don't want to have that conversation with Gigi. I don't like her and she barely acknowledges my existence, even though we live in the same house. Dammit though, I think we're going to have to talk because I can't trust her to let it go. I'll have to reassure her that I'm thrilled to forget what I saw.

Those were my thoughts on what was the worst day of my life – up until today, that is. Today's events stem from my inadvertent exposure to the steamy office affair.

Gigi set me up and her lie cost me my job and my home. I really didn't have any friends among my co-workers but we were all friendly until they saw me being escorted from Diedrich's office right through the building. My cheeks burned with embarrassment and the struggle to hold back my angry tears kept my lips tightly sealed. It was hard to keep my head high with Security tugging on my arm and Diedrich hissing insults about ingratitude and thieving bad blood.

But now, just a few hours later, I'm being driven in a fancy car to a home in the country to start a new life. Serafina Liriani, re-invented!

Mr Michaelson from the Home Sweet Home Agency is giving me plenty of silence and space to think my thoughts. I hope he'll be just as agreeable about answering my questions.

"I have some money in the bank, Mr Michaelson, but I don't think it will be enough to pay you your commission or whatever the fee is—" I begin but he cuts me off.

"Cirelli will pay, that's how these things work. We get a commission based on how long you work for him or until the specified amount of time ends. That's never happened, no one has lasted the length of the Cirelli contract yet. But maybe you will, hey? With other clients once they stop paying us they usually give the employee a raise. Antony Cirelli is a generous man, you'll do okay with him."

"I'm glad to hear I don't have to pay, thank you. And I'm glad too that you think it will all work out for me."

"I've got a good feeling about this. I think you'll be an excellent fit into the household with the family."

"When you say *the family* and wealthy Italians are you hinting that they're in the Mafia?"

"Mafia? Oh no, no, no, not Mafia, not really... well, maybe. What you could call *connected*. Is that an issue for you?"

"Not at all, I don't know anything about it. Has it been a problem before?"

"Hmm, maybe. I never really thought about it. Do you read sexy romance novels?"

"Umm I do, sometimes. I also like murder mysteries, especially the old-fashioned ones," I add, as if that will sound more respectable than admitting to female porn. Which I adore.

"Oh well never mind, I'm sure you'll still be fine. Apparently a lot of the romance novels feature handsome sexed-up Mafia types with hearts of gold and it's possible some of the women we've placed with the Cirelli's came with expectations. I seem to recall threats of harassment or scandal... hmm, Aggie Antonacci took care of it. But you strike me as a sensible person so we won't worry about that."

"I have no expectations whatsoever, Mr Michaelson."

"Good, that's good to hear."

After almost an hour's drive through beautiful countryside he slows the car to turn onto a side road. The area certainly is isolated but the fresh air and wide open spaces are wonderful. Every now and then we see big brick homes set well back from the road on their own acreages.

The Cirelli house is differentiated by an ornate fountain with cherubs spewing water and a statue of a naked female bathing in the basin. A circular driveway leads past the fountain and alongside a covered walkway with brick pillars and archways every few feet. I've read about *breezeways* and wonder if this is one? It certainly keeps you sheltered at the front door. Expensive town cars and sports cars are parked off to the side.

The house is a two-story red brick with green shutters and white trim around the windows. There's lots of shrubbery and mature fruit trees adding greenery.

"It's a very nice-looking home," I say.

"With all the amenities too. A swimming pool, putting course, tennis court, sauna, wine cellar, every bedroom has an en suite bathroom, and there are gas fireplaces for winter and air-conditioning for summer. The modern kitchen has every appliance imaginable because Antony Cirelli loves gadgets. Flat screen TVs and internet in every room, satellite and streaming of all the movie channels. Luxurious comfort in scenic surroundings protected by a state-of-the-art security system. I sound like a realtor trying to sell you the place, don't I?" he laughs.

"Oh I'm sold, Mr Michaelson!" and I'm delighted to discover I still can smile on this horrible day.

Antony

No matter was Jack Michaelson said I was determined to keep Serafina Liriani after just one bite of that delicious cupcake. I immediately wanted her to head into my kitchen and whip up another batch, two batches because everyone who had one would want two.

So I had to listen and nod and agree and promise that I and all the males in my household would keep their hands off the girl. I will guard her from them and, as Jack very well knows, she has nothing to fear from me. I was never the cause of the complaints from previous female employees.

To me Serafina is a very sweet girl with a beautiful face who seems younger than her twenty-one years. My Maria already had two boys by that age. I have no trouble giving Jack my assurances. But I'll have to make it clear to everyone else that they need to keep their distance from my new employee who I will treat like an adopted daughter, no! an adopted *grand*daughter.

Jack says I'll have to call Aggie as well and convince her that the girl will be safe here. I reply that I'm surprised they let her come out right away instead of making me jump through all their hoops first. That's when he explained the girl has been abandoned – he doesn't know the ins and outs of that story but does tell me all he knows from their conversation in the drive out here.

Serafina is in desperate straits. Now I'm twice as determined to keep her and take care of her. Her and her magic hands that bake so beautifully.

She's still sitting rigidly upright in one of the best living-room's chairs. Actually that's about the only you *can* sit in those things. We hardly ever use the *best* living-room.

"Put my cell number into your phone Serafina–" he begins but she interrupts to explain she doesn't own a phone. Both of us are completely knocked-back by that information. I mean, what young person doesn't have a mobile? It's unheard-of.

Fortunately I always have a few spares charged and ready to go so I tell them to wait a moment while I just run down the hall to my office. Of course with my physique running is an exaggeration but I hurry as quickly as I can. When I return Serafina looks a bit more relaxed so I'm glad Jack has those minutes to reassure her that she'll be safe here with me, with us.

She knows how to use a phone and gets it set up in no time. Now Jack's the one who needs reassuring before he'll go and leave her behind. Finally we get him on his way and I take Serafina to the big kitchen in the basement to meet the married couple who also live in, Fred and Eileen Finch.

I'm happy to witness Serafina's delight when she looks around the kitchen and wish I could demonstrate all the gadgets to her myself, but it's more important to get the family together and warn them all off.

"Serafina I'll introduce you to all this stuff, it's my pride-and-joy, but first get acquainted with the Finches, have a bite to eat, and I'll be back to see you after I've spoken to the guys."

I pull out my phone to message the family on our chatting app to come to my office right away. Sometimes I refer to the room as my study but when I call it my office everyone knows serious business is at hand. I hustle back there to be ensconced in my chair, behind my desk, to look as imposing as I possibly can as I threaten them all.

Three

Antony

I'm finally on my way to the kitchen to find Serafina. Giorgio waylaid me after I paused the family meeting. He's reciting a litany of dire predictions because I have, once again, brought a young female into the house.

I begin by stating: "Gino learned his lesson—" "

After the third complaint of harassment," interrupts Giorgio.

"Well, those first two... you can't really say..." but I don't get to finish.

Giorgio jumps in saying: "And what about those sons of his? Hmm?"

"They're all away at school and besides they're older now, more mature."

"Like their father, you mean?" He crosses his arms over his chest, knowing he's made his point.

"Look, Serafina isn't like those girls, she's not the type to lead anyone on. She's not here with dollar signs in her eyes hunting for a rich husband."

"You can't possibly know that."

"I believe I'm a good judge of character, Giorgio and in Serafina I see a young innocent who needs help that I'm more than willing to provide."

He wisely holds back whatever criticism he was planning to make knowing he lives here as a courtesy. Instead, he goes back into my office snorting his disapproval.

Arriving in the kitchen I fetch Serafina from where she's sitting stiffly over a cup of coffee with the Finches. She jumps up when I enter the room and I decide to ignore the chilly atmosphere. It doesn't mean anything, it's just their way, and they'll get along well enough in time, I'm sure.

Giorgio is right about us having had quite a turnover in female staff so I guess to them Serafina is just another young girl who won't stay long.

I invite Serafina to join me in meeting the rest of the household. I can tell she's nervous but I give my reassurances saying: "Don't worry, nobody bites!"

Walking into a room full of men can be intimidating, I guess, but this is my family and I know they're all good boys. Still there are eight of them waiting and all are looking at us.

"I won't stand on formality, instead I'll start with a general introduction then move round the room. Everyone, this is Serafina. She creates the most exquisite desserts and we'll all need to rack up some gym time to balance all the extra calories we'll be enjoying." I hear a snicker and realize the younger boys are teasing me about my sweet tooth so I pat my tummy with a theatrical sigh.

Starting on my right I bring Serafina forward to meet Gino.

"This is my brother Gino, he lives on the third floor with his four boys. You won't see much of them but you'll definitely hear them when they're at home! Cesare and Vittorio are both in college but they're home now for the holidays."

Both of my nephews give Serafina an approving smile at her pretty face but apparently don't appreciate her full-sized figure because their eyes run down her body without interest. Good.

"Next are the twins, Luciano and Lorenzo, who are still away at boarding school. Again, just home for the holidays."

The twins also shake Serafina's hand, all four boys have been taught their manners, with one saying *Call me Luke* and the other adding *I'm Lorrie.*

"Here we have another L, this time it's my youngest boy Leo who is at the same school as his cousins. I'm quite sure the staff is thrilled to be getting a break from the three of them.

Now you have to be careful around Leo because he's an absolute genius at gadgets and tech-y things. He gets his love of these toys from me, you've seen all the counter-top appliances in the kitchen, but Leo here can actually fix them if they break. So if you have any problems with your phone or laptop or anything like that he can take care of it. But be warned, if you have any secrets on said devices he'll discover them."

"Oh Dad," says the handsome boy aged fifteen or so. He holds my hand a moment too long and I feel him exerting all of his charm when he greets me. "Don't listen to him, he thinks it's magic that I can unlock his phone after he's forgotten his password – again."

"Well I'm thankful for Leo's skills and proud of his ability, but I have to confess I'm a little frightened of all that smart home technology, it's probably an age thing. Or maybe it reminds me too much of an old movie called 2001: A Space Odyssey."

Serafina has no idea what I'm talking about and just looks at me politely. I realize I'm rambling.

The next male I introduce to Serafina is my brother Giorgio. He's the oldest of us, with a thin build and gray coloring. Compared to the others he seems worn-out and faded. My wife died, and Gino is divorced, but the two of us did experience the joy of marital bliss – for awhile at least – whereas Giorgio never married.

I think that lack has made him older than his years... it's certainly soured him. Funny because Gino isn't bitter at all, even though his wife, Lee, ran off with one of the boy's teachers years ago. I think their marriage must have been over long before it actually ended. I know Gino enjoys being a single Dad.

Giorgio bows his head acknowledging Serafina but doesn't speak to her. I feel his disapproval coming off him in waves but I ignore it.

"Last but not least here is my son Remo," and as I turn to Serafina I see she's absolutely staring at my oldest with a dazed look on her face. The way Remo says her name tells me the attraction is mutual.

"Pleasure to meet you, Serafina." Taking her hand he holds it in both of his and their eyes simply feast on each other. I interrupt their exchange to take her upstairs to get settled in her room.

"I know you've had a long day, my dear, so I'll let you get to your bed."

Looking around to make sure everything is in order I point out the alcove where the fixings for an early morning coffee or cup of tea are stored. "That tin holds cookies and dried fruits: raisins, apricots, mango, if you need a nibble before bed, or even wake up hungry."

"Everything is wonderful, thank you Sir."

"Oh call my Antony, really."

"Then please call me Fina."

"Fina, hmm... it's nice but Serafina is such a beautiful name. I think you'll have to indulge my little whim if I call you by both. Now, goodnight and sleep well."

"Goodnight, Si– Antony," she replies, giving me one of her shy smiles.

Serafina

I'm living in a house full of hotties! I think as I putter around the room getting ready for bed. I have embarrassingly little to unpack and even when I pick up the rest of my stuff from Dietrich's carport it won't amount to much.

Today has just been one long rollercoaster ride of ups and downs in real life and emotionally. I am beat but my mind's racing so I know I won't be able to sleep just yet.

Coffee won't help but I fill the kettle from my bathroom to make a cup of tea. A warm drink will be soothing, and I'll investigate the cookie tin, too. I've never had mango but I love dried apricots, and raisins are okay.

I get different vibes from everyone in this house. Antony is a sweetheart, a cuddly teddy-bear, and the Finches are reserved but polite. With all the boys still in school It sounds like I won't have much to do with them but the men live here all the time. Gino seems nice, Giorgio seems... not so nice, and Remo is drop-dead gorgeous! I felt my insides do a little flip when he held my hand. A real hunk, what they call a Book Boyfriend in the eBooks I read. The kind I never buy from the used bookstore because I'm a bit snobbish about romance. Well, I don't want the salesclerks feeling sorry for me or thinking I'm pathetic.

That Remo though... he is like the ideal of a man. Literally tall, dark and handsome with strong features. Dark brown eyes, finely molded lips, strong jawline... there's a hint of masculine dominance there or maybe that's wishful thinking on my part?

Not that it matters... a man who looks like that will never be interested in someone like me. No, I picture him arm-in-arm with a tall blonde who is a high-powered executive or super-successful realtor or even a doctor. A woman of substance. I'm a girl who works in the kitchen and I'm grateful to be there! But he was really nice to me.

I've really been lucky coming to this beautiful home and having such a nice boss as Antony. I could have been hanging out in an all-night coffee shop, headachy from the buzz of florescent lighting, terrified of falling asleep and being robbed or worse. I've really landed on my feet here.

It's comforting to know there are people around, I can hear them moving about closing doors, having showers, and flushing toilets. I wonder if I should lock my door? I noticed there is a good lock on it, not the usual bedroom door locks that you can open with a hair pin. I'm sure I'll be okay but it would probably be sensible to lock up.

But what if Antony comes by with a cup of coffee in the morning? will his feelings be hurt if my door is locked? I can't imagine Mrs. Finch serving anyone anything in bed! I wouldn't hurt Antony's feelings for the world so I just leave the door as is.

Hours later, when my bladder has woken me, I lock the door on my way back to bed.

Four

Dominic

The cane whistles through the air cracking down sharply on the boy's skinny butt-cheeks. I've got the stripes lined up nicely, four so far which means two more to go.

"Stop shrieking Peter, you little bitch! Schoolkids in England get *six of the best* with the cane so I'm pretty sure you can take that many, too."

"No, no more Dom, please! I'm begging you, it really fucking hurts!" he sobs.

"Number five coming right up," and with a wicked slash I place another horizontal welt right where his ass meets his thighs. He's really howling now.

"You can spare yourself a lot of pain if you'll just do what I say and bring your sister to me. Just catching sight of her was enough to really whet my appetite and I can't wait to meet her. I don't want to wait. You can trade me her body for yours and she'll take your punishment instead of you."

"I've told you before she's not my sister, she's just somebody my mother kind of adopted. My parents knew her parents," he shouts through his tears.

"Even better then. Nothing for you to feel guilty about."

"Yeah but you can't do this, this kind of whipping, to her. If I introduce you two you can't hurt her."

"Oh of course I'm going to hurt her, Peter, stop pretending you don't know the score. The only question you should be asking is am I going to hurt you too? I mean, I don't have to, you can trade your ass for hers, but if you deny me then you both get it. Anyhow, let me just get finished up here and then we'll talk some more."

I really wind up with all my strength to lay the final stroke diagonally so it cuts through the other lines and blood wells at each junction. Peter is crying out so loudly he can't catch his breath. The funny gasping sound he's making makes me laugh.

I've got him tied over my desk and figure I might as well enjoy fucking his red-striped ass before I free him. I'm sure his dick is hard.

"If this was a real punishment I wouldn't be using lube so count your blessings little Petey," I say as I grease up his hole and my cock before plunging in deeply. Looking down I see streaks of blood on my thighs where I've pressed up against his ass. "Ha! bitch, it looks like I took your ass virginity but we both know you lost that long ago, long before you met me anyhow. Hey, is your sorta-a-sister still a virgin, Petey? I'd like that."

"I don't know, I told you I don't... oh, uh, uh fuck, I don't see her much, I... I, omigoddddddd," he stutters.

I've reached around his skinny hips to stroke his skinny cock with one hand and massage his balls with the other. Just as I thought the caning made him rock-hard, despite his tears, and now his orgasm leaves him utterly spent. I'm still hard as I pull out so I stroke myself until I shoot ribbons of cum over his sore and bloody ass.

"It's a shame that your sister caught my eye, Peter, because now I've become obsessed with her and you know that's never a good thing. You think telling me she's an innocent will save her? that only fuels my appetite even more. I want to *annihilate* that innocence. I'm totally into debauchery and sin and vile corruption."

I know he will bring the girl to me because he's a cowardly little fuck who's half in love with me. Or at least as much as a lying, cheating, stealing junkie can be. He'll weigh up the value of whatever it is he gets from her versus what I can take from him. He might even delude himself enough to think *I'll* owe *him.* Stupid twat.

My voice is low but menacing when I tell him: "I want Serafina, I dream about her Peter, and you have to bring her to me. No more fucking around or I'll stop going easy on you." He shudders as my threat sinks in.

Still leaving him secured to my desk I turn my attention to my next problem. The whore Christine stole from me by setting up one of my dealers with a fake robbery while she was fucking him. So now he owes me for the missing product and cash, and she owes big time for trying to play me. Now I've got her crying and squirming on the floor tied hand and foot. It's time to collect and I'm really looking forward to this.

Peter

My old man kicked me out of the house when I was sixteen. Yeah sure, I sneaked his car out of the driveway but it was just joyriding. I don't even think that's a crime. And okay the accident sucked but nobody got hurt except a telephone pole. It's a real fucking rip-off how much they charge for one of those things. And the reason there was no insurance is because Father wouldn't put me on his policy so that's on him. Except he blamed everything on me.

My mother was no use. She wouldn't go against Father no matter how much I cried. But she did slip money to Fina to give to me, and she got me that crummy job at the car wash. I let on that I was homeless, but I was actually shacked up with some older guy who let me stay at his place for blow-jobs on demand.

It must have been soon after that that Mom got the cancer diagnosis. I know she went for treatments and surgeries and that all took a couple of years or so. But eventually they reached the end of the road and Fina quit school to stay home with Mom all the time. Fina adored my mother. She told me Mom begged my father to let me come and see her but he refused. What a fucking prick he is.

I went to the funeral, though. I knew he wouldn't kick up a fuss in front of all the relatives and his friends but he made a point of letting me know there was no money coming my way. That surprised me, but Fina got a legacy which I convinced her was mine by rights so she gave it to me. I knew she would.

I also told Fina that since I'm her boyfriend what's hers is mine. I'm four years older than her and she's always looked up to me. She gives me most of her paychecks too. Well she doesn't need the money: she's fat so no point spending it on clothes, and her face is truly gorgeous so she doesn't need any make-up. A bit of spending money is enough to buy coffees and those dingy, ripped-up paperbacks she gets at the used bookstore.

Just my luck that Dom had to see me out with her. She'd come to meet me at a Mickey D's and I remember ordering a lot of food. I guess I was starving and stoned. A fish sandwich and a cheeseburger plus two large fries while Fina sipped on a milkshake.

Maybe it was the sight of her sucking on a straw that caught Dom's eye? He doesn't frequent fast-food joints, not even the drive-thrus, so he must have seen us through the window from the sidewalk. He wouldn't have been able to hear her prattling on about her boring life with my mother. No wait, he had to have seen us after Mom died, when Fina was living an equally boring life working for my father, otherwise he'd have started bugging me about her long ago.

Yeah, that's probably what happened. And if I try to see her from his point of view well, sitting in a booth he'd only see the top half of her: great hair, a beautiful face, big boobs. And, as usual, she'd have a huge fucking smile like she actually had something to be happy about. Whatever. Now I'm caught between the two of them and I can't say no to Dom.

I mean, I know he wouldn't *really* hurt her or anything, no matter what he jokes about, but he will hurt me. I need to find a way to get Fina to meet him. He's a really handsome guy although he looks a little freaky with the smudged eye-liner and nail polish. Definitely fits the *bad boy* mold and isn't that what all the girls want? If I introduce them and she falls for him well then... problem solved.

Even if, by mistake, he does hurt her it won't be really bad, especially when he finds out she is a virgin. I'm sure she is, she must be because I'm her only boyfriend and I've never touched her. Well, I did a little exploring out of curiosity but chicks don't do it for me, they aren't my thing. I definitely didn't fuck her and I can't imagine she's had any other opportunities.

I'll have to try to get out to the industrial plaza and get hold of her at the plant. It's too easy for Father to spot me if I hang around his house and he'd probably call the cops. Or shoot me, I wouldn't put it past him.

Serafina

I was heartbroken when Dietrich threw Peter out of the house. Partly because my twelve-year-old self was in love with Peter but mostly because of what it did to Marta, Peter's mother.

I still think all the stress and worry she had over her son's well-being brought on the cancer. Our research taught us that everyone has cancer cells but it take a trigger of some sort to activate them. We discussed it and decided the problem likely stemmed from the Peter situation. She worked hard at calming herself and doing her best to take care of him from a distance.

I was a one-way conduit of money, essentials, and loving concern. Peter took it all with resentment, always believing his mother should be doing more. But even I knew that Dietrich's word was law and he wasn't above raising his hand to his wife if she disobeyed him. So a whole relationship was conducted in secrecy. I'm sure Dietrich had his suspicions but maybe he didn't want to know the truth.

When Marta died I was devastated. We'd become so close in the two years that I spent as her caregiver. Finally she told me it was time for her to go and I had to let her do so. I cried buckets when it happened but was dry-eyed from numbness at the funeral. It wasn't possible that my Marta was in that shiny white coffin or that we were sending her into the flames.

Dietrich had a very formal meeting with me after the funeral. He explained that Marta had left me some money but it wasn't enough to set me up in a place of my own or train me for a career but I could start working in the office at the manufacturing plant, and of course I would continue to make this my home.

"I'm very grateful for the kindness and devotion you showed my wife during her illness, Fina. I realize you took on a hefty burden at a young age and I appreciated it every day," he said in his usual stiff manner.

I met his gaze and replied honestly saying: "It was never a burden, Dietrich. I loved Marta, I always will."

So changes came about but much remained the same. I still slept in the room I'd had since coming to this house at the age of seven, and I still cooked Dietrich's dinner each night except now that happened after my day's work in the accounting department at the plant. The meals became simpler as a result.

As Marta's time drew to an end food held little pleasure for her and it was a challenge to tempt her tastebuds. Sweet treats proved to be the answer and I took great pleasure in creating fancy desserts that she'd sample.

Marta herself had been an excellent cook and taught me everything she could. We'd sit with cookbooks and discuss what recipes to try. She told me I had the all-important light hand necessary for pastry and worked with me to develop that skill.

Cooking isn't just a way to a man's heart, Fina, proper technique and presentation is a marketable skill. All these years later her words come back to me like a prophecy. She was one hundred percent right.

I often wonder what she would think of how quickly Dietrich replaced her. Gigi, a ridiculous abbreviation for Angela, joined the company about six months after Marta died. The office shares typists and clerks but Gigi managed to finagle her way into a permanent position as Dietrich's secretary. He'd never needed one before, and after they married she pretty much stopped working but never bothered to find a replacement for the job.

She's in and out of the office most days but I've never known exactly what she does, or what her title is. Gigi spends her time redecorating, attending advertising and design meetings, and showing the new sales staff the ropes. At least she does if they're good-looking men.

I still can't believe Dietrich actually married Gigi after having the love of a woman like Marta.

My thoughts are all over the place, wondering and speculating. Thinking about Marta makes me think of Peter. I wonder if he knows I no longer live at the house or work at the plant? I have no way of reaching him. He never gave me his phone number, and I didn't both to ask since I've never had my own phone anyhow.

So far I love living in the countryside, but I have to admit it's isolated and there's no way he can just *drop in* on me way out here. Should I try to get hold of him? He is my boyfriend after all.

I'm sure Antony will give me a day off but I can't drive so I'd also need a ride into the city. I know Peter's address because Marta used to send him money in cards. He doesn't have a car so the car wash where he works can't be too far away from there. I'm sure I can find it, it's a place to start. I'll search car washes online and check the route to the apartment too. I need to give all of this some thought. I expect he'll want some money as well.

Five

Serafina

I'm happily humming as I crumble the pastry between my fingers until it reaches the perfect consistency. This is such an enjoyable task, so calming. I know the end result will be delicious. Life here in the Cirelli household is great, no more than that – it's wonderful.

The Finches aren't friendly but they're okay. We all do our work and manage to get along well enough. Johnny, Antony's chauffeur and handyman, is a flirt but Mrs Finch warned him off me so he won't be a problem. Besides, he's like twice my age or something.

Antony Cirelli is a terrific boss. Family members and friends are always dropping by and everyone has been so nice and friendly. Giorgio never did warm up to me but he's only one out of many so I just ignore him right back.

The decor of the house is pretty over-the-top with lots of gilding on vases and mirrors, crushed velvet in china cabinets and curio tables, and long-fringed tassels on everything from cushions to drawer handles. But the furniture is all high-end and everything is comfortable. Well, except for those spindly brocaded chairs in the living-room. One of the living-rooms, that is.

My room is huge. It holds a queen-size bed, loveseat with coffee-table, and a small writing desk plus bookshelves. The en suite bathroom has both a tub and a shower which has a rain-head faucet. The few clothes I brought look lost in the walk-in closet. That's where the dresser is, too, which is a good use of the space. I only need two drawers and truth be told I could have made do with one.

The only personal ornament I have is the single photo I have of me and my parents. We're all dressed up because it's my First Communion. It shows how my parents are such a handsome couple with Dad quite dark and Mom so fair. I don't remember who took the picture, it happened shortly before they were killed in that car accident, but I remember they refused to pose formally.

So here we are with Dad sitting down and Mom perched on his knee while I'm standing in front with Dad's arm around my waist and Mom's hand on my shoulder. We're all wearing white but I've got the full regalia on: floral headpiece with veil, puffy embroidered dress with chiffon sleeves and white gloves, white socks, even white slippers. My grin shows a missing front tooth but we're all too happy not to smile hugely.

This photo is my treasure and on my tenth birthday Marta bought a sterling silver frame for it but told me not to tell Peter that it was real silver. He was struggling even then.

I spend most of my day in the kitchen and it's to die for. Seriously. Every possible gadget with ideal workspaces lit to perfection. I make myself a different fancy coffee every morning choosing between latte, cappuccino, macchiato, espresso.

Antony has an amazing capacity for eating sweet treats and I'm in my element. Mrs. Finch tends to all of the plain cooking, but I'm in charge of pastry-making, souffles, crepes, and desserts. I bake at least two varieties of cookies daily, in addition to cupcakes, cakes, and snacks like Brownies and Nanaimo Bars. And I make all of our bread and buns. The kitchen always smells great.

Hearing someone enter the room behind me I glance over my shoulder and see young Leo. He's grinning and I smile back at him.

Such a handsome boy. He's home for ten days or so while the school is on a break for the holidays.

Leo comes up to the table to see what I'm working on but he stands too close. Just as I'm asking him to back up he steps even closer, right up against me, and I feel his hot breath on the back of my neck as his arms come around me and his hands grab hold of my breasts.

"Leo! Stop that! Stop right now, what are you doing?" I hiss, not wanting to make a scene.

"You feel so good Serafina, you're so soft and round and I bet your bare skin feels even better," he says, his adolescent voice cracking in his excited state. "You like this, right? You want me to touch you."

At the threat of him slipping his hands under my clothes I holler out a loud *"NOOOOO!!!!"* not caring if I do disturb the Finches, and am so relieved when someone comes pounding into the room. Leo is yanked away from me and I turn to see him struggling to get free of Remo who's grabbed his younger brother by the neck of his jersey.

Leo calls out, "Let go of me, what the fuck's your problem–" before Remo cracks him across the face with a resounding slap.

"You watch your mouth and you watch your hands. If I ever catch you touching Serafina like that again I'll beat you black and blue."

Tears of pain fill Leo's eyes and being embarrassed makes him angry. He mutters, "She's only a servant, what do you care?" and when Remo lashes out again Leo ducks and flees from the room.

Remo turns to me apologizing. I feel my hair has come loose and when I reach up to fix it I smear flour across my face. "Oh!" I exclaim seeing my messy hand and Remo's lips quirk in a smile he can't suppress. A giggle escapes me and he takes my hand, rubbing it gently, while asking if I'm sure I'm okay.

"I was startled more than anything," I explain anxiously. "I'm so sorry I overreacted."

"No, you didn't. Leo was so far out of line doing what he did and then saying what he did? Geez, if that's the kind of attitude he's picking up in his fancy boarding-school then maybe Dad should reconsider sending him there. Anyhow, we're the ones who need to apologize, not you!"

"Oh I'd rather just forget about it, Remo. I think Leo will behave himself now."

"So you're not going to swoon or burst into tears and flounce out of here?" he teases.

"I'm not really the swooning or flouncing type, you know."

Remo gives me a beautiful smile and I feel my insides flip over. I can't help imagining how I'd enjoy it if he'd been the one to creep up behind to enfold me in his embrace. I'd like to feel his hands fondling me and when I think of him touching my bare skin my face blushes hotly. I can't think like this, I have a boyfriend.

Remo goes still for a moment and it's like he's looking right into my head and clearly seeing my foolish thoughts. I want to close my eyes to keep him from knowing too much but instead I say: "I'm not much a crier, either."

"No, I don't imagine you are. You're a strong young woman, Serafina."

"Oh please call me Fina. That's what I prefer, actually."

"Fina. Yeah, that suits you. Okay, Fina it is. Now if you're sure you're okay..." his words trail off and it's obvious to me he's eager to leave so I quickly assure him that I'm fine.

"I have to get on with the meal. This pastry is ruined so I'll need to make a different dessert now."

"Oh no, I'm sorry about that."

"It's your father who will be sorry, he had his heart set on... oh well, he's a very understanding man. I'll just say a draft came through the kitchen and it collapsed the soufflé."

At the dinner table that night Leo sits sullenly with a purplish bruise on his cheek and Antony is disappointed at the change of dessert until he tastes my chocolate meringue pie and declares it his new favorite. He says that every night. I smile at his compliment, but it's the wink from Remo that warms my insides.

Leo

I want to hate Serafina but I can't. She didn't tell Dad about what happened and she just acted normal to me at dinner. She's been nice, she is nice.

Before school broke up for the holidays the guys were all talking about how they were going to make the moves on servants and local girls and any friends of their sisters' who happened to be around. Everyone was confident they'd *get some action* and from what they said I figured Serafina would be up for it but... Remo made me feel like I was a rapist or something.

He came to my room immediately after my run-in with Serafina and he sat down and talked to me quite seriously, like I'm a grown-up. One thing he said really stuck with me: that no matter how strong and fit a woman might be she's no match for a man. Oh sure if he's old and decrepit but the average guy has way more muscular strength and stamina than women do. It puts them at a real disadvantage.

"That's why they should all learn self-defence, because plenty of men treat them like they're prey. Don't try to be one of those guys, Leo, because you'll never know the real joy a man and woman can share intimately and respectfully."

So here I am coming down the stairs to the kitchen, making plenty of noise so she knows I'm not trying to sneak up on her, to apologize. She was wrapping up food to put it away but now she's stopped and is just watching me. I guess that makes sense, she has to keep an eye out because she doesn't trust me.

This is so hard to do but it's clear she isn't going to break the silence between us. I huff out a breath and speaking quickly on the inhale say:

"Serafina I'm so sorry about how I acted earlier I had no right to do that or to say the things I did and I'm very sorry it happened."

Phew, it's done. Now I'm not sure what to do next. Do we shake hands and call *truce*? She nods her head, acknowledging that she's heard me, then gestures to the table motioning me to sit down. I do so, a little worried she's going to start yelling at me but a moment later she serves me a another large slice of that gingerbread and peaches cake we had for dessert. One of the desserts, I should say. It was warm then, and with whipped cream, but I take a big bite and discover it still tastes good cold.

Serafina has carried her coffee over to the table and sits down across from me.

"I really appreciate you coming in here and apologizing to me, Leo. I didn't expect it, I know that must have been hard, but you're more mature than I thought."

Then she gives me a big sweet smile and suddenly the awkward feeling I had is gone and everything is okay with us. What a relief.

I tell her how I never knew my mother, she was killed in a car crash when I was just a baby. I was with her but she'd had me strapped in a car-seat in the back so I was safe.

There were nannies but it was like a revolving door they changed so often. Uncle Gino and my Auntie Lee were still married then so they didn't live here but it was still an all-male household. And of course my school isn't co-ed so I don't know many women and obviously I don't know how to act properly around them.

"Remo came to my room after and set me straight but then he said he was sorry he'd hit me and I figured if he can apologize to me then I should be able to do the same with you."

"Oh I'm glad you and your brother aren't on the outs because of me. Now we can all put this behind us."

"You're being really nice about it, Serafina."

"Oh call me Fina, Leo."

"Okay I will. Fina. That's a nice name, too. If you ever need me to help you with anything, when I'm home like, just say so."

"Thanks, Leo, I'll keep that in mind. Now, I'm going to send you on your way so I can finish up in here. Again, I appreciate what you've said, that was a real grown-up thing to do."

I get up and carry my used plate to the dishwasher, something I don't usually do, but I feel good. Saying good night to Fina I head up to my room, taking the stairs two at a time.

Remo

I listened in to Leo and Fina's conversation and I'm impressed with both of them. He really did show maturity in apologizing and she accepted so graciously, treating Leo as an adult. That's smoothed things over really well and there won't be any awkwardness.

Dad warned us all off pestering Fina but I'm just checking in on her, making sure she's okay. Nothing creepy or stalkerish about it. Except I stood behind the door so Leo wouldn't see me when he left.

I make a point of clomping down the stairs so I don't startle Fina. She's setting the dishwasher to run and looks up at the noise I'm making. Her sweet smile of recognition stirs something inside me.

"I know you want to finish up your chores so I won't stay long," I reassure her. "I heard a bit of your conversation with Leo and it sounds like you two have everything sorted?"

"We do," her smile widens when she adds, "He really is a nice boy, he just acted on some wrong information from the boys at his school."

"Well you've been great about the whole thing, Fina."

She blushes and I can't resist stroking her creamy cheek as it reddens. Her skin is incredibly soft, amazingly so. I lose myself in the moment of touching until she gently places a hand on my wrist and stepping back says:

"Remo, I have a boyfriend."

That brings me back to real time with a jolt. Now I'm the one who is blushing as I stammer out an apology. Dammit, Dad warned us to keep our distance.

"No harm done, you couldn't have known."

She's so nice about it and yet, having recently suffered betrayal myself I'm the last person to put anyone else through that horrible feeling. Learning the person you've committed to wants more than you're providing is a sobering and saddening thought.

Now I'm uncomfortable and I just want to get out of the room as fast as I can. I back up and half-turning when I get to the stairs call out *goodnight, Fina* without looking her way.

Six

Peter

Buses service the industrial park that houses the Strutt manufacturing plant but they only run early in the morning and late in the afternoon. I have to hitchhike and walk which means mostly walk although I do get a lift when I'm almost there. *Typical* I think, curling my lip.

I can tell that the driver regrets picking up someone as bad-tempered as me and I hope he decides to never help out anyone else. I'm doing him a favor, it's a pretty risky thing to do.

The only thing pushing me on is how much I'm afraid of Dom. I mean I love the guy but he terrifies me. I have to show Dom results or the ensuing punishments will just get worse and I've seen too much of Dom's brutality vented on others.

Like Christine last night. My whole body shudders at the memory and out of the corner of my eye I see the driver shifting his body away from me. He probably thinks he's picked up somebody with the flu or something.

Christine is savvy enough to know you don't steal from Dominic Ferragamo. So she probably did deserve to die but... sometimes the need is just so great. I can understand it but she's still a stupid cunt. Or she was.

When I see her the clothes she has on are all messed up. It looks like she's been picked up in the middle of turning a trick and the fight she put up didn't improve anything. Her bra is pushed down around her waist, her black stockings are shredded, and her arms aren't even in her blouse even though it's still wrapped around her neck. Her skirt has been lost somewhere on the way and she isn't wearing panties.

She's lying on the floor of Dom's office, on the far side of the room where the floor is concrete and the walls are plain cinder-block. She's been crying quietly the whole time and her eye make-up is streaking through her face powder. Christine always paints her face in a very pale, ghostly look like she's a vampire or something with her long black hair, black clothes, even black nail polish. Just like Dom wears.

He's in a great mood after beating and fucking me and leaving me still tied to his desk. I know it's because he's looking forward to disposing of Christine.

He sashays over to where she's lying on the floor and looks down at her tut-tutting before repeating her name *Christine, Christine, Christine. What am I going to do with you?* and then he puts the boot in. Concentrating on her body rather then her head he gives her a nasty kicking. The sickening snap and crunch of breaking bones is closely followed by piercing screams that echo through the room.

Then Dom picks up the bound and battered woman and swinging wide hefts her hard against the wall. Another stomach-churning splatting sound and then, stunned to silence, Christine slides down to the floor again leaving a trail of blood behind. Studying his victim for a long moment Dom picks her up and this time swings in the other direction throwing her other side back into the brick. She's no longer making any noise. Dom gestures with a nod to one of his men who hurries over and kneeling down he checks Christine's pulse.

"She's still alive, boss," the man says in surprise.

Dom taps a finger against his lips obviously trying to recall something when suddenly he snaps his fingers and shows us all a mean grin.

"Put her to bed in the cells, Rico."

"I don't think it's safe to move her–"

"NOW Rico."

The man doesn't even answer, he just calls another guy over and between them they lift Christine and carrying her awkwardly stagger out of the room. We can all hear her groaning in pain but Dom has already turned his back and finding the contact he's been searching for on his phone he makes a call that has gives me chills. Probably everybody else who heard, too.

"Mister or is it Master? X I have a prospect I think will interest you greatly. I'm afraid I can't deliver, I doubt she'll last a journey, but if you hurry over here you can play with a broken body before she breathes her last. We can discuss the price later, time is of the essence if you're to get any enjoyment out of her."

He listens while the man he's called asks some questions. Dom nods before replying: "Some blood, probably internal bleeding, but most of the damage is broken bones, a few of which are protruding, having pierced through the skin."

After a truly evil chuckle Dom says, "Yes, I thought you'd like that. I'll leave word at the door so you're taken straight to Christine as soon as you get here, and I'll see you when you're both finished."

He ends the call but it still smiling and giggling quietly to himself. I can only imagine the look on my face. Whatever it's showing makes Dom laugh out loud.

"Oh Peter, you have no idea how far I'll go. You probably think Christine only deserved a beating and a bullet, right? Well I might have agreed with you if she hadn't been in my bed three nights ago promising me her undying loyalty and devotion.

I thought we'd shared a moment but the truth is she'd already ripped me off and was laughing at me. Thinking she'd *pulled a fast one, gotten one over me, took me for a ride...* what else, um... oh yeah, *played me for a fool.*

So I think combining me being angry-mad with my client being crazy-mad is a fitting revenge. And I'll make a lot of money because he doesn't often get the kind of product he fantasizes about."

Looking around the room at the assembled men all paused in their work but refusing to meet his eye he claps his hands and hollers: "Chop, chop duty calls." And as usually happens after one of Dom's brutal punishments no one argues or questions or forgets the lesson learned.

He's still wearing that crazy grin as he stalks towards me, pulling his hard cock out of jeans and fisting it. Now I know why he's left me tied down and helpless. "No lube this time Petey, I'm feeling mean."

I've been so wrapped up in the recent horrible memory I don't realize the car has stopped and the driver is eyeing me anxiously. Yeah, I've definitely cured him of picking up hitchhikers. Sucks to be the next guy, boo-hoo. Under my breath I mutter a *thanks* and get out of the car. I've barely closed the door before he's pulling away sharply.

When I was still in school I worked here at the plant part-time. I don't kid myself that any of the people like me but I've got two things in my favor. One, they hate my father even more, and two, there's always the chance that I'll inherit this place someday.

No matter how unlikely it seems right now I know my old man and he's full of Teutonic pride – his words, not mine – and no doubt he thinks he's building a dynasty. As if.

I stretch after getting out of the car and see Jimmy Johns, the warehouseman, coming out the side door having heard a vehicle.

I lift a hand in greeting and he grudgingly acknowledges me saying *oh, it's you*. As I get closer he says people have been using the plant's dumpster for their own garbage so he's trying to keep an eye on it during the day. What a lame excuse! anyone sneaking round a dumpster would do so when it's dark. He's just a nosy bugger, coming out to investigate, but a gossip and a good source of info.

Looking me up and down he comments that it's been awhile since he's seen me and I agree then ask how things are going and he says so-so. All the usual bullshit but it's a necessary dance before I can come to the point.

"I haven't spoken to Fina lately so I thought I'd drop in to see her."

"You haven't heard the news, then?"

When I shake my head his eyes light up over having a juicy tidbit to share: "Fina got caught forging a check and was fired. Your father kicked her out of the house, too. Nobody knows where she is."

"What the fuck? Fina's gone?"

"No one's seen or heard from her. But I'll tell you right now that charge against her was trumped up. That girl wouldn't forge anything, she's not a thief or a crook, not by a long shot."

"She sure isn't... what happened exactly?" By now we've turned and are walking back towards the warehouse. I'm hoping Jimmy might give me a cold one from his beer cooler. He often stays late relaxing with a drink and we all know it's to avoid going home to his nagging bitch of a wife. He gestures to the seating area he's created at the edge of the loading dock but doesn't offer any refreshments.

"Well, I wasn't there myself so this is just secondhand but the story goes that someone in accounting spotted the discrepancy. A check, made out to Fina to refill the petty cash float, was altered by a thousand bucks. The check hadn't even gone to the bank, it was just lying on Fina's desk, and whoever that someone was they took it to Dietrich and he fired Fina on the spot.

I heard he didn't even let her speak or ask any questions, just told her to get out and to come get her stuff from the house before garbage day otherwise he'd toss it all."

"He's such a fucking prick."

"Well, he's the boss so I really can't say anything about that but..."

"But you know exactly what I mean and you agree. Shit, where could Fina have gone? she doesn't have any friends so there's no one to go to. When did this happen?"

"A week ago. Whaddya mean she doesn't have friends? she's a real nice girl."

"Yeah, she is, but she lost touch with any friends she had when she dropped out of school to look after my Mom. The old man had already kicked me out of the house by then but I still knew that Fina was with Mom 24/7. That was until Mom died, and then Fina came to work here. As far as I can remember nobody here socializes much. When the shift bell rings everybody just punches out and heads home."

"Yeah, it's not a very friendly bunch because that's how your father wants it. He doesn't encourage friendships among the workers and there's never been staff picnics or Christmas parties. Nothing like that. Everybody's just here for their paycheck. I never noticed Fina spending any time with anyone in particular. Besides, they say Dietrich marched her out of here I don't think anyone would have dared to ask after her."

"So where's she been for the past week? I've got to get hold of her."

Scenting intrigue Jimmy asks: "Is something wrong?"

"Oh no, no just somebody I know wants to meet her. It would be a good thing for her, a chance to improve her life, so..."

"Well I don't know for sure but I heard when Fina left here she went straight to that coffee shop two blocks down, on the corner, and she's friendly with Sherry, the woman who works there. Maybe she could tell you more?"

"What about Father's new wife, Gigi? Is she mixed up in this stupid business with Fina?"

Jimmy's eyes sparkle at the chance to spread some malicious tittle-tattle. Dropping his voice to a dramatic whisper he answers: "Just between you and me? that's what I heard and I have no trouble believing it. No sir, no trouble at all."

There's a knowing look on his face and I'm feeling the same vibe. This whole set-up just reeks of Gigi covering up with one of her farfetched ideas.

"I guess I'll try this Sherry woman then. The coffee shop's two blocks away, you say?"

As Jimmy nods I spy a 10-speed bike propped up against the warehouse wall, the chain-lock looks easy-peasy to break, but Jimmy is watching me. I can tell he's reading my mind so I can't steal the bicycle. I sigh and turn in the direction he's pointed. I feel his eyes on me, watching, until I'm safely away from the warehouse.

Fina getting fired and disappearing is a real set-back. How the fuck do I find her now? and what do I tell Dom? Where the hell can she be?

The walk to the coffee shop hasn't made my mood any better but I have to flirt with the girl who works there because she's my only chance to get a lead on that idiot Fina. I really don't think she'd try to forge a check but... maybe she was trying to get some extra cash for me? Well I wished it had worked because I need the money.

Right now, I need information. I revise my plans about flirting when I see the shop employee is a woman, not a girl, and I'll have to do a good job of laying on the charm because she looks like she's been around the block once or twice.

"Hi, I'm glad to see you aren't busy just now because I'm not a customer but I do want to talk to you–"

She interrupts: "I'm not the owner so don't waste your sales pitch on me."

I read her name tag and start again saying, "Sherry, right? Sorry I gave the wrong impression, I'm not a salesman well, I am, but not in coffee shop products. Actually, I'm trying to track down my girlfriend and found out she was last seen here a week ago. I've been out of state and just got back. I went straight to her office but got the news that she's left there? So now I'm worried and hope you can help me out with what happened."

Sherry narrows her eyes, thinking over what I've said, before asking: "Where's your car?"

"At my place. I cabbed from the airport planning to get a lift home with my father and Fina."

"So you're Peter?"

"Peter Stutt, yeah, Fina talked about me?"

"Oh yeah, I've heard your name." Her lips thin when she says this and I realize she's overheard the warehouse crew gossiping.

"I can see you're smart enough not to believe everything you hear, Sherry. But seriously, do you have any idea where Fina's gone? She doesn't have anyone but me so I can't figure it out."

"Maybe she's gone to your place, then? You wouldn't know if you've been away." I pause to make it look like I'm considering her suggestion before she snorts out a *Huh!* Adding: "Fina never even mentioned you when she was in here trying to figure out her options."

"What did she decide on?"

"Peter I'm not sold on your story or on you for that matter but... I'll tell you what I know because it isn't a lot and if I hear from Fina I'll let her know you've been looking for her."

She's a sharper old broad then I'd figured so there's no point trying to change her mind. I feel my mouth twist into a smirk and wait for her to tell me what she knows - or at least as much as she's willing to share.

After an explanation that takes much longer than it should I finally hear about the Home Sweet Home Domestic Employment Agency.

That sounds out of my league but probably not Dom's so I'll take this information to him and hope he doesn't whip me again. Although I won't say no to the sex... not that he'd stop if I did.

Everything works out even better than I imagined when I finally get back to the city. I got lucky when a talkative trucker picked me up and rattled on the whole way leaving me to plan exactly how I'd explain all this to Dom to make it look like I'd really had to work hard to get this info.

"Oh good work, Peter," Dom says with a grin. "Home Sweet Home is Auntie Aggie's place, well she's like a third cousin or something but still an honorary Aunt. I'll get Fina's contact info out of her, no problem. Then I'll get to know your little sister a whole lot better, Petey."

"She's not my—" he shuts me up with a kiss before I can explain, yet again, that Fina isn't my sister. I wish he hadn't, he bit my tongue hard enough to draw blood before pushing me to my knees to suck him off. My tongue throbs and hurts like a bugger, but he likes to see my blood-stained teeth dragging along his cock. Dom gets off on the weirdest shit.

Seven

Serafina

The house is strangely quiet. With so many residents there's always some sort of sound usually male voices arguing, running water, different music genres competing... but this afternoon there's no noise.

I've already completed my day's work and sought out Mrs Finch to see if I could help her with anything. She manages this huge place with only her husband's help and I had no idea how until I learned that once a month a big cleaning crew comes in and sweeps through every room vacuuming, dusting, mopping, and scrubbing. We all have to vacate the house that day to let them get on with their work.

Still, looking after nine men is a lot of work. Clothing discarded everywhere, rooms left in disarray, muddy footprints tracked everywhere... show plenty of evidence of their slobby sloppiness.

Mrs. Finch stares silently in that disconcerting way she has before giving me a brief smile.

"If you wouldn't mind delivering this laundry that would be a help, Serafina," she indicates a couple of carry-cases holding fluffy cottons. "Four towels and two washcloths in each of their bathrooms, please."

Antony is escorting me to the city tomorrow to buy a dress for his upcoming party and to visit Sherry so I figure helping out today is the least I can do.

I pick up the canvas totes and start on the ground floor so it'll be a lighter weight as I head up the stairs. Antony and Giorgio each have suites on the ground floor. Marco and Leo are on the next floor along with my bedroom and a guest room. The top floor belongs to Gino and his four boys: Cesare, Vittorio, and the twins Luciano and Lorenzo. Ten connected bathrooms altogether.

I leave one tote on the second floor since I plan to finish up in my room, and carry the full one to the top. The boys' rooms are so untidy but I'm not prepared to make beds or hang up clothes belonging to adults.

I discovered that the Finches are the only live-in help because the men couldn't keep their hands off the female employees. It's their own fault if they have to live in untidy surroundings. After delivering and hanging their towels I head back downstairs.

Leo's room is tidy enough, he's only been home a couple of days, and when I move on to Remo's I'm not at all surprised to see it's very neatly kept. He has a king-size bed with navy linens that match navy black-out drapes. Persian runners sit on dark hardwood floors that match his brown furniture. A very masculine but comfortable combination.

I'm just placing one of the washcloths in the shower stall when I sense a presence behind me. Turning quickly I see Remo filling the doorway between bedroom and bathroom and I feel a guilty blush as if he's caught me spying in his personal space.

"I-I'm just giving Mrs. F-Finch a hand," I stammer.

Remo smiles slowly but doesn't say anything as he stalks into the bathroom, crowding me. Placing his hands on the counter he traps me against the vanity and looms in close sniffing at my hair.

"You smell so good," he rumbles quietly in his deep voice.

"Oh! um, I, uh... thanks?" I respond foolishly.

Now his lips are gently brushing up and down the surface of my neck. Little hairs stand up as I shiver at his touch. His mouth is warm as he kisses my skin, sucking lightly over the pulse in my throat. Encircling my shoulders with one hand he holds my head with the other, running his fingers through my thick curls.

Remo tilts my head back forcing me to meet his eyes. His gaze is intense with his pupils hugely black, barely showing the chocolate-brown color of his iris. My whole body heats up in the warmth of his gaze.

I'm utterly entranced, so drawn-in I'm hardly breathing. He leans forward pressing his forehead against mine. His right hand moves from massaging my scalp to tugging at my bottom lip and slipping a finger into my mouth. I don't know what to do with it so I give a gentle nibble and his groan is so seductive.

Suddenly his big hand is cupping my chin and his lips are pressing hotly against mine. His tongue invades my mouth and claims mine. He pulls it between his teeth, tenderly holding it in place, while his tongue swirls against the tip. My mind is so full of the sensation I'm not even aware that his hand has crept down to stroke my arm from shoulder to wrist, up and down several times kneading my muscles, before sliding across to cover my breast.

I gasp when he squeezes and moan a little when his grasp tightens. His thumb flicking my nipple sends a thrill of excitement thrumming right through my whole body. My hands are free, I could stop him, but instead I'm reveling in the pleasure of his caress.

An urgency takes him and he spins me round until my back is pressed tight against his chest and we're looking at our reflections in the mirror. I'm wearing my usual work garb of an oversized men's shirt on top of leggings. I kid myself that the big shirt disguises the size of me, but I'm vain enough to acknowledge how the leggings show off my shapely legs.

Remo gets most of my shirt unbuttoned before I half-heartedly move to stop him. He easily pulls my hands away and tucks my arms behind my back, trapping them between our bodies. Now he can finish his task. Opening my shirt he discovers that my guilty pleasure is sensuous, sexy lingerie.

Today I'm wearing a concoction of satin and lace in pale pink. The bustier is laced tightly to hold my big breasts in comfort which makes an enticing package of soft swells and deep cleavage. The appreciative sounds he makes while running his hands over my skin has me panting. The overflow of flesh pushes to escape and he slips in a finger to pop a nipple free of the fabric.

"Brown!" he exclaims with pleasure. My nipples are brown, the aureoles a light tan and the nipple a darker shade. He pinches and I squirm, closing my eyes until he orders me to open them and watch. He's got fingers pushed inside my bustier pinching both nipples. I watch us in the mirror and feel oddly detached between what I'm seeing and what I'm feeling. Me and Remo, unbelievable. That can't possibly be me with this gorgeous man. He's so tall and his shoulders are so broad, his arms so muscular, his hands so big...

"Watch my hands touching you, teasing you, and... teaching you?"

My cheeks flame red when I see he realizes how inexperienced I am. Peter and I have kissed, and one night he came to my room and lifted my nightgown to expose my body so he could see it naked. He poked around long enough to satisfy his curiosity about what I looked like, but he didn't caress, stroke, or grope. His touch didn't make my lady parts tingle or my breath quicken, but thinking about him has reminded me that I have a boyfriend. I blurt that out, again, and Remo curses.

Meeting my eyes in the mirror he asks: "Do you want me to stop?"

I can't help when a groan escapes because because saying *yes* is a lie, but it's the right thing to do so I bite my lip and nod. His eyes focus on my mouth before drifting back to my half-naked chest. He grinds his hips into my backside and I can feel his hard length. My blush deepens when I think about how I've aroused him but I don't press backwards and with a deep sigh he pulls the edges of my shirt together and lets my arms loose. A final kiss to the top of my head and he's gone.

I feel bereft, empty, but after a few moments I get my feelings under control and button up my shirt with shaky fingers. I'm ashamed to admit – even to myself – that I'm so turned on. Looking in the mirror I see my high color and want to splash cold water on my face but decide to wait until I'm in my own bathroom. Remo is gone when I exit through his bedroom. *He wasn't supposed to be home* I think, remembering that I saw him leave earlier.

Back in my own room I lock the door and before lying down on the bed I close the drapes. A movement outside catches my eye and I see that it's Remo walking towards the house. It looks like he's just parked his car in the driveway but that can't be right. I wasted more time daydreaming than I realized.

To my relief he looks up giving me his fabulous grin. I'm so glad things are still okay between us and that there won't be any awkwardness. I've heard boys can get really pissy if you tell them *no*. But, I guess that's another one of the differences between boys and men. Remo is a man.

Pulling up the afghan I keep over the foot of my bed I slip my leggings and thong down to my knees. I get a delightful shock of pleasure when I touch my clit. I'm already wet from the top to the bottom of my slit and I rub my fingers up and down enjoying the sensations that brings. I tap at my entrance but I've never put my fingers inside my hole, I don't even wear tampons. For some time I've been thinking it would be nice to have a dildo to use, but even nicer to have a boyfriend who wants to make love to me.

As usual my fantasy is the image burned into my brain of Andre's tight butt flexing as he pumps his dick up and down Gigi's throat. Except it's me, not Gigi, who's swallowing him up, and it's me whose breasts he's squeezing and massaging, and he's Remo, not Andre. It's so easy to fantasize about being in the act with Remo. That picture is so hot I'm verging on orgasm really quickly, way faster than usual, and I rub my clit round and round until I explode. The tremors are wonderful but leave me gasping and aching for more. In the middle of the afternoon in broad daylight, too!

Remo

I grin when I see Serafina at her window and chuckle when she waves back with great enthusiasm. I didn't even realize I'd looked up there. I've gotten used to her being in the house and I guess I'm always looking to see her, but I've got to stop teasing and flirting. Things can escalate too fast.

She's such a pretty girl but so young. There's probably only six or seven years between us but it seems like more. I really have to keep my distance, I'm not the kind of guy who gets off on corrupting girls. I don't know her full story but from what I've learned she's led quite a sheltered life. It's made her sweet and shy, naive, innocent... virginal.

Something about her makes me feel very protective, and I want to get to know her better while keeping everyone else at arms-length. Hypocritical, I know. Anyhow, she's made it clear she has a boyfriend.

Dad read us all the *Riot Act*, as he calls it, telling everyone to keep their distance and their hands off, Serafina. Uncle Giorgio snorted and from the sideways look he gave Dad I can tell he's thinking the worse. But Giorgio's dirty thoughts aren't Dad's. I can tell that Serafina brings out his protective instincts too, but in a different way. He won't want anything driving his skilled baker away!

Eight

Antony

Although she demurred at me buying her a dress for the party Serafina's eyes are sparkling as we're sitting in the car while Johnny drives us into the city to go shopping. We'll stop afterwards so Serafina to visit her friend at a coffee shop.

When she asked if she could get a ride I shuddered at the thought of Johnny having her alone in the car for a couple of hours there and back. Definitely not a good idea.

That's when I realized I could use her visit and a shopping trip as an excuse to accompany her. Serafina won't be attending the party as a guest, but she will be serving and on hand to answer any questions about the food, so she'll need something appropriate to wear. Her everyday garb is practical, but I need her to look impressive.

I'll find her something that shows off what a pretty young girl she is but also clearly states *hands off, her!* I'm not falling for her or anything but... I wouldn't mind if Remo did. I'd be happy to see Serafina move from the role of adopted granddaughter to daughter-in-law. Although she is awfully young.

Meanwhile I'm having a pleasant afternoon in her company. We'll get a dress and then matching shoes that are dressy but with a comfortable heel. She won't need a matching handbag for the party but I'll buy her one anyhow. I see she only carries a change-purse. A handbag will make it easier for her to carry her money and the phone I gave her.

Once all that's done we'll go visit her friend *Sherry at the coffee shop*. I get the impression there's a young man somewhere in the picture too, but she hasn't been very forthcoming on that subject.

Serafina

I can't stop staring at my reflection. This dress totally transforms me. In the mirror my eyes meet those of the saleslady and I can see she's delighted at my surprise. My shock, would be more accurate.

She had to come in with me to organize the built-in bra attachment. I'm doubtful it will fit, but she assures me this model is for *full-figured women* as she puts it. The neckline of the dress is so widely scooped you can't wear a bra without the straps showing. I know some women do that as a fashion statement but I can't pull off that kind of style.

When I remove my blouse - I dressed up a bit for Antony's sake - she admires my bustier and comments on how it's pretty but still supportive. However we both agree it won't work with the neckline of this dress. The bustier holds my boobs up in such a way that I'd be flashing everyone.

The dress is maroon with three-quarter sleeves, a fitted bodice, and what the saleslady called *a girdle* of brocaded fabric in maroon, gold, and dark blue. It's a gorgeous piece of tapestry that helps hold my stomach in before the dress flares out over my hips down to knee-length. When I move the material swings. I feel like a queen.

"Serafina? What's taking so long? Let me see," calls Antony from outside the dressing-room. The saleslady indicates I should leave my clunky shoes off and go barefoot to model the dress.

It's an expensive and exclusive boutique so Antony is comfortably sitting in an armchair drinking a coffee while balancing a plate of cookies on his knee. He almost spills everything the way he sits up so sharply at the sight of me. It makes me giggle, from both pleasure and shyness.

"Oh Miss Serafina, you are an absolute picture! That dress is perfect on you." He smiles at the saleslady complimenting her choice and telling her to ring up the sale.

"Are you sure, Antony? It costs a lot of money–" I begin but he interrupts me to ask:

"Do you want it?"

I bite my lip and hesitate only a moment before saying: "Yes!"

Antony claps his hands saying: "Good girl! now we need to get the perfect shoes and you'll be all set." He tells me to take a ginger-snap even though *they don't hold a candle to yours.* I happily munch while the precious dress is folded and wrapped in tissue paper before being stowed in a pretty bag with streamers on the handle.

While I'm admiring the packaging Antony spots a sparkly phone case in girly-pink that he picks up telling me to slip my phone in to see how it looks.

"It's gorgeous!" I exclaim, and he buys it for me as well.

I try on seven or eight pairs of shoes before Antony decides which works best. He's stuck between two pairs and wants to buy both but I refuse his offer, it's simply too generous."

"Then you must let me buy you the bag that matches the shoes, hmm? That's only fair," and he looks so determined that I give in gracefully with thanks.

Johnny stows my packages in the trunk while Antony and I settle in the backseat for the quick trip to see Sherry at the coffee-shop.

Johnny keeps glancing at me in the car's rearview mirror but when our eyes meet he immediately looks away. I realize he's spying, trying to catch me doing something... something with Antony? Oh my, Johnny couldn't be more wrong. Antony has no interest in me that way. I'm naive about a lot of stuff but I do know when a man is looking at me with... special interest. Antony behaves like a father, not a *Sugar Daddy*. Johnny's mind is in the gutter.

There are a few customers at the coffee-shop but they're already settled at their tables with their orders so Sherry is free to visit with us.

She and Antony banter like they've known each other for years and, I suppose, they recognize a certain type with certain expectations of behavior. He flatters her outrageously and she acts like he's a naughty boy full of charm and mischief. The two of them are instant pals. I'm happy to just sit back and enjoy the exchange.

Finally Sherry breaks away from the flirting to tell me there's been a bunch of drama at my old office. She heard some of the staff talking and asked them outright what was going on, explaining I'm her friend. They were happy to have an opportunity to gossip and righteously declare that they'd *never believed it of Fina in the first place.*

Turns out Gigi's nagging at Dietrich to bring me back home, due to her guilty conscience, aroused his suspicions. He bullied her into admitting she'd altered the check to discredit me but that's all she wanted to do, she didn't want him to turn me out, she just wanted me branded as a liar so no one would believe any accusations I might make. Well he was onto that in a flash and she finally confessed to her *momentary indiscretion*. That being her version of the semi-nude-groping and face-sucking with Andre that I witnessed.

Dietrich has a short fuse and he especially hates being in the wrong. Knowing he'd kicked me out without giving me a chance to defend myself wouldn't have gone down well once he found out the truth. The entire office heard the yelling followed by Gigi's sobbing.

I'll bet he gave it to her when he had her alone at home. He'd hit Marta a time or two that I was aware of before she got sick and now that Gigi's tumbled off her pedestal I'm sure she'll feel the effects of his wrath.

I can't pretend to feel sorry for her. I realize how extremely fortunate I was to find Home Sweet Home and get placed with Antony Cirelli. I could have ended up in the homeless shelter or even sleeping outdoors. What would have happened to me then? The thought is frightening, I'm not a tough, street-smart girl.

Sherry and I speculate about the whole situation and she wonders if Dietrich will try to track me down. That reminds her that Peter stopped by trying to get some information about me.

"Peter? Who is Peter?" asks Antony.

"Peter is... uh, well I guess he's my boyfriend," I answer.

"You guess?" both Sherry and Antony say in unison.

"Well, he just always has been, I mean I've had a crush on him since I was a kid. He was my big brother but so much more than a brother, he was my everything. When his father threw him out of the house at sixteen I thought my heart would break and I think his mother's did. I was the go-between for the two of them until she died, and Marta always said I was good for Peter and she knew I'd always help him. I promised I would."

"Huh. Death-bed promises are so unfair, Fina. You never mentioned Peter and when he came by here well frankly? I wasn't impressed."

"You don't sound very sure about him," puts in Antony.

I look between my two friends and seeing their concerned looks realize my ideas about Peter being my boyfriend might just be all on me. Maybe Peter doesn't think the same way. I do help him, with money like Marta wanted, but I've never been able to do anything good for him. I guess we need to talk.

"Did Peter say how I can get hold of him, Sherry?"

"He didn't leave a number because, well he knew I'd just throw it out. I really didn't take to him, Fina. You can do better."

"If that's your opinion Sherry, then I'm sure Serafina can. Just forget about this boy, you don't need to get in touch."

"But I do feel obligated Antony, I promised his mother."

"Yes, but was it fair of her to ask that of you? How old were you at the time?"

"Well, I was young but... you know, I really do need to talk to Peter. Maybe I've been on the wrong track all this time, I need to find out for sure."

"I think you're right," declares Sherry adding: "about talking to him, not about the obligation bit. Anyhow, he said if I do hear from you to ask you to leave a message for him at a nightclub called *Malavita*."

"Malavita? you're sure?" Antony interjects.

"Yeah, it means *bad world* or something, right?"

"Underworld, but the literal translation is *bad life*. It's owned by well, I guess by my uncle-in-law - he owns a lot of businesses - and it's run by my nephew Dominic. Serafina, I guess your Peter knows or works for Dominic. Small world!"

"Isn't it just!" exclaims Sherry before continuing: "Fina, you need to get hold of that guy and tell him he's toast. Seriously. He hasn't been a good boyfriend to you so cut him loose, am I right Antony?"

"Well *I* think so, Sherry, but it really isn't our decision to make." he turns to me with a half-smile and I know what he wants me to say.

"As far as I know Peter works at a car wash. I guess I need to call that Malavita place and make some arrangement to meet–"

"You don't have to dump him in person, he'll try to twist you around his finger, just do it on the phone. Or better yet, send him in a text," Sherry counsels.

Fina is shocked saying, "That sounds cruel!"

"Pfft, he's done nothing to show he deserves any better, has he?"

"Still... that's not the right way to do it. I have to see him. He's been part of my life since I was a child and I hope he always will be, although not as a boyfriend anymore, I guess."

I know Peter will want some money, but I don't tell them that because I know they'll tell me I'm a fool. I also know that they'll be right to do so.

"Do you have the number for your nephew's place, Antony? If so, Fina can call now and get it over with."

Antony's face goes blank, shuttering his emotions, and he replies in a flat tone that there's a rift and he's deleted Dominic from his contact list. I have no idea what that's all about but before I can ask he continues, saying: "Call directory assistance, Serafina, and get them to connect you."

I've got my phone safely stored in my new handbag which I'm carrying even though I'm not wearing my new shoes yet. I do as Antony suggests and when a woman answers the phone saying *Malavita Nightclub* I ask for Peter Stutt.

Nine

Peter

I'm watching Dom torment Sapphire, one of the topless waitresses who work here at his club. Her tits are small compared to the rest of the servers and she wants Dom to buy her a boob job. He's done that for some of the other girls.

Instead, he paid to have her nipples pierced and ornaments them with some heavy hanging jewelry he's bought. Now he's tapping the pendants, making them swing, and her nipples have turned dark red from pain or passion or both. He only stops when the landline phone rings and he nods at her to answer it.

"Malavita Night Club," she says then listens, frowns, and repeats: "You want to speak to Peter Stutt?"

That makes me sit up but before I can say a word Dom takes the receiver from her and asks into it *may I ask who is calling for Peter Stutt?* The answer pleases him because he turns to me with a huge grin announcing, "Peter it's your girlfriend Serafina!"

Thank Christ she tracked me down, maybe now I can get Dom off my case.

"Fina? Is that you?"

"Peter! yes, I'm glad I got hold of you. Sherry, from the coffee shop? she told me you'd been in and passed on your message so I thought I'd call and... well, things have been happening with me and–"

"Yeah what's up with that? What happened at Father's place?"

"Well I don't know for certain but I'm 99% sure that Gigi set me up to make it look like I was stealing from petty cash–"

Again, I interrupt asking: "Why would she do that?"

Fina pauses for a long moment before giving a big sigh. "I saw something that–"

Dom snatches the phone out of my hand so I don't get to hear Fina's explanation.

I hear him say: "Serafina, instead of chatting on the phone with Peter why don't you come and see him here, in person? because I'd love to meet you as well. Peter has spoken about you, you see. Let's set a date, when can you come here?"

Fina explains that she's a live-in domestic at her employee's home on an acreage out of the city and she has no transportation. Dom assures her he'll send an Uber on his account. Next I hear him say that he'll hang on while she asks her boss when she can get away. Knowing Fina she'll be flustered and feeling pressured. After a long time I heard Dom say "Excellent! We'll see you soon!" and he hangs up.

I wasn't expecting this to happen. I blurt out: "Where is she?"

"Living out in the country but she's in town now and her ride is going to bring her over," he replies.

I haven't even prepared what I'm going to say to Fina and I don't like the thought of Dom being there when I talk to her. I know exactly what to say that'll work on her and he'll just interfere. I'll have to see about getting her on her own for a bit first.

Dominic

Serafina phoning here has put me in a good mood. Ever since I caught sight of her with Peter I've had that girl on my mind. Not all the time, but thoughts of her and what I'm gonna do to her, are always hovering in the background.

I look at skinny Sapphire with distaste because there are no curves to her, just jutting-out hipbones and small tits.

I pull her onto my lap and ask: "Do you still want a boob job?" and her face lights up as she exclaims that *yes, yes she does!*

I nod and contemplate for a bit, enjoying her anxiety. She wants me to agree but is afraid to push. She should be afraid, she's worked here long enough to have an idea of what I'm capable of doing... especially when I'm in a temper which happens a lot considering I'm surrounded by idiots.

"Okay I'll tell you what. I'll give you the same deal I gave Trixie," I say and smile when I see her go pale under her thick face make-up.

"But Dom," she complains, "I'm a dancer, I'm not a prostitute."

"Sure you are, hon. Anyone who earns money off their body is whoring themselves and that's exactly what you do."

"B-but..." she tears up and I enjoy hearing the quaver in her voice as she struggles not to cry. "I don't want to fuck strangers."

"You will if I tell you to, right?"

"Well... Dom you know I... I'll do anything to make you happy but–"

"If I tell you to fuck somebody, Sapphire, I expect you do it. I don't have to buy you a boob job to get your obedience. You want to do whatever I tell you to do, right?"

Cowed, she casts her eyes down when she answers me *yes, Dom*. I see Peter watching us carefully and decide to give him a bit of a show.

Unhooking the ornate earrings I'd hung on the rings in Sapphire's nipples I attach them to the ring through her clit. Her eyes fly open because the two earrings are too heavy for that tender flesh. Immediately she squirms and whines wanting me to take the pendants off. Instead, I fish around in my pocket until I find a bullet vibrator. It's just a cheap one, not controlled through Bluetooth, so I flip the switch to high and shove it inside her.

The vibration makes her cunt shimmy and the earrings tinkle and clank against each other while tears stream down her face. I lean forward to lick that salty liquid but my eyes are drawn back to the sight of her red, swollen clit all dragged down with the weight of the gaudy costume jewelry.

"Pleasure and pain," I murmur and nobody argues.

Ten

Serafina

Antony has Johnny drive us to the nightclub. He tells me he has a few phone calls to make but hopes I won't be more than half-an-hour. I assure him I won't, I just want to have a word with Peter.

We arrive soon after. It's a big building with lots of neon lighting, even the club's name on a huge sign, but with all the lights turned off in daytime it looks deserted. Then the door opens and Peter comes outside. I get out to meet him and when he sees that the car isn't leaving I explain I can only visit for a few minutes.

"But I've got a phone now so let me give you my number and you can call when you've got time to chat."

Peter pulls his mobile out of his pocket and taps my number into his contacts. He doesn't offer his and I don't ask for it. I find I'm studying Peter with a critical eye. He's a good-looking guy, but a bit on the thin side, and he seems awfully young. Compared to somebody like Remo he's just a Peter Pan kind of guy.

With relief I realize I'm over him.

The door opens again and a tall, well-built man steps out, unapologetically knocking Peter out of the way. At first I think that him wearing eye make-up is kinda weird but it suits his very handsome face. His gaze is very intense but not in a scary or angry way, more like he knows a secret and is just dying to share it.

"You must be Serafina!" he enthuses. "I'm Dominic and this is my place, please come in."

"Hi Dominic, I'm sorry but my ride is waiting so I can't stay right now."

"I thought I recognized the car," he gives a wave but Antony doesn't acknowledge him. Because I'm facing the car I don't see the way Dom's expression goes cold and his eyes narrow but his voice doesn't change as he adds: "I'm afraid I'm in his bad books – again! Never mind, we'll have Peter bring you by for a proper visit soon, does he have your number?"

I nod, saying "Yes, nice to meet you, Dominic."

"Dom," he replies. "And it's all my pleasure. I've looked forward to meeting you," and taking my hand he kisses the back of my fingers which makes me giggle. "I hope we can get together before too long, Serafina."

"Just Fina is fine."

"I'll say she is!" he smirks, and when my eyes widen at the compliment his face breaks out into a charming smile.

I get in the car and the drive home is mostly quiet. I have plenty to think about but my thoughts are all over the place.

Meeting Dom has been fun, he's so hot and we flirted! but I think I should feel badly about Peter. Except... I didn't want to flirt with Peter the way I did with Dom. Peter didn't even seem interested when Dom was eyeballing me and he sure didn't object when Dom kissed my hand. He acted like he didn't care and he would care if I'm his girlfriend so...

Time to face facts, I guess. Peter no longer wants to be my boyfriend so ending things between us is okay. I'll be sad but only because it's always sad when things change. I know I'm not going to cry. Maybe he won't even bother to call.

Once we get home I thank Antony for taking me out today and for my new dress and shoes, and for taking me to meet Sherry and then Peter.

He just chuckles at my lengthy thanks and says it was his pleasure, especially meeting Sherry because *she's a real firecracker.* Then he tells me he's got a bit of work to do before dinner and leaves.

I guess I'm making a funny face because after hanging up my jacket in the foyer I see Remo who greets me with his devastating smile asking why I look so perplexed. I don't want to talk about my confusion over Peter so I just say the first thing that comes to mind and blurt out: "I met your cousin Dom."

Immediately he scowls, his face turning thunderous, and now I really am perplexed.

"Stay the hell away from him, Serafina," he insists.

"What? Why?"

"He's really bad news. Just... just do what I say, all right?"

Remo's gripping my shoulders but he isn't aware until I pointedly look at his hands and then he quickly pulls back.

"I'm serious, Fina. Stay away from Dom."

His demanding tone of voice makes be feel defiant. Remo has no right to tell me who I can and cannot see. He's just my boss's son, not my boyfriend. Peter, my ex-boyfriend doesn't care if I see Dom so why should he?

"I really don't think my friendships are any of your business, Remo," I say trying hard to sound bored and snooty but there's a slight quaver to my voice. Remo has that effect on me. It's not fair that he acts hot and cold, sometimes even caressing me while standing well back the rest of the time.

"Now you listen to me, Fina–" he begins but I turn my back and run away. Suddenly I feel teary. I don't know why that is, but I sure don't want him to see me cry.

In my bedroom, after putting my new outfit away, I sit down at the vanity and stare at my reflection. The urge to cry has passed but it doesn't seem like it's very far away.

Why am I so emotional? Maybe I'm getting my period, it's roughly due. I've never had a carved-in-stone schedule, not like Melanie who worked alongside me in the accounting office. She'd always know exactly when she was due and would book off her first day. There was some old employment regulation that allowed women to take off one day a month. I never needed to make use of it. My periods are irregular but have never been particularly painful. I look at my face closely to see if a telltale pimple is forming but nothing shows.

It's been quite a day all told. Antony was wonderful and so generous shopping with me, and then meeting up with Sherry at the coffee shop, and so patient waiting while I saw Peter and Dominic at Malavita. He's such a nice man and I know his feelings for me are 100% genuine friendship, nothing more, despite the funny looks and odd remarks his brother Giorgio is always making.

I wish I knew what happened with Antony and Dominic, but I have to wait for one of them to tell me, it's not my business so I can't ask. Although I want to!

Anyhow it's time to work with Mrs. Finch to get the evening meal served. She takes care of all the main dishes and I'm in charge of dessert. I baked several different types of pie this morning and now I need to whip up some cream so I can offer a variety of toppings.

I'm walking down the hall and so deep in thought I completely lose my head and start screaming when I'm hugged from behind. It's Remo, he sneaked up on me when I came out of my room.

To make things even worse when he quickly covers my mouth with his hand I bite him! Not hard, thank God, but enough to make me feel like an utter loser idiot. He just laughs it off because he's such a nice guy but still... I feel so stupid. Here he is trying to make things right between us and I'm acting like a long-tailed cat in a room full of rocking-chairs, as Marta used to say.

He apologizes: "Fina I'm so sorry, I didn't mean to scare you. But I should have realized... damn, I'm thoughtless."

"No, it's all my fault," I tell him. "You were just playing a prank, teasing me, and I totally overreacted. I'm such a drama queen!"

"Tell you what, let's both apologize to each other with..." He pauses and I swear I'm holding my breath until he says, "with a kiss."

He puts his hand behind my head and gently pulls me close to press his lips softly and then more urgently against mine. He tastes slightly minty – toothpaste? – and then his lips open and his tongue pushes into my mouth and licks mine. It feels cool against my tongue, maybe the mint is from mouthwash? A moment later I forget all about mint-anything and concentrate on the delicious sensations stemming from my mouth right to my lady parts. I blush even thinking about where I'm feeling this tingling sensation.

Remo makes me feel all kinds of new and interesting things.

One hand remains cradling my head which he palms my cheek and grips my chin to hold me steady for a thorough kissing.

I wasn't aware I moved but next thing I know I'm standing on tippy-toe with my arms snaked around his neck. My breasts press against his chest. He runs his fingers through my long hair as his hand moves from the back of my head down to my waist to pull me in even tighter. It's inevitable that this kiss will draw our bodies even closer together. Attached at the lips, breast and chest, now belly, hips, groin, thighs.

I feel his hard length pushing against me and I jerk back with a gasp. Remo blinks at me as if coming out of a dream then quickly apologizes before brushing past me to go into his room and close the door.

You're such an idiot! I tell myself. *Now he'll think you're just a scared kid."*

Remo

I'm a pretty straightforward guy and I only mix myself up when I start trying to figure out what other people are thinking. Even so, I know I fucked up with Fina this evening. Instead of trying to lay down the law I should have told her what's going on with Dominic.

I know we're all keeping quiet to let Great-Uncle Tonino look into things without drawing attention, but she should know. Dom is pure poison. When he's around she should run as fast as she can in the opposite direction.

Damn. I'm never going to get to sleep with all of the conflicting thoughts racing around my head. I get up and head downstairs to pour myself a drink. Maybe if I just sip on a whiskey while sitting quietly I'll be able to untangle my thoughts and figure out what to do.

I wonder what Fina wants? It sure doesn't sound like she's getting whatever it is from her boyfriend. I mean, seriously, what kind of man would let Dominic Ferragamo anywhere near her? Yet it sounds like this Peter introduced her to Dom.

After dinner Dad told me about them meeting up at Malavita. He stayed in the car because he doesn't want anything to do with my cousin. He doesn't know what they said to each other but it was a short conversation. Thank God.

Fina is exactly Dom's type: innocent. He'll be all over her, and somehow he'll hurt her. It's what he does, it's what he's always done. I could never understand how he and Marco became so close, and yet he destroyed him in the end. At least as far as we know.

I have to save Fina from him but... how can I intervene when she's made it clear that she's got a boyfriend and isn't interested in me?

Antony

As usual, when I settle myself to sleep I let my mind review the events of the day. Overall today was very good with only a couple of niggling concerns.

I have to admit I wasn't happy to hear Serafina has a boyfriend. She arrived on my doorstep in desperate circumstances with literally nowhere to go so what kind of boyfriend is he?

Well, not much from what Sherry said and I have to agree!

Sherry's quite a character and I enjoyed chatting with her. I'm glad Serafina has someone like her to talk to because Sherry is down-to-earth with plenty of common sense. I like her forthright way of speaking.

It's years since I've had the chance of a shopping expedition with a young lady and it was fun. Serafina is so childlike in her enjoyment and that's a lovely thing to witness.

That reminds me that I want to have a word with Johnny. I wasn't pleased with the odd looks I caught him giving Serafina. I've warned off my relatives and now it seems I need to have a word with my chauffeur as well. Serafina must be treated respectfully by everyone. She's under my protection.

The only real worry I have about today is that Serafina met my nephew. I regret not involving the police at the first sign of trouble but between Tonino and Remo well... I did agree not to say or do anything while the matter is investigated within the *famiglia*.

But Dominic Ferragamo is the last person I want to be anywhere near Serafina.

Eleven

Remo

I stayed in the shower far too long but I still feel knotted up. It took me more than one drink to relax enough to get to sleep last night.

Now I can't see my reflection in the mirror so I open the bathroom door to let some of the steam escape. The glass clears and my pained expression looks back at me. Yeah, this troubled feeling shows.

Quickly towel-drying myself I walk through to my closet but there, on the bed, sits Marco.

I'm so shocked I ask him a whole bunch of questions all at once: "Are you okay? Have you seen Dad yet? What the fuck are you doing here, man? What's going on with you? Are you insane or something?"

"No," comes a voice from beside me and turning I see Dominic. "I'm the one who's insane *and* something, I'm *something else*."

He's grinning widely like the maniac he is. Despite the dark make-up rimming his eyes I can see clearly enough to spot the glint of his particular madness.

"Oh you're fucking something else all right. You can get out of here right now but Marco, you stay."

I have no time for their bullshit antics. Why are they even together? I make a warding off gesture with my hands but next thing I know Dominic has propelled himself on me driving both of us on top of Marco on the bed.

Being naked puts me at a disadvantage until my damp skin proves too hard to grab hold of so I manage to slip free. A moment later I'm captured again. I twist and struggle but I'm no match for the two of them. Them being fully dressed makes me feel especially vulnerable.

Marco has pulled me tight against his body by curling his muscular arms under my armpits and around my shoulders wrapping his hands behind my neck. I'm wearing him like a backpack. He falls back down onto the bed again, taking me with him. I try a head-butt but he can see it coming and dodges effortlessly.

Dominic holds my legs letting Marco hook his around them. My hands and feet are free but they can't reach anything with all four of my limbs secured. I'm thrashing my head back and forth trying to connect with Marco's face, nose... but Dominic grabs my chin in his tight grasp and holds me steady.

Through gritted teeth I spit out the words: "What. Do. You. Want?"

Instead of answering Dominic straddles my hips and with his free hand starts stroking my chest, tugging at the hair there, flicking my nipples. His hand starts trailing lower and he gives me a wicked smirk. Now I understand the expression *seething with rage* because my anger is boiling over and I can't even get the words out to threaten him.

I feel his warm hand wrap around my cock and squeeze. He starts pumping his fist up and down my length. I can't believe he's touching me and Marco's helping!

"This is nice, Remo but I'm disappointed not to see any piercings, that's not very considerate of your partner is it? I have a pubic piercing of a *captive bead ring* but with three beads instead of the usual measly one. I'm definitely rubbing that clit when I'm balls deep into a babe.

However, you are neatly groomed and with silky smooth skin, especially here at the head. If I tap the slit will I get some pre-cum from you? That always works for me so let's find out."

I can't even glare at him because he's not meeting my eyes, he's looking down as he plays with my cock.

I can't have anyone hear us so through my clenched jaw, I call to my brother: "Marco! Stop him, stop this!"

"No, Remo. It's time to *widen your horizons.* You're so sure about everything and you know it all, don't you? You've got right and wrong all figured out. We could have had fun with Shelby, you know, lots of fun but you got all righteous. Well we're going to show you another point of view. Maybe then you'll stop being so uptight and rigid and—"

"Oh he's definitely rigid," interrupts Dominic with a chuckle, and to my utter shame I realize I am getting hard. I can't control it, my cock can't help but respond to Dominic's skilled handling. When two fingers slip down underneath my ballsack and press up at a sensitive spot my hips buck and I'm suddenly fully tumescent. I'm angry and ashamed and a little scared, too. My cousin is psycho and I can't figure out what Marco's up to.

"Oh goody! I want a taste of this," exclaims Dominic in a sing-song falsetto.

"Don't you fucking dare!" is all I manage to shout before he does dare exactly that.

A hot wet mouth, lips firm around my shaft, and tongue stroking while Dom swallows me down his throat. He starts making exaggeratedly loud *mmm-mmm* sounds and I feel Marco's laughter vibrate through my body.

This is demeaning and shaming. There is nothing sexy or fun about this, it's out-and-out assault. We're not boys exploring, playing a game, it's the deliberate sexual assault of me by my twin and my cousin. Dom isn't gay but obviously he's bi. But this isn't about sex, it's about power: theirs versus mine.

"You're both dead men," I grind out.

"Did you forget, Remo? I'm already dead," states Marco.

Dominic pulls his mouth free from my cock with a loud pop adding: "And I'm the fucker who killed him, remember?"

I stop fighting to free myself and let my body go limp. I won't give them the satisfaction of winning. Keeping my eyes closed after some time I feel Dom step away and then Marco releases me. Dom hovers until Marco gets out from under me safely. I refuse to look or speak again. I refuse to acknowledge them in any way.

I sense the two of them moving away and hear the bedroom door opening. Marco pauses to say: "You can't fight us when we stand together, bro. No one can. You better figure out quick that you need to join us."

I still don't respond and hear the door shut sharply. A lot of things make sense now. Several times I've felt Marco was close by. Some of the comments and looks other people have given me – as if we had a conversation I don't recall – and catching his scent and glimpses out of the corner of eye.

I never did accept that he'd been killed. Sure, I can believe Dominic would kill someone but I'm also sure I'd know if my twin died. I always thought we were so close but in the last year or so we've really gone in opposite directions.

Obviously Marco and Dominic cooked up this scheme together but why? What is Dominic after? and why is Marco helping him? His disappearance devastated Dad.

I'm the oldest by seven minutes and that's always bugged Marco although I don't know why. I never rubbed his face in it as the *older* brother, and it's not like I'm in line for a throne or something.

Still, there's always been a one-sided rivalry with Marco wanting everything I have. Like Shelby, although she's certainly not the first girlfriend of mine that he's come on to. It's just that, as far as I know she's the first who responded and kept responding even after she knew the truth. When I found out they invited me to join in. That killed all the feeling I ever had for my beautiful ex-girlfriend model.

And then there's been his deepening friendship with our cousin Dominic who we used to make fun of...

This assault makes me feel I've been betrayed to the very depth of my soul.

Marco

Remo and I are physically identical in every way. The way we look, the way we sound, our mannerisms, even our illnesses. So when I'm holding his naked body against me it's like I'm holding myself. It's a real struggle because of course we're evenly matched. Same height and bulk, same muscular development.

I can't imagine what it's like to not have a twin. The relationship I have with our younger brother Leo is nothing like this. Remo is a part of me and has been since our inception. Separating us is inconceivable and I don't understand what he's trying to do and why he's being so stubborn about it. First with Shelby, now with Dom.

Dom's plan is a good one. It doesn't matter if Remo doesn't want to be part of the *famiglia*, he is part of our family and so is Dom. We need to stick together, help each other out.

Our mothers were sisters and Dom is our cousin. Sure, I know the man is way out there – in fact calling him a psychopath isn't a stretch, but... none of that matters right now.

Well, I guess *right now* it does matter because Dom's way of doing things is certainly attention-getting. I thought we might slap Remo around but Dom has other ideas.

It's a neat twist on Remo's recent good and bad, right and wrong, black and white stance. It'll do him good to learn something about the grays. He's pretty pissed, though.

I almost lose my grip when Dom actually sucks Remo's dick, that's unbelievable! I didn't think he'd go that far and I had to laugh from the shock of it.

The really funny part is that Remo can't help reacting, no matter how much he might hate the idea, and when I feel his body stiffen up I get hard in response. We spent our adolescence masturbating together, even jerking each other off at times, but this is something else. Dom is definitely something else. I shake my head smiling in memory.

I'm a little envious. I've never had the opportunity to get a blow job from someone who knows exactly what a good cock-sucking feels like and how to do it. I guess I would have had opportunities if I'd only been open to them, I mean I must have gone to school with gay or at least bisexual guys.

Oh hell, now I'm speculating about Dom. I've been hiding here at home a lot but mostly I've been hanging out at his place which means I've been spending way too much time with him. Now he's making me detour past the kitchen hoping to get a glimpse of Serafina. He can't stop talking about her, but he says he doesn't want her to see him so we're only going to spy a bit.

She's not my type, Shelby is, but I have to admit that Serafina's thick, soft skin felt damn good in my hands yesterday when I held her for a kiss. She's got a hell of a rack and everything jiggled when she jumped and screamed as I crept up on her.

Twelve

Serafina

I can't really say I was surprised when Peter phoned. He did ask me for money and reminded me, once again, of my obligation to him. Somehow that made it easier to end our so-called romantic relationship.

"That obligation you speak of Peter, is as much for Marta's sake as yours. I mean, we were boyfriend and girlfriend but that's no longer that way it is. I will Venmo you something as soon as I hang up."

"Okay, good. How much?" He doesn't say a word about us breaking up, he's only interested in the money.

"I'll have to check my bank account and see if your father put in my severance pay, but even if he didn't there still should be some money."

"Okay, thanks. We're still friends, right? You and me?"

I hear that familiar neediness in his tone and my voice softens with relief as I answer: "We always will be. There are so many memories that I treasure."

"Good, oh and Dom? my boss? he'd like me to bring you to the club some night to show you what it's like here."

"Oh no, I can't come at night. I'm too busy here. But I can visit during the day."

"I don't know if that will... well, I'll talk to Dom and let you know."

He ends the call without saying goodbye but that's typical Peter, he's not mad at me or anything.

Peter

Fucking Fina. Dom took it out on me when I told him she wouldn't come out at night. He practically strangled me, hanging me from a rope and letting me gasp for air. He said my mouth looked like a fish mouth. Asshole. And he kept doing it until I really thought I was gonna die but afterwards he just laughed it off saying people do that to themselves all the time to have stronger orgasms when they jerk off.

Then he pinned me down and wrapped his big hands around my throat which already hurt like hell and he squeezed and squeezed. I couldn't fight him, he's way stronger, and I got scared. I couldn't help crying but then he freed up one hand, still choking me with the other, and got his hand down my pants and started massaging my cock. He did it in a rhythm of choking and stroking and fuck if I didn't get super-hard. So I'm horny and crying, and hating him and wanting him – all at the same time.

"It's all about oxygen deprivation, Petey. It gets you half-high and the pleasure intensifies. And it's also about the fear because you do fear me, don't you? as you should 'cause I'm a nasty fucker. But I give a mean hand-job so just take a deep breath because we're going to finish this and get you off."

By now I don't care if he ends my life so long as my dick gets serviced first.

"I'll have to rethink my plans for Serafina but I can make it work. We'll have a nice daytime visit and that should soften her up, get her feeling safe and comfortable with me. Then we can move on to the next step. I have lots of plans for that girl and I'm going to need a whole night. At least one night."

I barely hear Dom talking because I've briefly passed out from the lack of air and then zoned out from the sheer joy of explosive sex. He slaps my face hard enough to get my attention and demands that I get Fina here tomorrow or the next day at the latest.

Dominic

I'm salivating at the prospect of playing with this adorable pet but know I have to play it *calm, cool, and collected* so I don't scare her off.

Petey-boy came through and we arranged for Fina to have lunch with us. I sent an Uber but had to promise we'd drive her home in order to get Antony to agree. Jesus, you'd think he was her father instead of her boss.

We settled for an Italian lunch because Serafina has no idea if she likes my first choices of sushi or Thai. I start getting pissy but control myself because she can't help her lack of worldly experience. In fact, it's not just her body built for sin but that same sheltered existence which makes her so desirable. Her oh-so-corruptible innocence.

A nice guy would savor her delight at new experiences, tastes, and sensations but that's not me. I crave her tears and pleas, cries and screams. I want the whole orchestra with lots of *sax and violins* as I once heard a BDSM novel politely described.

So we ate our spaghetti and veal milanese, drank Chianti and espresso, and now we're back at the club ready for just a sweet taste of dessert.

"Let's begin with an experiment that will help me get to know you, Serafina. Are you willing to explore your psyche with me?"

"Uh, I guess so Dominic, I mean Dom."

"Delighted! Okay so I think you'll find some light bondage a stimulating way to break out of your shell. Nothing silly like spreadeagled on a bed. No, no. Just your arms – not even your hands – but like this."

I take hold of Fina's left wrist and gently press it back towards her shoulder explaining the rope will wrap her forearm and upper arm together, from elbow to wrist. "It's called Shibari, the art of Japanese rope-tying."

"And what does this do?"

Plenty for me! I think but aloud I answer: "It's psychologically freeing when the body is restrained in a comfortable manner in safe surroundings. You do trust me, don't you?"

She smiles and nods, more intrigued than doubtful, so I push my advantage, adding: "Now your shirt will probably get wrinkled, maybe dirty but it won't tear or anything. Still, should we take it off?"

"Oh no. No, I'd rather not do that," she quickly replies with her voice dropping down to a whisper.

I smile brightly and taking her right arm this time I assure her: "Then we won't bother with that. Okay, now let's get your arm pushed back again, yes, just like that. Good. Hold the position a moment while I get started."

I've used this particular tie many times so it doesn't take long to have the rope neatly wound immobilizing her dominant arm. I lace my fingers through that hand and squeeze, checking that the binding isn't too tight.

"No it's fine. It just feels kinda funny having my arm tied up," she answers.

Taking hold of Fina's weaker left arm I take a step back to survey her and unbuttoning her shirt comment that *this really doesn't work*. Of course she protests but she's too polite to make a fuss and it only takes my quick fingers a moment to have the shirt open and pulled off her left arm. Pushing it round her back there's only a bit of white fabric showing on her right shoulder. The rope fully covers the sleeve.

Fina presents a breathtaking picture. Her olive skin is enhanced by the black clothes she's wearing. A black camisole type of undergarment and black leggings. They expose how round her belly is and the curve of thick thighs but also showcase shapely calves and dainty narrow ankles. Stepping around for the backview I'm entranced at how the thin material clings emphasizing her round ass cheeks. I think of an old song about *fat-bottomed girls*. This plumpness might not be fashionable but most men enjoy it and I especially love it.

"Fina, I'm fascinated by this black thing you're wearing. What is it? and what's it called?"

"Dom, please, everyone can see me," she hisses in an embarrassed whisper.

I look around as if I'm just noticing the men and chuckle to see their eyes glued to this girl's luscious body. They'd all love a piece of this but I'm taking her first. Afterwards... maybe. I'll see.

"Oh don't pay any attention to them, they're just admiring you. You're showing less than you would in a bathing suit."

"But I'm not at the beach!" she whisper-shrieks.

I just ignore what she's saying and tell her: "You should be proud of your assets, Fina. Now, explain to me all about this thing." I gesture to the black satin contraption that appears to be held together by hooks.

"It's called a bustier and it gives me lots of support, see these panels on the side? without having thick straps cutting into my shoulders."

"Yes, I see. What a wonderful invention." I stroke the soft skin from her naked shoulder to neck. "No red marks at all from a bra having to carry a heavy load." I look down a her smooth flesh bulging over the edge of her bustier. A frill of lace hides her nipples but I can see that they're hard and turning reddish brown with the erectile tissue blood-engorged. It takes all my restraint to keep my hands off but I need to wait until I can get the opportunity to properly tie her up. This is just a taste, for both of us.

"And is this lingerie comfortable enough?"

"Oh yes, it's so much better than a bra or going without a bra."

She blushes beautifully over the last phrase. I imagine she would get sore with those full breasts swinging heavily. I'll find out later. Now I need to secure her left arm but that's only a minute's work then I hoist her on top of the bar and nudging her legs apart stand directly in front. Now her eyes are level with mine and I stare into hers.

"Look at you holding so still and doing such a good job for me. You're such a good girl, aren't you Fina?"

Her eyes light up at my praise and I smile inwardly at discovering yet another kink. While letting my gaze feast on her half-naked torso I hear her breathing quicken and notice that the swell of breast flesh overflowing the top of her bustier is trembling as she pants.

I can't resist that smooth expanse and drop my face down into her cleavage. Soon I'm rubbing my cheek from her neck right down to the frilly lace. I pretend not to see her hard nipple. Today is an introductory session only, just enough to get me into her trusted circle. I've already gone further then I should have but I'll get her stoked with more compliments.

"You're skin is so soft, Fina, it's incredibly soft. And it smells so good."

Her voice hitches as she replies: "It's only soap, I don't wear perfume."

"And I'm so glad you don't because perfume masks a woman's unique odor, the smell of her skin and the scent of her arousal. You smell so clean and fresh. So let's see, today you've explored light bondage and I've witnessed three senses: sight, sound and smell. We'll savor taste and touch another time, hmmm?"

"What do you mean by sound?"

"Ah, your breathing sweet thing. Those little gasping breaths give me a very clear indication of your feelings at being tied and helpless. We've learned a lot about your inner thoughts from this brief exploration even though you aren't completely restrained. But again, that's something for another day, I hope?" I turn the last bit into a question and she just gets lost staring into my eyes. She is utterly delectable.

"Now tell me Fina, how do you undo this bustier? It looks like it's skin-tight and your body was poured into it."

"Don't undo it!" she gasps.

"No, no I wouldn't with all these people here." Lowering my voice I lean close to her ear to whisper that I'll want her all to myself when that happens.

She giggles and explains it's quite easy to get out of. She just expels the air out of her lungs as she leans right forward from the waist and quickly pulls the hooks apart. To put it on she lies flat on her bed and just pulls everything together, similar to zipping up a tight pair of jeans.

I run my hands over the entire bustier and plant a kiss at the top of each breast. A blush of arousal spreads across her chest and her lips have fallen open enticingly.

"Your mouth is an unusual shape for someone of Mediterranean descent," I tell her. "Your upper lip is thicker than the lower. Italian girls are more likely to have a plump lower lip while this kind usually belongs to pale blondes like Scandinavians or some English girls."

"My mother was German, not Italian.

"That explains it then. It's a very intriguing look, you know. Pretty overbites are so sexy."

Now the flush on her chest spread upwards over her cheeks. Since I've told her I won't be tasting or touching she's relaxed a little, but every bit of praise I give ramps up her arousal. She's also very aware of the men in the room and how they keep sneaking glances, or even openly staring, at her. I think Fina might be a bit of an exhibitionist, although she's unlikely to be the type who thrills to *nude in public* action. It's serendipity that humiliating a sex partner is one of my kinks.

"You've been bound for more than half-an-hour so I'm going to release you now. You've done so well and I'm so proud of you. I know it isn't easy to give up control, even minimally like this, but you've been a real champ, sweetheart."

She shakes out each arm as I free it from the ropes and gives a wince of pain reaching back to find the left sleeve of her shirt. I massage the sore spot on her shoulder and then help her get dressed, lingering over each button. Once I'm finished I lean forward and brush a gentle kiss across her lips but she keeps her mouth closed. When I pull back she tucks her chin down towards her chest and tells me:

"Dom, Peter was my boyfriend for a long time and this feels... funny. Especially with him here."

I glance over at Peter who looks bored out of his mind. I force my fingers to uncurl from the fist they automatically formed at the sight of him. I don't want to upset Fina so I give her a chaste kiss on her forehead and compliment her again for being such a beautiful and good girl.

I'm happy to hear that my voice is steady when I say, "Come on, Peter. Let's drive Fina home now."

I'll enjoy making him suffer when we get back but no, I've got a better idea. Once we're about halfway home I'll make him get out of the car to walk the rest of the way. Yeah, that'll work.

Besides, I've got a hot little bartender who's been shorting my cash register and I've been really looking forward to dealing with her.

Serafina

I have so much to think about and my head is spinning. I probably drank more wine at lunch than I should have, plus I never drink during the day. Actually, I hardly drink at all... but I can't pretend I was too drunk to know what was going on.

My cheeks flame at the memory but it's desire, not shame, that spreads the heat through my body.

Dom, with his two-tone hair of platinum and black; his eye make-up; his nail polish; his drop-dead gorgeous face and physique, is pure trouble. Is that why Remo has tried to warn me off? I know Dom's manipulative, I sense he's dangerous, and I suspect he's crazy! Yet my body is telling my mind and my heart to just shut the f up. Geez, Fina, time to grow up - you can at least say the swear words in your thoughts: *shut the fuck up!*

When he tied up my right arm it wasn't painful but there was some discomfort. My forearm bent back like that was an unusual position but it didn't hurt. Binding up my left arm – not even thinking about how he'd opened up my shirt – really made me feel helpless yet strangely also in control.

I mean, I couldn't cover my chest or strike out or anything but being put on offer, so to speak, made me so aware that the bindings lifted up my breasts and they really are the kind men love to look at and fondle. It turned me on to know the effect I was having. So despite being the one in bondage it was me that everyone looked at, ogled, admired, and fantasized about.

Everyone except Peter, that is. It felt strange to see him standing silently beside Dom who was full of praise. Peter made me feel like a specimen of some sort, like a butterfly pinned to a display-board, while he studied me with a critical yet dispassionate eye. His lack of lustful interest proves to me that he truly is no longer my boyfriend.

Speculating about whether or not he thought we were an item is just a waste of time. I was young and I believed something, now I'm older and able to figure things out better. I've gotten judgey, and Peter falls short of my expectations.

Dom, on the other hand, showed an intense interest. I could practically feel his eyes crawling all over my skin covering every inch to savor me like one of my delectable desserts. He didn't lay a finger on me, well except for his lips, but oh boy, my panties were soaked. My nipples tingled like they'd been zapped by a taser or something. Okay I know I'm exaggerating but everything that happened today was so new, so exciting, and so arousing.

Did I feel this horny when Remo unbuttoned my shirt to have a look? He touched me too, just my nipples but still... I stopped him because I had to be faithful to Peter. Or at least that's how I felt, even if I feel kind of foolish thinking that way now.

Although even if I was kidding myself over what kind of relationship I was in the real point is I *thought* I had a boyfriend and I couldn't let anyone else touch me so intimately.

But I did touch myself at the first opportunity that afternoon, and I didn't have to masturbate for long before I orgasmed while thinking of Remo. My most powerful orgasm ever, too, but maybe that will change tonight when I'm alone in my bed thinking of Dom and what happened today.

Dominic

I made Peter wait until Serafina was safely through the front door before we drove back to the city. Her little finger-wave and over-the-shoulder smile was so cute. She's a pretty, winsome, charming little girl who makes me ravenous. I need to enjoy this anticipation because so often it's way more pleasurable than the reality although I'm sure Serafina will fulfill her potential.

She's already proven herself to be a bit of a show-off, well so many girls are. They love to wield their power over men. All those strippers and starlets, influencers and models, working jobs based on their looks – faces and bodies – and how well they attract and hold the eyes of their audience. Performing, showing off, cock-teasing...

I plan to give her much more than just a taste of real humiliation and degradation, publicly shamed for her nudity, arousal, and pain. But first I'll have hours of delightful destruction while I break her and make her mine. It's important to crush her down first. That will be private, and it will be my memory alone, mine.

I remember as a young guy, maybe eleven? scrolling through the links in the search history on my mother's laptop. I was looking for evidence against her latest boyfriend, back when I still believed my opinion counted and my wishes might sway her.

I found a series of exquisitely obscene pencil drawings. Just light colored lines on a white background, but beautifully executed and vibrant with detail. Sketches showing naked girls being tortured to death.

Each image depicted a different girl and a different way to a slow dying. They were utterly horrible but equally fascinating. Such detail, from the meticulous rendering of every coir in the rope to the glint of light in the victim's running tears. The artist must have lived and dreamed through hours of inspiration and creation, pouring a very black soul into each stroke of graphite.

Pornography isn't photos of various body parts entering various holes simultaneously, in tandem, or individually. No, true pornography is violence and degradation and I revel in the victim's shame. Those drawings I saw at a tender age didn't warp me, no, they called out the darkness already lurking inside.

I long to hear Serafina's shrieks of pain, pleading cries, and desolate begging. Her agonized whimpers will make me way harder than cooing whispers of love. Like the French say *chacun à son goût,* and I can't wait to claim her.

Suddenly I'm struck by a memory of myself at thirteen, almost fourteen. In my mind's eye I can clearly see Biagio, my tutor, leaning forward with such an earnest expression on his face as he lectures me. That's the last time I saw him.

He was a huge man: tall, muscular and broad-chested. He was also gay and I was naive enough to imagine all gays were pedophiles and I could easily seduce him. Nothing was further from the truth. I tried and tried but got no reaction at all. I even remember studying my face in the mirror wondering why I didn't look beautiful to him.

Biagio was telling me goodbye, explaining it was his last day, when he became very serious and stern. He told me my blatant attempts at flirtation only cheapened me and disrespected him. He'd seen through every *accidental* touch. He mocked how I'd gazed up at him through my eyelashes while biting my bottom lip. Seeing myself through his eyes made me ashamed and I hated that feeling, hated him.

But then he lightly tapped my forehead and told me I had a powerful intellect and that was an incredible gift.

"All those tests, tasks, and assignments I gave you were measuring your IQ and gauging your aptitude for critical thinking, your ability to reason, and Dominic you're brilliant.

However, I am very concerned that this," he points to my crotch, "Will destroy any chance you have to exploit that brilliance. I think the most important lesson you need to learn now is how to control your impulses. Especially the dark ones."

I couldn't believe he even knew I had dark thoughts but... he mentioned them so obviously he did. It was too late, of course, in fact way too late, but at least he tried.

I feel a half-smile forming on my mouth as I remember my oh-so-sexy tutor. Once I take over the Ferragamo *famiglia* I'll have the resources to track him down. Seeing him again will be... interesting.

Smirking now I follow through with my plan to make Peter stop the car and switch places but I leave him standing stupidly at the side of the road while I peel rubber racing away. The look on his face is hilarious. He'll be bitchin' the whole way home but really, he should be grateful, after all he's escaped my attention for the rest of the night.

Poor Desiree with her sticky fingers is going to find it hard to steal without finger tips. Or maybe I'll leave her digits intact but break every joint and knuckle? Or scalded or skinned or nail-less? Decisions, decisions, it's like picking off a dessert menu when the truth is I want it all.

Thirteen

Antony

Serafina was in a bit of a state when she got home last night so I followed her into the kitchen, pretending I was looking for a hot bedtime drink. Just as I thought she took the opportunity to pour her heart out.

What she told me was good and bad news, the good being that she's ended things with that useless boyfriend. But she's obviously intrigued with Dominic, the way she spoke of him with her eyes sparkling and her cheeks blushing pink, and that's very bad indeed.

Dominic Ferragamo, as manager of the money-washing and drug-running nightclub, is quite high-up in Uncle Tonino's *famiglia*. A man like him should never be involved with a lovely girl like Serafina.

In addition, Dominic has serious mental health issues. I know it's fashionable to jokingly label people as *psycho* or *maniac* but in my opinion he truly is dangerously ill. Dangerous to anyone who thwarts him, and to anyone he lets get close.

My Ella saw it first, back when the boys were all very young, and she always kept a watchful eye. Talking about him with her sister did no good so she warned our sons to be careful. Since her death I've managed to keep contact between the families to a minimum but there are still occasions that my boys are expected to attend.

At this point I don't think it's wise to reveal too much to Serafina. Unfortunately the young tend to gravitate to the very things they're told to avoid. I don't want to drive her closer to Dominic. Instead,

I commiserate about the relationship that failed and let her tell me about her feelings at its ending.

"I guess, mostly I feel relief? I mean, it was always just the way it was, an understanding or something. Peter was my boyfriend and I never questioned how or why that came about. I think it must have been Marta who first told me he was. Yeah, that makes sense because I always listened to her. I mean, it's not like Peter ever made any grand gestures to sweep me off my feet or anything."

She pauses to laugh a bit but it's a sad sound and I feel so sorry for this inexperienced young girl. She isn't suffering from heartbreak but disillusionment and a feeling of loss.

"No, it was more like a situation that was just there and, especially after Dietrich threw Peter out of the house, Marta grew more and more insistent that he and I had to take care of each other. So, I'm not really unhappy and definitely not mourning the end of the relationship but I do have to adjust to not having a boyfriend anymore."

I feel a surge of resentment towards this dead Marta who burdened poor Serafina with such an obligation at a young age. But the dying are often unfair and demanding. I won't say anything, she obviously idolizes the woman.

I will tell my boys to ease up on teasing Serafina since she'll be a little fragile right now after breaking up with her boyfriend. A roundabout way of letting Remo know she's free. After all, the living can be quite manipulative too.

Serafina

I can't wait to see Antony's face when he tastes this! I think, so excited over how well this difficult dessert turned out. Too light and airy to hold its consistency until dinnertime I'm bringing it to Antony now as a mid-morning treat. *He's gonna love it.*

I'm pleased to see his office door is half-open so I can just push in with my shoulder instead of having to find a table where I can place the tray in order to knock. I wouldn't dream of holding the tray and kicking the door with my foot, that would mean Antony having to get up from his chair.

My eyes are watching my hands to make sure the dishes and cafetiere don't slip or spill so I'm halfway into the room before I realize Antony isn't alone.

"Oh I'm so sorry!" I gasp, mortified at interrupting. It's kind of an unspoken rule not to disturb men when they're at their business.

The visitor asks, "Who is *this*?" with emphasis just as Antony waves at me saying: "Come in, Serafina you must meet my uncle. And what do you have for me?" His face lights up with a greedy smile. I thought I'd detected a certain tenseness in the atmosphere when I came through the door but it's gone now.

Looking at the little monkey of a man I nod a greeting before quickly leaving, calling over my shoulder that I'm fetching another cup. I hear the men protest but I hurry and am back in less than a minute with an extra mug, plate, and dessert fork.

Antony has already cut into the fluffy concoction murmuring in appreciation. I take over from him, setting out the plates, napkins and cutlery on the table. Pouring two cups of coffee I push the sugar bowl and creamer towards Antony before removing the tray.

"I hope you like this, Antony. It's an old recipe that I've enhanced and I'm sure you'll enjoy the blend of flavors." Stepping back I watch him as he takes a bite, his eyes widening and his lips smacking with pleasure at the taste.

Then the little monkey man exclaims: "This is delicious!" drawing our attention to him.

"Uncle, my apologies! Let me introduce Serafina Liriani to you. Serafina is my new kitchen treasure, she's an absolute wizard when it comes to baking and desserts."

The old man bows his head as Antony turns to me adding: "This gentleman is my uncle, Tonino Ferragamo."

He really does have simian looks with his heavily wrinkled brown face, age-spotted bald head, and bright inquisitive eyes of nearly-black color. His ears stick out and his nose looks like it's been broken more than once but despite all that there's nothing comical about this man. In fact, I'm struck by the air of menace that surrounds him.

I can't pinpoint it exactly, but there's a stillness and a watchfulness that makes me very aware that he's registering every single thing about me. Like he has a computer in his brain that's inputting, calculating, and storing all my data. All this despite his wide smile.

I respond: "Pleased to meet you, sir," and back away towards the safety of my kitchen but I'm not allowed to escape yet.

"Liriani... Liriani. The name rings a bell, but why? Hmm, let me think a moment. What's your father's name, my dear?"

"Oh, uh, it was Pietro. He passed."

"Pietro Liriani," he pauses a moment, his expression giving no indication of his thoughts before he meets my gaze adding: "Car crash. Him and his wife. Sorry for your loss, my dear."

He knew my parents? or, at least, of them? That's odd and it makes me uncomfortable. Again I nod and lifting the tray indicate I need to get back to work.

"Yes of course, Serafina. Go back and create some more culinary magic for me. Thank you for this, it's scrumptious and I swear I'm getting a hint of Amaretto? Yes? I knew it, but there's something else I just can't quite... I'll work on it and let you know. Uncle, you'll see Serafina again at the family party."

I can't help but smile basking in the warmth of his praise. He's such a wonderful boss.

I later learn that the feeling of danger I experienced around Tonino Ferragamo was more than justified. As the head of the Mafia for this region that old man's hands were drenched in blood, death, and destruction.

Antony

After delivering my tray of *elevenses* this morning Serafina is fidgeting and I know she's got something on her mind. Lifting my coffee cup I gesture towards one of my visitor chairs and tell her to sit down and talk.

"Well, it's a bit awkward because it's none of my business but... well yesterday I met your Uncle Tonino and..."

"And he's a bit scary?"

"Yes! I mean, he's elderly and looks kinda frail but there's a, hmm, how to explain? a power or strength or something that just comes off him."

"That's very perceptive of you, Serafina. Uncle Tonino, my late wife's uncle actually, is a very powerful man and, I'm afraid, not a very nice one."

Her voice drops to a whisper when she asks: "Is he in the Mafia?"

I only hesitate a moment before answering truthfully *Yes*. It's best that she knows exactly what's what for her protection and ours

"We don't actually mention it, though. And, in case you're wondering, I'm definitely not in the *famiglia* and neither are my brothers or sons or nephews. Well, not the nephew's who live here, the ones on my side of the family. Dominic, well, he's a Ferragamo so..."

Her pretty face is frowning while she thinks through the implications of what I've said. There's no need for me to further explain that Tonino Ferragamo is the Don for a vast area, his control is unchallenged – despite his age – and his viciousness is legendary. I'm not part of his world except when he wants a favor, like hosting a get-together at my home. I can't refuse him and in all fairness he's never given me any reason to want to do so.

Still wearing a slightly puzzled expression and speaking tentatively Serafina asks: "Since you're not in the mafia why did he let you marry his niece?"

This is one of my favorite stories so I smile hugely when I answer: "Because she was such a slut."

Serafina's eyes and mouth form wide O shapes as she loudly cries: "WHAT?"

Just then Remo comes in the room and sensing the excited atmosphere between us asks: "What's going on?"

Serafina turns bright scarlet and that makes me laugh with delight when I reply: "Serafina just asked how your mama and I got together–"

"Oh no wonder you're in such good spirits!" Turning to her he explains: "This is Dad's favorite story to tell and I always love hearing it, too."

He helps himself to one of the saucer-sized cookies from the tray and pulls up the other visitor chair. Serafina is completely baffled by our reactions.

"Elenora, Lenora to her family but Ella to me, had a terrible reputation. Her father was killed when she and her sister were just girls and since her mother couldn't cope with such headstrong children they ran wild. But my Ella was the worst!

By time she started high-school she was already staying out all night, riding on the backs of motorcycles, and skipping classes. She got expelled and never graduated, instead she got a job at a barber shop. Not even a hairdressers. She dyed her hair and facilitated the drug-dealing that happened out of the backroom.

Although she was picked up by the cops several times no charges ever stuck once her uncle made a few phone calls. Her behavior didn't exactly endear her to Uncle Tonino, though. She told me he took his belt to her on the last occasion so she was very careful not to get in trouble with the police again.

"I don't think I knew that detail, Dad."

"Probably not, she hated remembering that beating. I gather it was quite an ordeal. However she did shame him and the family name and, as we both know, he could have solved the problem by killing her. Instead, he let her marry me.

I met my Ella at a wedding my cousin took me to. I don't remember whose wedding but you know how it is with us Italians: everyone's welcome to bring guests.

I was a good-looking guy, if I say so myself, and I could dance. Something many of the other young men couldn't, or wouldn't, do. Oh, they could managed the disco tunes – this was a few decades ago! – but they couldn't waltz, samba, or foxtrot. Ella loved to dance and she had great rhythm. It only took a few steps for her to pick up a new dance.

That night, at that wedding, we danced until we were both so hot and sweaty we collapsed into chairs to drink and laugh before dancing some more. I held her in my arms and knew I never wanted to let her go.

At some point my cousin pulled me aside to tell me I was making a spectacle of myself because everyone knew about Lenora Ferragamo. She'd been with lots of guys, she was a tramp, and I should keep my distance."

"Oh no!"

Remo leans over and takes hold of her hand, comforting her by saying: "Don't worry, Fina. Dad punched him in the mouth!"

"Really?"

"Really and truly. Cosmo was so angry with me. I'd hit him hard enough to split his lip and I can still see him with blood running down his chin as he spit curses at me. We caused quite a scene but fortunately the bride and groom had already left the reception so it was just the die-hards left. The same ones who are always so full of gossip.

I could see them casting sideways looks at Ella and hear nasty comments so I challenged the room, daring anyone who had anything to say against her to say it to my face. Such a tough guy I was, eh Serafina?"

I stop there and I'm sure my eyes are twinkling because Serafina is completely swept up in the story, a story I love to tell. I notice she hasn't pulled her hand out of Remo's hold and that's something I particularly like to see.

"And did anyone say anything?"

"Her Uncle Tonino had been sitting at a table smoking cigars with a group of older men. He waved me over and even I knew who he was so of course I went. Ella insisted on tagging along too. As we drew closer I grabbed hold of her hand and she squeezed back so tight. I was determined to protect her.

Uncle Tonino asked me my name, where I came from, and what type of work I did. After I answered his questions he thought for a bit, nodded, then announced I had his blessing. All the people muttering behind their hands quickly shut up and I felt like I'd won the lottery when I turned to see Ella's eyes shining with happy tears. I wanted to kiss her so badly but no way would I push my luck that far!"

I chuckle at the memory and then sigh with pleasure as I recollect the rest of that evening. How we continued dancing until the band packed up for the night. I was determined to take Ella home but realized I'd come in my cousin's car so I had to call a taxi although I assured her I did have a car of my own. Nothing fazed her, she just kept smiling and smiling, everything was good, great, wonderful."

My mind is still living in that time forty-plus years ago and I hear Remo pick up the tale. It's a story he's heard so many times over the years.

"Mama and Dad got married quietly in a Registry office. She'd basically been kicked out of the Church and didn't have any close girlfriends. Nobody wanted their daughter tainted by association with her, her reputation really was that bad."

"I didn't care. My own parents were doubtful, they'd heard some of the stories, but witnessing the two of us together made them change their minds. They both fell in love with Ella and attended the wedding along with her mother and uncle. A wedding that happened after hardly any dating at all. We both knew that first night that we were meant for each other.

Uncle Tonino's wedding present was enough cash to make the downpayment on a house. I was flabbergasted, but Ella explained he was paying me off for providing a respectable marriage. I couldn't have cared less about that. She was my Ella and I loved her so deeply."

"Oh, that's such a sweet story," sighs Serafina.

"I haven't told you the best part," I say, smiling in anticipation of her reaction: "My Ella was still a virgin. She'd never even fooled around."

Now Serafina's mouth falls open in shocked surprise: "Really?"

Remo laughs as he picks up the story as his mother told it to him: "Mama said she was afraid Dad would be disappointed so she tried to pretend she was just as experienced as he'd imagined but she couldn't stop gawking and gasping as she put it."

"She could kiss, but once I started to caress I felt her trembling and at first I thought it was just love and lust but soon realized she hadn't a clue. It was all so sweet and I felt so... tender, I guess, towards her. So I went along with it, pretending I was fooled, but she knew I wasn't and called me out on it.

When I asked why she didn't correct the people who called her awful things you know what she told me? She said *To hell with them, I don't owe anybody an explanation and they can believe whatever they want.* And she was absolutely right.

She was strong-minded and strong-willed, matched with a deeply caring heart. I'm making her sound perfect and of course she wasn't but my Ella was the only woman for me."

"Oh Antony that's such a wonderful story. Thank you for telling me."

Serafina's face shows her emotion, she has a tender heart. This girl is a real find.

"Thank you, Serafina, for reminding me. Now scoot, I need to talk to Remo."

She has to tug on her hand to get him to release it but they're both smiling at each other the whole time. It takes Remo and I about forty-five minutes to finish up our business and then he leaves me to return to my memories of my Ella...

Despite her struggling to hold it in a gasp of pain escapes Ella when I push through the tight membrane. I'm right, she is a virgin. I have to push through quickly, like ripping off a band-aid, so she can start to relax and hopefully enjoy. No, I'll make sure she definitely enjoys this.

It's funny now to remember I was worried about not measuring up to her other lovers since I wasn't all that experienced myself. But I was determined that this lovely and wonderful woman will not leave this bed until she's wrung out from orgasms and pleasure. I just want to kiss and nibble, caress and massage, stroke slowly and deep, pound fast and hard, I want to give her every fantastic sensation. I can't believe my luck in having Ella as my wife.

She runs her fingers across my chest and tweaks my nipple, rubbing it between her forefinger and thumb. I laugh at her expression when she catches on that I'm mimicking every move she makes. Once she does she leans in and sucks my nipple into her smiling mouth. Of course I do the same but Ella's nipples are far more sensitive then mine and she soon abandons toying with me in order to give full access to both of her lovely breasts with their erect nipples. I can almost cover one breast with one hand so I straddle her and use both hands to massage both. I rub just my palms across her hard nubs and she lifts her chest up to push into my hands, craving more. When I bend to kiss and suckle first one nipple and then the next I slip my hands around her throat and grasp firmly while my mouth is busy moving back and forth. Pinning her in place while I take my time to play has her pleading to feel me inside her again.

Our honeymoon only lasted a long weekend, spent in a cabin by the lake, but despite the beautiful scenery we hardly got out the door. Huh, we hardly got out of the bed!

Ella learned quickly and I got an education, too, since she wasn't shy about telling me to do something again or to rub faster or push harder. I never wanted to go down on a woman before so Ella was my first taste of pussy – I felt so worldly and adventurous! and she was so sweet and delicious. She learned to suck my cock deep into her throat and the sight of her mouth stretched wide around me is a picture I cherish. I never wanted to try another woman.

We could say anything and tell each other everything. Together we explored our passionate natures. It was so much fun to have her play with me, exploring my cock and my balls, to see her looking up at me with her big brown eyes sparkling with mischief... But while we both enjoyed that I only let her take charge for awhile before firmly holding her in the position I chose. We were both turned on by the way she squirmed and struggled. My Ella was quite the little actress playing coy or timid, shy or tough.

After all these years I miss her so much it still hurts but I'm thankful I got to have her in my life. I hope each of my sons can find the same love I felt with their mother.

Fourteen

Dietrich

I'm a big man and I never hesitate to use my size to intimidate. Truth is, I rarely hesitate ever. That gets me in trouble sometimes, and the whole Fina thing is a perfect example. I couldn't help it though, when Gigi showed me that altered check I just saw red. Once I lose my temper there's no reasoning with me. It's a failing, I know, but I'm not about to go to Anger Management classes or anything.

At work I'm always in Boss mode. Sure, I let the staff call me by my first name and we have Casual Fridays in the office but that's where all familiarity ends. So when it looked like an employee had altered a check, and made a really poor job of it, too, I didn't care that Fina had lived in my home as an adopted daughter for more than a dozen years. All I saw was the deception of someone trying to cheat me; and the ingratitude of someone I paid a salary to every week.

I completely lost it. God knows what I actually said, all I remember is that I said it at the top of my lungs. I recall shouting and ranting as I followed the poor girl being led by Security out the front door.

Because I'm *strictly business* employees don't drop by my office for cozy chats so I never get told gossip – but I do overhear it. And I heard the whispers about how impossible it was to believe that Fina would do something like that yet how easy to imagine Gigi doing such a thing.

Once I calmed down I realized Fina wasn't a stupid girl so why would she choose such a stupid method? and, if she really did need a thousand dollars, why wouldn't she just ask me for it? I'd want to know why, and there's no guarantee I'd say *yes,* but surely that would be the first place to start?

After having lived most of her life under my roof she'd certainly know my feelings on trust, responsibility, and thievery.

Not only that but Fina proved herself to be a valued family member, more so than my son, when she nursed my first wife Marta through her final bout with cancer.

Thinking of Peter, my son, made me wonder if he was behind this since stealing from me would be nothing new to him. But again, Fina would ask me for the money first even if it meant lying to cover up for Peter.

These thoughts about what Fina would and wouldn't do led me to thoughts of Gigi, my second wife, of whom I know there's very little she won't do.

I married Gigi for the sake of my cock, she married me for my money.

Her looks are exactly my type: a slender blonde with long legs, narrow hips, nice tits – even if they are fake, and a pretty face – even if her lines have been filled with Botox, her eyebrows tattooed, and her lips plumped with filler. She's a high-maintenance gal from the tips of her ridiculously long bejeweled nails to the diamond stud in her front tooth. Spa days, lunch dates with her girlfriends, outrageous spending on clothes, but a waxed and willing pussy whenever I want it.

If she'd been younger she could have held out for a wealthier man but the silly girl married her high-school sweetheart and it took her ten years to dump him. I got her in the end and since I devote a lot of time to Gigi's orgasms we both enjoy fucking each other.

For a while there I suspected Gigi as having an affair but luckily, for her sake, it turns out she was only acting guilty because of this nonsense with the poorly forged check. Gigi did that because Fina saw the new salesman give my wife a kiss.

I knew she'd be relieved to get the truth out in the open, no more hiding, and I was proven right when she quickly crumbled at my accusation. I called her into my office to confront her with my suspicions. I have no problem humiliating my wife but only for my private entertainment. No doubt the staff were all whispering their gossip regardless.

Now I have to apologize to Fina and get her back home, and I have to punish Gigi. I'm quite looking forward to that. Her pretty hairless cunt has given her way too much confidence and it's past time for her to be humbled. By me. Tonight.

I do miss having Fina at home cooking our dinner each night. The girl has always been handy in a kitchen whereas Gigi struggles with the simplest meals. I've told her we're foregoing dinner in favor of dealing with her bad behavior.

"Specifically, your lies about seeing Fina alter the check and then finding it's hiding place. Your punishment for lying is to have your mouth washed out with soap."

"Dietrich, no! You can't do that to me—"

"It's happening. Secondly, your manipulation of the check means your hands need to be punished. Using my belt I'll strap your palms six times."

"No way, I'm your wife I'm not a schoolgirl—"

"Yes, you are my wife, totally dependent on me and subject to my rules and my discipline. And, since you're behaving like a naughty child your punishment will also include some time spent standing in the corner reflecting on what you've done."

"I won't!" Gigi's actually stamping her foot and proving what a spoiled child she is. Doesn't she realize how dangerous my anger is to her well-being?

I grab hold of her chin and squeezing her lips I tight hiss at her: "Oh yes, you will."

When I let her go she pouts and I can see a thought running across her brain like she's broadcasting it. Her mouth twitches into a smirk and her eyes glint with calculation. She's decided she'll seduce me to get out of her punishment. I love how transparent she can be.

Poor girl has no idea how I've been longing to punish her, how much I enjoy it. I've held myself back because I know I went too far with my first wife. Thinking about my lovely blonde Marta causes a pang of loss. If I could go back in time I would treat her better than I did. We were both young and I didn't have the same self-control I do now.

When the business had growing pains and we were struggling I often took out my fear and temper on her. It relieved the pressure but... huh, I'm having a flashback to an angry little girl with a frown on her face and her hands on her hips telling me to *stop hitting her!* meaning Marta.

Little Serafina was quite a fierce defender, doing more than Peter ever did. Of course I didn't stop and Serafina didn't go unscathed either, but she only got a shaking, my fists were for my own flesh and blood.

"Prepare for your punishment by getting naked, Gigi. Everything off." I half-expect her to coo an *ooooh!* a la Marilyn Monroe at me. She strips with sexy moves, shaking her shoulders to drop her bra straps down her arms which makes her tits sway. I let her see that I appreciate every movement. Once she's buck naked I order her into the bathroom and to get there on her hands and knees.

Her eyes widen at my command but she quickly drops to all fours and begins to crawl in a very enticing manner, rolling her hips and stretching her whole body. In the bathroom I order her to kneel and she's quick to obey with her mouth already half open, expecting to service my cock. Instead I insert a large chunk of soap and then hold her lips shut so she can't spit it out. Her whole body convulses in revulsion and she tries to stand up but I easily hold her in place.

"Just hold that soap right there on your tongue, covering your tastebuds, coating all over the inside of your mouth," I instruct while she makes angry and anxious sounds. Her face gets red and her eyes tear up which makes her nose run. Drops of mascara start beading around her eyes as she blinks furiously. When her nose is snotty enough to impede her breathing I haul her up to the sink and gasping for air she spits the soap out and starts cursing me through her sobs. I fill up the drinking cup and tell her to rinse. She knocks it from my hand and sticks her mouth right under the tap. She's a beautiful mess of red-faced crying and spitting. Not feeling very seductive now I'll wager.

Still keeping her in the bathroom I slip my belt through the loops and doubling it up take hold of her hands and place them side-by-side palm up. Stepping back so I can get a good enough swing to strike both at once I bring the belt down.

"OWWW, that hurts!" she screams at me.

All I say is: "That's one. Put your hands back in position."

"No, I won't."

"You're getting six swats, Gigi. If you want me to start the count all over again I'm perfectly happy to do so. The choice is yours."

She peers into my eyes trying to figure me out. When she's convinced of my intentions she reluctantly lifts her hands towards me. I make a minor adjustment and then swing the leather down and again she yelps but doesn't pull her hands away so I strap her again.

"Halfway through," I announce and see her looking at her red palms. Her fingers have curled and I straighten them out, warning her not to make a fist because the belt can inadvertently do real damage with a mis-hit.

After the fourth strike her whole body is shaking with her sobs and I marvel at how weak she is. How pampered her life is. I deliver blow number five and she pulls her hands behind her back and shaking her head at me keeps saying *no more, no more, no more* but of course there is that final stroke to administer. I wait about fifteen seconds then ask if she wants me to start the count at one again. With her eyes screwed shut she holds out her hands and I smack as hard as I can and predictably she shrieks out a loud *fuuuuuccckk*. For a moment I toy with the idea of washing her mouth out again.

"Go back into the bedroom and stand in the corner beside the armoire with your nose to the wall."

Although her eyes are awash with tears she still manages to throw a look of reproach my way and I have to hide my grin. *Not so proud now, are you Gigi?* I think to myself.

She stands as I told her but for a greater psychological impact I have to correct her stance. I nudge her further away from the wall which arcs her lower back and thrusts her ass out. Then I place both of her hands flat on the wall. She flinches at the contact with her raw palms.

No doubt she can't understand how I'm immune to her charms. Actually I'm not but I'm saving up my pleasure for bedtime. Gigi's always a willing partner, up for anything. It's good to make her wait.

"You stay like that, thinking about all the harm you caused and the mess you're given me to clean up, until you're ready to give me a heartfelt apology."

"I'm ready now," she insists but I just laugh saying I'll have a seat and smoke a cigar while I contemplate the sight of her nude body. I'm pleased to hear her quick intake of breath. Sitting down in the armchair I do light a cigar although I don't smoke in the bedroom as a rule. However, this is an exceptional circumstance. Gigi's a beautiful and passionate woman and I'm lucky to have her in my bed each night, pleasing me in every way.

This is what I'm thinking as my eyes enjoy her nakedness but not even five minutes later I see she's having trouble staying still. She's pressing her thighs together and that's making her pretty behind quiver. When I see the muscles in her bum move I know she's trying to rub her clit.

"Oh Gigi, Gigi, tsk-tsk. You can't possibly be thinking thoughts of contrition when you're trying to pleasure yourself. I had hoped that your physical punishment was over but obviously I was too soft on you."

"What?" she spins round and questions me with wide-eyed alarm. Feigning regret I stub out my cigar and standing I lead her over to the bed and push her face down, her hips over the edge and her long legs sprawled across the carpet. I've still got my belt in hand so I hold her down and lay a stripe across her bottom. She shrieks and I quickly strike again, this time on her upper thigh. Several more swats and

Gigi is struggling so hard I have to pin her with my knee on her lower back and my hand gripping the back of her neck.

I keep spanking her with the belt until my cock feels like it'll explode and then I pull her legs apart and freeing myself quickly I push into her very wet cunt. With one hand still holding her down my her neck I use the other to pinch and rub her clit until she's writhing with pleasure. My balls tighten and I let loose just as Gigi orgasms, our voices harmonizing in hoarse shouts.

"I've never punished you before, Gigi, but you deserved that. I let your little indiscretion slide and I think that might have been a mistake."

"Oh Dietrich I am sorry, so sorry for all the trouble I caused, but you know I was only thinking of us. I really did it for you, I didn't want you to get the wrong idea over just a kiss."

She gives a hiccuping cry and I kiss her face and soothe her saying: "I know baby, I know. I believe that's what you thought. Huh, if I thought you'd ever let another man do more than just kiss you I'd... well, I'd beat you until you broke."

She shudders violently and I'm sure she's enjoying an orgasmic aftershock.

Fifteen

Serafina

I came up to my room to use the toilet and seeing my phone blinking on my dresser realized I'd left it behind again. I'm not used to owning a cellphone and keep forgetting to carry it around with me.

I remember to charge it because I use it to set my alarm each night and that reminds me. Not that I'm using much battery power, I don't get any calls. Until now.

Although I'm curious I need to get back to my kitchen first because I've got chocolate melting in the double-boiler. Once I get that off the heat and poured into the molds I turn my attention back to my phone. There's no reason I can't carry it around with me, all of my oversized shirts have two smock pockets.

Leo helped me set up my outgoing message and I know how to retrieve my messages. I dial, enter a passcode, and learn I have one new message.

"Hey Fina, it's Sherry. Are you there? If you're there pick-up, it's Sherry. Sherry from the coffee shop. Okay well I guess you're not answering right now. Anyhow, Dietrich Stutt your ex-boss and ex-family-whatever came by and wanted to get in touch with you. He's really bossy, you know. Insisted I give him your phone number and when I said *no* he told me to call you right away but it was busy and I didn't want to call you with him hanging around. Figured he'd grab my phone outta my hand. Anyhooo I waited him out.

But first I gave him a piece of my mind and I told him that, too. I said *I'm giving you a piece of my mind because you treated poor Fina like she was scum*, and then he goes *oh no, it was all a misunderstanding* and now he has to talk to you to make it right. You know, over the years I've heard his employees talking about him and boy, they weren't exaggerating. The guy's a prick.

Anyhooo, I guess that's that. So call him. And say hi to that cutie Antony for me. Tell him there's always a free espresso waiting for him here. Hey, your machine hasn't cut out yet.. but I don't have anything else to say. Take care of yourself, kiddo and let me know what happens with that Dietrich character. Buh-Bye. It's Sherry, by the way. Bye."

I'm in stitches by time I finish listening to the message. Oh I have to share it with Antony, he'll get a laugh too. Sherry's such a sweetie and I can just picture her cracking her chewing gum in Dietrich's face. That would be priceless!

I'd better find Antony now so I can talk to him and get his advice about Dietrich. I actually don't want to phone him but if I don't he'll harass Sherry, so I better call.

Checking that everything's under control in the kitchen I see that I'm covered for the next forty minutes, plenty of time to head upstairs to Antony's office. The door's ajar so I knock and enter. He smiles when he sees me but gets a disappointed look on his face when he realizes I'm empty-handed.

"Oh Antony, I'm in such a tizzy I forgot to bring you a snack."

"That's no problem Serafina, what are you in a tizzy about?"

"Well, I got a call, a message actually and– hey, we can have this conversation in the kitchen. I've got red velvet cupcakes..."

"You've got a deal!" he's grinning now as he jumps up to follow me.

Once we're settled in the kitchen with coffees and cupcakes I tell him about getting Sherry's message.

"You have to hear it, it's hilarious, but I think I better come clean and give you a bit of background about me and how I came to be here first."

"Serafina you don't have to tell me anything you don't want."

"Oh Antony, you're such a great boss and such a nice man. No, it's time. I did nothing wrong and have nothing to be ashamed of.

The day I came here you saved my life, seriously.

I went into work that morning, my job was in the accounting department at Stutt Manufacturing, and everything was normal until Dietrich Stutt called me into his office and presented this check that had so obviously been altered it was laughable. It was made out to me for Petty Cash and an extra thousand dollars had been added to the written amount.

So he fired me, without even giving me a chance to ask any questions like *where did this check come from? who found it?* He just had Security escort me out of the building, marching me right through the whole office with him following and yelling at me in front of everyone."

"Serafina! what an awful experience for you. I don't think much of your Mr. Stutt," Antony is indignant on my behalf.

"And what made it even worse is we lived in the same house. See my parents died and I went to live with Marta and Dietrich, their best friends and Dad's business partner. So I lived there most of my life and now that I was fired I no longer had a home either."

Antony is tut-tutting and he's reached over to take hold of my hand. Mrs. Finch comes in but stops when she sees us. Antony waves her into a chair saying:

"Sit, sit Irene, you'll be wanting a chance to get off your feet. Serafina's just telling me about her previous boss, an awful man."

I jump up to fetch Mrs. Finch a coffee and bring another plate so she can help herself to a cupcake. She nods her thanks but, as usual, has nothing to say.

"So, you don't have a job and you've been thrown out of your home. My God. What then?"

"Then it was Sherry from the coffee shop to the rescue. I didn't know where to turn but I needed a pick-me-up and thought of her. Also, I knew I could get Wi-Fi there because I needed to get online and start job hunting.

Sherry listened to my story and helped me out and I ended up at the Home Sweet Home employment agency and then here. That's why I said you were a life-saver! Anyhow, that's the story up-to-date now you've got to hear this phone message from Sherry."

I key up the message and place my phone on the table between the three of us.

Antony interrupts at the beginning, "Pick up? Oh she thinks she's talking into an answering machine!" and later when she mentions him he blushes and smiles.

"So now I have to call Dietrich because if I don't he'll just pester Sherry but I don't know what to say to him. What do you think I should do?"

"Sounds like your friend is capable of putting that one in his place all by herself," comments Mrs. Finch which surprises both Antony and me. He asks me to play the message again and he listens to it carefully. After thinking for a minute he says:

"Serafina, I think you should call this man and invite him to come here for a meeting with me. We'll meet him together. I don't think you should be alone with him because I suspect he's up to something."

"Like what?"

"I really don't know I just have a sneaking suspicion... what Leo calls my *spidey sense* and for some reason I think money's involved. I also think that if you tell him everything that's happened since he kicked you out he'll act all worried about your safety out here and that's why I want you to invite him to meet us and see you in your new home."

"Oh I would really like that, Antony. Thank you."

"Call him now, the sooner we get this dealt with the better."

I have the phone number of Stutt Manufacturing memorized. Having to remember numbers is one of the benefits of never owning a cellphone, I guess. I dial and click the speaker setting on.

I'm surprised when Melanie answers but it turns out she's covering the reception desk while Annie has a meeting with HR. I ask to speak to Dietrich and when she hesitates I smooth over the awkwardness by saying I got a message to call him.

After waiting long enough to wonder if I've been disconnected Dietrich's voice booms at me: "Serafina! Thank God, we've been worried sick." Startled, I stare at Antony but his face is expressionless as he listens to the call.

Antony

I've taken an immediate dislike to this Dietrich Stutt. First off learning how he treated Serafina, putting her in danger the way he did, and then hearing his smarmy voice. I'm flattered she's asked me to be present at their meeting. Not that I'd have stayed away but this way we present a united front.

He told her he wanted her back where she belongs – in her home and at her desk in the office – and he has something important to relate her which will help her understand why.

"Serafina, do you think Dietrich wants to make a match between you and his son Peter? Your ex-boyfriend?"

"Oh I don't think so, Antony." She really does look doubtful as she says this. "Dietrich threw Peter out of the house years ago and has never shown any interest in him or his well-being."

"But he's getting older now and with his wife gone, and the two children grown up and gone, maybe he's changed his mind?"

"Oh Dietrich isn't alone! No, that Gigi I mentioned? she's his new young wife. Antony, I'm going to confess something – not something I did but something I know – and that will help explain things.

One day at the office I was moving old files to the storeroom in the sub-basement. It's a dusty and dark place where no one goes. My arms were full and I was concentrating on not dropping anything when I opened the door and walked right into the room before I saw them.

Gigi was half-naked and... well in a... well, a sex act with our salesman Andre. All the women in the office thought he was really something to look at. I had no idea he and Gigi were meeting secretly. I don't know if that was the only time or if they were actually having an affair. Anyhow, they saw me. They didn't speak to me directly and I was just trying to work up the courage to let Gigi know her secret was safe with me–"

"You wouldn't have said anything to Dietrich?" I probe, interested in her reaction.

She sighs deeply before continuing: "First of all I'm terrified of Dietrich. He's one of these big men with a big voice and just a *commanding* presence. I would never voluntarily stir up his anger!

I know I live – lived - under his roof but I don't feel I owe him anything. I've always worked around the house for my keep, cooking dinner every night, and I do a good job at the office. He's not a man who inspires loyalty or devotion. I mean, it's not up to me to protect Gigi but, well maybe I'm optimistic but I think bad behavior does eventually catch up with people."

"Meaning karma will – or won't – take care of Gigi and it's nothing to you either way?"

"Yes! exactly that. She's a grown-up making her own decisions and it's not my job to tell her what to do. That would be presumptuous. And, maybe, I feel Dietrich was asking for trouble when he chose Gigi as his bride. He keeps himself in shape but he's older than her by decades. She's a few years older than me but she gets all the treatments for fake everything: hair, skin, lips, boobs, tummy... you name it. His first wife, Marta, was a real lady. I'll always be grateful to her, and I miss her all the time."

"So what do you imagine this compelling reason is all about?"

"I can't think! In the past Dietrich's been able to make me feel guilty about them taking me in – the poor orphaned daughter of his business partner – but I took care of Marta for a long time, instead of finishing school even, so any debt to him has been paid. I feel differently about her."

"Well this should turn out to be an interesting meeting, then. I suspect money is involved and I'm further going to speculate that it's money that Dietrich and Gigi don't want to give up. If they still have it, that is."

"Oooh that sounds ominous!"

She's laughing at me and that's okay, in fact it's more than okay because Serafina smiling and laughing is a delightful sight.

"You know, I did get a small legacy from Marta, it was so kind of her to remember me."

"Then you'll have a bit of money to fall back on when we get your schooling sorted out–"

"Oh no, the money's long gone. Peter... well, he got left out and as he pointed out I'm not blood or anything, so..."

"So he wormed your legacy out of you?"

"Gee, when you put it like that it makes me feel stupid."

"Oh no, my dear. You just have a kind heart that's easily manipulated. You need to find a man who will protect from all those sharks out there and I'm confident you will."

"It's a funny thing, you know. Because I always thought Peter was my boyfriend I never really looked at anyone before and now..."

"Now?"

Her laughter bubbles forth as she says: "Now I'm living in a house full of hotties!" and I can't help but join in. My mind immediately goes to Serafina and Remo. For a while I thought he and Shelby were... but she hasn't been around for quite some time now now... hmmm. I'd much rather see him with Serafina.

Dietrich Stutt is coming to the house at ten tomorrow morning. He seemed to be in two minds about whether or not bring this Gigi with him. I'm betting myself that he won't, he'll prefer to keep the spotlight on Serafina and this Gigi sounds like a woman who always wants to take center stage.

I'm determined that he won't browbeat or guilt-trip Serafina into doing anything she doesn't want to do. I believe her when she says living here os the happiest she's been as far back as she can remember. I'll see to it that she gets to stay.

There's a knock at the door and Remo comes in but halts when he sees us saying *sorry! I didn't mean to disturb you* but I wave him in. He's always friendly with Serafina but in a distant, polite sort of way. I bring him up to date on tomorrow's scheduled visit, advising:

"Serafina's ex-boss is going to try to spirit her away but we'll do our best to hang on to her."

"Do you want me to be here?" he asks me the question but is glancing at her to gauge her reaction. She looks hopeful but I quash that.

"No, thank you son but I don't want to overwhelm the man. Plus, he strikes me as the type – from what Serafina's told me and how he sounded over the phone – he won't easily accept losing and I think the less of an audience to that the better."

Remo nods that what I say makes sense but suggests that maybe he could be near the front door about 11:00 to try and get a look at this guy.

"I mean, he threw Serafina out of her job and home without the slightest regard to what a young, innocent girl would do out on the street on her own!"

I look at Serafina telling her to remember that when Dietrich Stutt tries to turn on the charm or the guilt.

Serafina

It's so strange to see Dietrich here in Antony's study. I've only just now realized that we never went anywhere, not as a family, because our home, the office, and Marta's funeral were the only places I ever saw him. Even his wedding with Gigi happened in our backyard.

He seems somehow... diminished. Now his loud commanding voice sounds bombastic and listen to me – it's like I'm pulling my words from all the Gothic novels I've ever read. I guess it's just because this all feels so strange and different.

I wasn't sure if Gigi would accompany Dietrich but I'm glad she didn't. Her presence would somehow taint this environment. This is mine and I couldn't bear to see her walking through the rooms with her eyes toting everything up like a cashier.

It's just the three of us in Antony's study and he's the only one who is calm. I served up plates of sweet treats and poured coffee and now I'm fidgeting, crumpling my napkin, and dabbing up crumbs from my plate.

After exclaiming over how he's missed my baking Dietrich has balanced his plate on the arm of the chair and has his hands wrapped around the china mug, alternately blowing on then sipping his coffee.

Antony has just begun speaking when Giorgio saunters in without knocking or anything. Antony speaks sharply before standing to usher his brother out of the room explaining he's having a confidential meeting.

Grabbing this opportunity to speak privately with me Dietrich leans in close and asks if I'm really okay here.

And right then all my nervousness vanishes and I reply with assurance: "I am, Dietrich. I feel very fortunate to have ended up here with the Cirellis. They've all been very good to me and I'm doing well."

His mouth twists as if he's gotten a bad taste but Antony returns before he can say anything further.

"My apologies, Mr Stutt–"

"Oh Dietrich, please."

"Thank you, Dietrich, I didn't introduce you to my brother or he'd never have left us alone. Now, you wanted to visit Serafina in her new home to reassure yourself that she's being looked after," he pauses for a reply.

"Yes, that's true and you have a very, very nice home. Fina tells me she's doing well here."

"She is indeed. Serafina is a real find for a foodie such as me." He directs a warm smile and a wink my way then turns back to Dietrich asking: "But there's another reason you wanted to meet, isn't there?"

"Ah, well yes I did want to have a word but it's really a business matter..." he trails off but Antony doesn't take the bait, he simply tilts his head with an interested expression and waits until Dietrich is forced to continue: "Well, a family business matter. I don't know how much you know?"

"Assume I know nothing," Antony replies.

"Ah, well, hmm. I guess, ah, in a sense you are an interested party. Interested in Fina's welfare and, well her uh future." Dietrich comes to a stop, unsure how to continue. Finally he takes a deep breath and comes right out with an amazing statement.

"Fina you know your father and I were business partners but what you don't know is that arrangement didn't end with his death. His shares, mine as well, were held for our family with a partnership agreement governing the running of the business."

I'm sure I look absolutely blank because he hastens to explain further: "You have money, in shares in the company, that you can sell at the end of your twenty-first year. That's this year. You don't have to sell, you can keep the money invested in the family firm, but if you do sell I get the first option."

"Subject to a third party evaluation, I imagine?" asks Antony.

His tone is mild but Dietrich immediately puffs up as if offended saying: "Absolutely. And every penny will be paid promptly."

"I'm sure the company has flourished under your stewardship, sir."

Dietrich preens a little at the compliment and I'm certain that he has done his best for the company, and consequently me, and that everything will be aboveboard. He is a successful businessman whose only lapse in judgement has been his choice of bride in his second marriage.

"So, Fina, if you are planning a wedding or to purchase a home then you'll probably want to realize the value of your shares but otherwise, of course it's entirely your choice, you can keep them in the company and your investment will continue to grow."

"Thank you for taking care of this for me, Dietrich. At the moment I'm not planning a wedding or moving but–" I catch a slight movement of Antony's head, "But I would like an assessment – is that the right word? so I can make some decisions about my future. This is actually wonderful news. I barely remember my parents but to know that they set up this legacy for me is... well, I think I'm going to cry but it's happy crying." And at that I burst into tears.

Both men begin fussing over me when there's a knock at the door and Remo's poking his head in to see if we need anything. I quickly wipe my face, I don't want him to see me in a state, but his frown shows his concern.

"Remo, come in son. Meet Dietrich Stutt, Serafina's adoptive parent and ex-employer. He's brought her good news."

I'm able to get my emotions under control and watch as the three of them, each one a businessman, handle the introductions with equanimity.

I'm so relieved everything has gone smoothly and I'm so glad Antony insisted on being present because if he hadn't been here with me I suspect Dietrich would have had me committing my shares to the company for years to come.

Sixteen

Serafina

Dietrich was invited to stay for lunch but he declined. I'm sure the meeting didn't go exactly as he'd planned but all is well from everyone's point of view.

I let Dietrich know that I'm confident he's handled my shares and account honestly and fairly but it doesn't hurt that Antony has requested a copy of the financial audit to review. Regardless, I plan to remove my money because if anything happened to Dietrich and Gigi or Peter ended up with control well... I can only imagine!

Besides, I have plans. More like daydreams but who knows? a lot depends on exactly how much money there is but... I've always dreamed of owning my own patisserie. There are already plenty of coffee shops and also fresh bread bakeries so I would offer just fancy desserts.

I guess I could put in one coffee machine for people who insist, but the goal is specialty sweets. A daily selection and then a made-to-order menu to choose from. Or maybe just the menu, no storefront, and I'd sell my services to catering firms? It's always been fun to plan and prepare and now... maybe that can someday become my reality?

It's amazing what a difference it makes to have money.

Even if it turns out there's only enough to pay for my education that's a start. Stutt Manufacturing does a lot of business and has a lot of employees but that doesn't mean the profit margins are high. It could be that every extra penny gets reinvested back into the company. I'll just have to wait and see.

Meanwhile I'll start with Leo to see if he can set up my laptop with everything I need to get my GED.

Leo

Time has been starting to drag, not that I miss school! but I'm glad Fina came to me. I feel good about being able to help her out.

She dropped out of high-school and wants to complete her diploma online but I was able to pinpoint what her goals are and give her some better ideas.

I was sitting in the den re-watching an action movie when she came in with her laptop and explained she wanted to study for her GED.

"Why do you want that?"

"To get a job, every place expects you to have your high-school diploma at least."

"Yeah, at least. I mean, a diploma is pretty much nothing nowadays, you need way more than a GED."

"But I have to start somewhere, right?"

"Not really, I mean you've already got a job. You can keep working for a bit and then enroll for something better as a mature student."

She stops to think about this and I can see the idea is totally new to her.

"I never really gave this much thought," she says, "I just always figured I had to have the GED."

"If you stop working here – and don't let Dad hear us saying shi-stuff like that – what would you want to do?"

"Oh, the same thing! I love baking and to do it as a career? that truly is the *icing on the cake* pun totally intended!"

She's got a great laugh and you can't help but join in. Then I notice I've been edging closer while she's been backing up on the couch so I make a point of shifting away. I don't want to give the wrong impression again.

"So you'll just stay here then?"

"Oh Leo, this is a great job and I never want to leave but I also dream of having my own pastry shop. A patisserie is just cakes and pastries, a specialty shop."

"Would a place like that make enough money to be a viable business? I mean, your baking is the best but can you, by yourself, bake enough and then sell enough to turn a profit?"

"Oh. I never really thought of it in those terms."

I give her a puzzled look and say: "What other terms are there when it comes to a business?"

I hear a chuckle and looking up see Remo lounging in the doorway. He comes in and sits on the arm of the sofa at Fina's end. When he smiles at her her cheeks turn pink and she looks really pretty. I notice that Remo is going all out too, he's got his laser focus trained right on her. Hmm, this is making me think.

"Leo is right, Fina. A business has to operate on a for-profit basis in order to qualify as a business. If you can't make money you won't last too long, not when you have to pay suppliers and overhead, etc.."

"Hey! what you need is to take an Entrepreneur course, Fina. Something that will teach you the basics of bookkeeping, profit and loss statements, inventory management, marketing, and stuff like that. You might have a real flair for business or you might discover that it isn't what you want at all."

"You can learn how to define and then research your target market so you can advertise directly to the proper people and–"

"Whoa, Remo and you too, Leo. Serafina's looking totally lost in this conversation that you two are very much enjoying!"

Dad comes in the room with a happy look on his face at seeing our enthusiasm.

"Now what's this all about?"

We all start answering at once and Dad waves his hands at us to stop. Pointing to Fina he says: "You start."

"Well. It started with me asking Leo if he could help me get set up to get my GED and when he asked why I wanted that I said I thought I needed it to get a job and then he suggested I go straight to the courses that will suit my future work."

"Future work? Are you leaving me... us?"

"No! no, but I told him that my daydream was to some day own a patisserie and, now that there might be some money I can maybe open one or at least take the training I need to get started."

"Then Leo spoke about entrepreneurial courses and I got a bit carried away since as you know, Dad, Sales and Marketing is my thing, so then–"

"Not then, first, we had to get Fina to understand that business is all about profit and how she'd have to learn to price out her costs and–"

"Wait!" interrupts Dad again. "This all sounds wonderful, really. Serafina, I would love to bankroll your business. I'll cover all the supplies and overhead because it will all happen here. I can't possibly lose you but you can run your new business from here and then we'll all be happy."

"OK Antony," she agrees with a big smile, "Leo and Remo can figure out what I need to learn and then you and I will sit down—"

"With the business plan we've created," I put in.

"Right, with the business plan and we'll take it from there."

Now everyone's smiling and all talking at the same time. It's exciting to have a project on the go, something to look forward to, and a way to help out a friend.

Seventeen

Serafina

"Oh Antony, a tuxedo! You look very handsome," I tell my boss with honest admiration. The bespoke tux turns his physique from stout to imposing, very obviously the man in charge.

In my mind I always think of him as a roly-poly kind of guy but the truth is he's tall and solidly built. No wonder Sherry enjoyed flirting with him! I see a teddy-bear of a man who loves desserts but she just sees a big man.

"Thank you, Serafina. And you look lovely. That dress is an inspired choice and the colors are perfect on you. But did I mention? this is going to be a stag affair."

He's wearing a worried little frown as he goes on to explain: "Not a stag party, like a bachelor party or anything like that, but it will be all men, no wives or girlfriends. This is primarily a business get-together that I'm facilitating on behalf of my uncle. You met him, Uncle Tonino.

It won't be a late night, the younger men will leave early to go nightclubbing and us oldies will sit around with cigars and brandy but not for too long. I just thought you should know."

"I know I'm not a guest, Antony," I reassure him adding: "And that's good because I'm way too shy to socialize with a bunch of strangers – especially all men!

No, I get it that you bought me this gorgeous dress so that I'll do you proud when I supervise the dessert buffet. You mentioned that the caterer's will be bringing their own wait-staff to serve drinks and the main meal, right?"

"Yes, and I've requested male servers not cute young things in skimpy outfits. I don't want any trouble with all the boys we've got in this house." He pauses, remembering an apparently unsatisfactory recollection. It reminds me of how Mrs Antonacci had reservations about me coming here. Although Mr Michaelson was correct when he said I wouldn't be bothered – especially if *cute young things in skimpy outfits* are what the boys want!

Remo comes down the stairs then and I'm sure I'm gaping like a country mouse in the big city because he's also wearing a tuxedo and rocking it. The custom tailoring shows off his body to perfection. He smiles when he sees me staring and I swear my heart is going into overdrive. Then his gaze sweeps down from head to toe and I see his eyes widen with interest. The dress is definitely a success! and now it's not just my heart that's throbbing. That thought makes me blush.

Leo comes racing down next. He's not in a tux, probably because he's still growing, but I bet he prefers wearing this very stylish suit anyhow. Such a handsome boy. He gives me a wolf-whistle and Remo half-heartedly cuffs the back of his brother's head.

Antony beams from one of us to the other, happy with the household he's presenting to his guests.

Although his brothers aren't related to the Ferragamos, except as in-laws to Antony's late wife, they've all been invited since the get-together is in their home. When Gino and his four boys come thundering down from their rooms on the top floor Antony sends them all into the living-room so the hallway isn't *crowded with testosterone* as he puts it.

Giorgio strolls in from down the hall saying: "I'm sure you aren't including me in that comment," then turning to me compliments my appearance adding: "You look very pretty, my dear Serafina."

He raises an eyebrow at Antony so I quickly speak up: "I'll just stand first in line here at the door so I can take your guests' coats before they come through to greet you, sir."

Antony's smile widens and I'm glad to see he's decided to enjoy his party. I know he was coerced into hosting it. And, he's unhappy that Dominic Ferragamo has been invited but Uncle Tonino insisted his great-nephew attend.

Antony told me that *even though his heart is breaking his uncle reminded him that there's no proof against Dominic.* I want to ask *what happened?* but it's not my business so I can't intrude.

I have to admit that I'm delighted to be seeing Dom again. If he flirts with me will Remo get mad? I'm tingling all over with excitement.

The chimes ring signaling that my door duties begin now.

Remo

Of course I see red the moment Dominic walks through our front door. If he hadn't come with Great-Uncle Tonino I'd probably kick him out.

It's not just because of Marco and what they did to me, but the way he looks at Fina just makes my fists clench. I'm enraged. How dare this perverted, corrupted pond-scum even *look* at her never mind hold her hand while leaning in to kiss both cheeks? I immediately intervene and I don't care if she glares at me with disappointment all over her face.

Fina's eyes are sparkling and her cheeks are rosy with a pretty blush and it's 100 percent wrong that Dom can elicit that kind of reaction from this pure, innocent girl. Can't she feel the contamination of him when his eyes crawl all over her body? He's vile and despicable and far too dangerous to be anywhere near our girl.

Great-Uncle Tonino sees right through me and huffs a laugh at my expense. I don't care. I glower at Dom until he moves away from Fina and I'm determined to intercept any moves he might make in her direction for the whole night. I'd question Dad's sanity for inviting Dom but I realize it's at Great-Uncle Tonino request so he has no choice. I'm sure the elderly man will enjoy watching his great-nephews trying to score off each other over a girl.

I'll do my best to make sure Fina stays hidden away in the kitchen for most of the night. Although that's where she was when Leo took advantage so I guess I'm going to have to keep her in view at all times. That's not a hardship, she's even more beautiful all dolled up in this dress and those shoes. I can tell that she feels it too, because of the way she walks giving a gentle sway that sets the hem of her dress fluttering around her shapely legs. It's best if she does stay out of sight as much as possible tonight.

Dominic

I'm practically giddy and I don't care how camp that sounds! I think to myself with a salacious grin I don't even bother to try to hide. Luscious Serafina! she brings out the wolf in me and Remo's thunderous looks turn my spirit animal into a werewolf. I want so much more than just defilement – I want to devour and destroy her. The fact that it will just about kill my sanctimonious cousin is simply the cherry on top!

I've only touched her hand and already I'm hard. And Great-Uncle Tonino's noticed. I guess spotting everything that's going on is how he got to the top of his very bloodthirsty organization. I want to be there, too. My Cirelli cousins aren't a problem, they're not part of the *famiglia*, they're only related because our mothers were sisters.

Remo once commented that *lots of the wives and mothers in this family have died.* The truth is some died naturally, like his mother, and some tried to leave and died unnaturally, like my mother. Regardless, they're all just as dead. Wives, and by extension mothers, are expendable in the Ferragamo dynasty. They can easily be replaced.

Someday I'll get hitched and when I do it will be to someone as innocent as Serafina. Maybe not as adorable because my marriage will be a business arrangement to keep the peace. I'll have so much fun tormenting the virgin offering of a rival family on our wedding night and every night thereafter for as long as I like. She'll learn to dread bedtime.

I'll terrorize her into knowing and fully believing that if she complains I absolutely will kill her brothers and sisters, and if she's an only child? I'll take out her mother and cousins. I'll only stop the torture once she births my heir. That will incentivize her to reproduce as quickly as possible. But that pleasure will have to wait until after I've solidified my position as head of the family.

I'm working hard towards that goal and Marco's helping. Once I've proven my right to rule by ruining my challengers I'll be at leisure to pick and choose a child-bride from the offerings.

Everyone wants to be on the credit side with the head of the *famiglia*. I'll be able to do whatever with whomever I please. No limits, no one to say *no,* complete freedom.

Meanwhile the delectable Fina is made even more delicious by the obvious interest Remo is directing at her, and the obvious loathing he's showing me. Happily, Fina is not impressed by his bad temper so pissing him off tonight is going to earn me brownie points with her.

I can't resist giving him a cheeky wink and letting him wonder if it's because of her or because of our encounter in his bedroom. I'm so turned on by them both that I can't help but grin!

Serafina

Getting the guests out of their overcoats and into the house takes much longer than I expected and now I'm rushing around in the kitchen to add the final touches. Presentation is an art and an important aspect of any meal. Especially tonight when everyone seems to be heavily invested in having a successful party.

The catering staff is all-male just as Antony requested. I'm far too busy to feel awkward at being the only girl, and besides, the kitchen is my wheel-house as they say. I'm in charge, I'm confident, and I'm more than competent. Luckily everyone is professional. I guess when the client is *connected* no one messes about or screws up.

The arrangement is buffet with service, so the guests simply point out what they want and a server fixes them a plate. Most of those are filled with fresh buns packed with cold cuts, hot meat on sticks, crunchy relishes, and strong-smelling cheeses.

The line moves quickly. Antony urges people to have seconds then contradicts himself by warning them that the desserts will be unlike anything they've ever eaten so they'd better leave plenty of room.

Once the diners have had their fill the catering staff clears away the remnants of food and collects all the used dishes. Espressos, cappuccinos, and lattes are offered while I set up the desserts, covering the long table with sweet concoctions. The guests are so full of compliments my face muscles hurt from smiling so much, and the head of the catering crew offers me a job! Every morsel garners praise and truly I'm over the moon. Nothing has ever made me feel this good, I feel like a star.

Silently I send a prayer of thanks to Marta who spent so much time talking food with me and sharing her techniques. She really did me a solid, no wonder I feel such an obligation towards Peter.

I put him out of my mind in order to enjoy my moment in the spotlight. When the visitors came through the door they were simply guests with coats I needed to deal with. I loaded up armful after armful of expensive leathers and mohair wool and never really looked at anyone. Now I'm face-to-face with those same people and their appreciative looks make me aware that these guests are men. Some are merely friendly as they thank me for a delicious plateful but others eye me as if *I'm* on the menu.

Antony sticks close by but as the host he's constantly having to deal with the things that come up like shushing Leo and his younger cousins when they get loud enough to attract grumbles from the older men.

Remo is trying to block Dom from getting anywhere near me but Tonino Ferragamo keeps calling him away making Remo fume and Dom smirk. I don't even want to think what Remo's reaction would be if he knew he wasn't the only one to see me in my lingerie since Dom did too. In fact, all the men – and there were several at Dom's club that afternoon – got an eyeful. That memory shouldn't make me feel as hot as it does but I'm enjoying the sensation.

Is Remo really interested in me? or is he just competing with Dom?

I've just taken a deep breath when I look up and catch Dom eyeing my rising chest. When he lifts his gaze to meet mine he winks! and gives me a very seductive smile. I bite my bottom lip to keep from grinning back at him and that's when I see Remo steaming towards me. Before I can react he's got hold of my upper arm and hustles me down to the kitchen.

"What are you doing? Let go of me, Remo!"

"I saw you and Dominic eyeing each other like teenagers," he grumps, adding: "I told you he's bad news, Fina, you need to stay away from him."

"And I told you that you don't get to tell me what to do. I like Dominic and I'll talk to him and I'll even ogle him if I want to! You aren't the boss of me, Remo."

"Well somebody should be because you won't listen–"

"Listen to what, cuz?" Dominic has come into the kitchen behind us. I don't know how much he's heard but from his smug expression I'm guessing most of it.

"Get lost," snarls Remo.

"No, I don't think I will. I think I'd like to stay and make sure that my friend Fina isn't being browbeaten by you, Remo."

"Fuck off, Dominic. Fina shouldn't be anywhere near a piece of shit like you. We both know what you've done and I will get you for that. I fucking hate you, Dom."

"Good. I want your hate, it nourishes me."

"Yeah? well then my fist in your face should positively enrich you–" but fortunately Remo is interrupted before any physical fighting breaks out by Tonino Ferragamo's raspy command for them both to stop.

I think Great-Uncle Tonino is a scary man but I'm so glad he's shown up and intervened. Fighting, even yelling and swearing, always frightens me. I'm surprised at the violence of Remo's words and body language. He never seems the type to lose his cool.

I know it's not really because of me so I guess it's whatever the secret thing is that Antony hinted at. I wish I knew what was going on but then, considering the nature of the Ferragamo business, maybe I'm better off in the dark.

Standing at the top of the stairs he lays into the two young men in Italian. Although that's my father's native tongue I've forgotten any of the words I knew once I was brought into a German household. Still, I don't need a translation to know he's tearing a strip off each of them.

Dom narrows his eyes but says nothing while Remo seems prepared to argue his case. The arrival of Antony breaks up the set-to and I'm thankful when he drags all the men away leaving me alone in my kitchen.

Antony

I'm thankful to get off my feet and ease back in a comfortable chair with a snifter of *Vecchia Romagna*. It's not the best brandy money can buy but I get it because it's Uncle Tonino's favorite, and I enjoy a taste now and then. I'm nibbling on one of Serafina's plain biscotti without icing to absorb the alcohol without sweetening it. She's done a wonderful job, I'm so proud of her skills.

Most of the guests, including the younger men and my brothers, have dispersed but Dominic will remain until Uncle Tonino is ready to go and Remo won't leave until his cousin does.

Remo, like me, doesn't trust Dominic in the least little bit. In addition I get the impression the boys are quarrelling over Serafina. I wonder what happened there?

Uncle Tonino sees me puzzling over my thoughts and interrupts to ask me what's on my mind. I smoothly ad-lib with a previous thought answering: "I was just thinking Serafina deserves a bonus on payday for putting on such a mouthwatering spread."

The old man agrees and with a sl y smile adds: "Serafina is a very capable girl, I think."

That sounds like he's saying more than just those words but I can't figure out what exactly he means. It doesn't matter, I always agree with the oldies to avoid arguments.

Uncle Tonino switches to Italian while chatting with his compadres over their cigars and I'm struggling to stay awake. I think I've been feeling stressed working up to this party and having to welcome Dominic into my house... that still bothers me, and as usual I ate too much so I'll just sit here quietly and rest my eyes.'

Remo

The catering staff are supposed to remove all the leftover food and pack up their dishes but I suspect Fina is still in the kitchen cleaning up. It's late and she should go to bed, she's had a long day, but I can't go check up on her without Dominic tagging along. Just being in the same room as him sets my teeth on edge. That thing with him and Marco... I'll never forget what he did to me.

Finally Great-Uncle Tonino indicates it's time to wrap things up. He's expressionless as he studies my sleeping father and maybe I'm imagining a hint of contempt but he's an old man and the elderly so often disapprove of the rest of us.

"I'll walk you out Great-Uncle," I say, blocking him from Dad so he doesn't wake him to say goodbye. I'm quite sure he'd never think of saying *thanks*.

He gives me a sardonic look, very much the mafia capo right now, but we understand each other even though his world isn't mine and never will be.

At the door I help him on with his coat while Dominic says he'll get the car. What he really means is that he'll tell one of the bodyguards that Great-Uncle is ready to go. Before he comes back into the house I push up close to him and whisper in his ear:

"Where's Marco?"

"Why ask me? He's my lover, not my prisoner."

"Fuck Dom, don't start with me because I'm this close–"

"To what? To fucking me? beating me up? killing me? Listen Remo I realize actually thinking out the solution to a problem might strain your brain but give it a try. Ask yourself *where's the best place for Marco to hide?*"

He pushes past me back into the foyer where he offers the old man his arm. I curl my lip at him, fighting the urge to snarl, while Dom just smiles saying *give Serafina a goodnight kiss and tell I'll see her soon.* Like hell I'll tell her that!

"*Andiamo!*" says Great-Uncle Tonino, and they leave.

I head to the kitchen, obviously not to pass on Dominic's message, but to chase Serafina off to bed. Just as I suspected she'd still cleaning up. Seeing her bent over to load the dishwasher gets my dick excited.

Fina's a full-figured girl and I'm imagining how great it would be to have her naked while cuddling up against her soft warmth. I think my lustful thoughts must show in my face because she startles when she catches sight of me. I'm looking closely to see if she's reciprocating but she quickly covers up any softness in order to give me shit.

"Why are you so rude to Dominic and so bossy to me, Remo?"

"Dominic is nothing but trouble and he's dangerous. There's stuff you don't know–"

"So tell me!"

"No, it's well... it's complicated and it's family stuff that's a big mess. Once we get things sorted I'll let you know. You should know the truth about him and I'll insist on telling you–"

"Oh you'll insist. There you go again, making demands and bossing me around."

I step up close, into her personal space, and look down at her upturned face. She really is a beauty.

"You not only need me to boss you around, Fina, but you want me to. I know you do," I've let my voice drop to a low murmur and I see her mouth go slack and her shoulders slump in surrender.

Unfortunately for me I also see how tired she is and I can't bring myself to push it. I pull her into my arms and resting my chin on top of her head I can't help but groan because she feels so good... but it's late, she's exhausted, and I can't take advantage.

"Off to bed, sweetie," I say regretfully pulling back. Just like a little girl fighting sleepiness she pouts and I can't resist tasting her lovely lips. Her mouth is as sweet and soft as I imagined and then she yawns which makes me chuckle. I turn her around and point her in the direction of the door.

As she climbs the stairs I land a hefty swat on her backside and she squeals with a giggle. When we get to the top we find Dad in the hallway, rubbing his chin as if he's trying to figure out where everyone went.

"Bedtime for all of us," I declare and he slips his arm across Fina's shoulders to give her a squeeze and congratulations on a successful debut. He leaves her with me while he heads down the hall, and I lead her up the next flight of stairs to our floor.

I ignore my aching cock and say goodnight at her bedroom door. Fina replies and hearing her voice husky with sleep almost breaks my resolve but I choose to be a good guy. And curse my good intentions all through a shower where I stroke myself to the memory of her body pressed tight in my embrace.

Eighteen

Remo

I replay Dom's words *where's the best place for Marco to hide?* and those words remind me of an episode of the very old Sherlock Holmes shows aired late at night. The answer is simple, *hide in plain sight.*

The best place for my identical twin to hide is anywhere near me. Any accidental glimpses or meet-ups can be easily misconstrued. Our voices even sound the same. Him and Dominic have probably been laughing their heads off, assholes.

So he's somewhere in this house. Fuck, he's probably even sleeping in his own room. Ever since his so-called disappearance only Mrs. Finch has entered the room to dust and vacuum.

Fina even referred to it as a second guest room. Of course she'd think that because no one's told her about Marco, dammit. She deserves to know the whole story. Dad will probably say something to explain the animosity between him and Dom, but I should tell her myself.

Fuck, Marco has got to come clean. I'll drag him out from under the bed if I have to but this ends now.

Marco

I told Dom to stay away from Remo but he wouldn't listen. He thinks because Remo's such a straight-up guy that he's weak and Dom couldn't be more wrong. Either could I. I should never have joined in with Dom to assault Remo. Things weren't supposed to go that way at all but Dom's always been unpredictable, the wild card in the deck. I guess that makes me the Joker. Now I'm having a hard time looking my own brother in the eye.

"Look Remo, man I'm sorry. Shit I know that's not nearly good enough but... it's like Dom's craziness is contagious or rubs off or something. I don't know, I can't explain it but I just always seem to be going along with whatever he wants."

"But why disappear? and in such a dodgy way? I mean, it looks like Dom killed you, or you just took off without a word to anyone. Either way you upset all of us."

"Yay, success. That's how it's supposed to appear, to make Dom seem dangerous, but only circumstantially so no charges are laid or anything."

"Listen, you fuck, you broke Dad's heart!"

"Broken is better than dead from a heart attack."

"What are you talking about?"

I tilt my head up to the ceiling as if the answer is written there. Anything to avoid Remo's demanding, questioning probing glare.

Exhaling a deep breath I begin: "Dom's blackmailing me."

"What could you possibly have done to make *this* the better alternative?"

I close my eyes in childish escape from the consequences. I'll tell Remo, I have to, but I can't bear the shock and disgust I'm going to see on his face. I've always wanted him to think of me the way I think of him.

"I raped an underage girl. Well, it was rape because she was underage but also... yeah, it was rape."

"Marco? have the fucking balls to look at me when you confess your dirty secrets. Now, how did Dominic find out?"

I do open my eyes and stare into a face that can just as easily be a mirror. Except I don't think I've ever worn such a cold, mask-like expression.

"He was there. He, uh, introduced us."

"And you tag-teamed this young girl? ran a train on her? A teenager? Marco I'm trying not to judge but man this sure as shit doesn't sound like you. Were you high?"

"Well yeah but, okay here's what happened. Dom told me all about this girl he knows who's a *Little*, well actually a *Middle*, and she's into all kinds of kinky shit so of course I'm intrigued."

"Of course you are, you've always been a man-whore but what's a *Little* and a *Middle*?"

"It's a role-playing thing, actually it's called Age Play. Any kind of couple can take on the roles of adult and child, male-female or male-male or vice versa, but it's almost always about sex. Not necessarily between the adult and child, sometimes it's just a stimulant. But everyone is a real adult playing a game.

The *Little* can act as young as a baby with binkies, onesies, a cot, diapers, enemas–"

"For fucksakes, Marco."

"That's not me, I'm not into adult babies. *Littles* are usually women pretending to be girls aged six to ten or eleven. Their Daddy bathes and dresses them, tucks them into bed and then joins them. Lots of cuddling and feel-good shit. The *Little* is totally dependent on the big strong Daddy for his care and protection which he in turn finds very satisfying. I get it, but that's not my thing either.

What turns me on is playing with *Middles*. They act between twelve and fifteen years of age. Bratty adolescents pushing their boundaries and getting spanked when naughty. I'm pretty sure all of the *Daddy Dom Middle Girl* relationships include discipline, you know punishments, varying from spankings to writing lines to standing in the corner."

"I don't get that at all."

"I know you don't but that's because you're normal, Remo. You've never had any doubts about your sexuality or needed to validate your self-worth by jumping from one bed to the next."

"Look Marco you *might* like having sex with men and you *definitely* like it with women and now, apparently, with women pretending to be children... fuck, that's... okay go on."

"It's way more common than you think. I mean, there's a whole generation raised by helicopter parents who've made their child the center of their existence but at some point the kid has to go out into the big, bad world and it can be pretty harsh. Maybe Mummy and Daddy want to spend their retirement cruising with fellow seniors, or maybe there's a divorce and the new step-parent isn't interested. For whatever reason there are plenty of twenty-somethings struggling and looking for a Daddy, sometimes a Mommy, to take care of them."

"Oh! So she wasn't really an underage girl?"

"No, I'm afraid she was. That's where Dom tricked me—"

"You mean he set you up!"

"He told me he knew this girl, actually a twenty-five-year-old, who wears her hair in pigtails and dresses in pink babydoll nighties. She role-plays as a tween in puberty with mood swings from playful and pouty to sassy and sullen. In other words half the time she wants to climb onto Daddy's lap for sexy playtime and for the rest she wants to be turned over his knee to get her ass turned red.

I gotta admit I was intrigued. Especially when he said her particular kink is dub-con - that stands for *dubious consent* - and means wanting to be forced, raped, and by more than one man. So that was the scenario and I was totally into it and having a blast. The girl acted her part so well I really believed in her tears and her begging and at some point I realized it wasn't a scene, it was all real."

This re-telling brings the memory back in vivid detail. Suzy was so hot waggling her ass in those frilly pink panties. She was sucking my dick when Dom pulled them down and smacked her hard. She flinched and my cock slipped another inch down her throat. Then Dom was fucking her doggie-style while I was fucking her mouth and I came so hard. He was really doing a number on her, smacking her ass and biting her back and shoulders.

"I saw her crying but thought it was just because I filled her throat with my dick so I pulled back to let her grab some air and that's when I realized the tears were something more. I stopped right away and Dom laughed when he realized I'd figured it out. Here was this poor girl, this child, with cum dripping from every orifice, exhausted and hurt and quietly crying. I'm a fucking monster, Remo. I laid into Dom and soon we were rolling around the floor punching and choking each other. He had the advantage because he wasn't sickened with loathing and he, well... he held me down and fucked me in the ass."

"He sodomized you."

"It was, um, consensual by time he was done and then I did it to him."

"Where was the girl in all this?"

"Once we started fighting she got up and got dressed then called for a ride on her mobile and, believe it or not, her fucking *mother* came and got her. Mommy Dearest also collected the payment from Dom. I think the girl was only thirteen."

"Okay so Dominic is totally complicit in this mess given that he hired the girl, God I can't believe I'm saying those words, and lied to you. He set you up, totally."

"He did, and it worked."

"But why? What does Dom get out of it? He's just as guilty and just as criminally liable as you are."

"Dom doesn't care. He doesn't have a conscience and if people find out what he did he'll just shrug it off as his business, not theirs. But I can't live like that, so I ran away from what I'd done. Which is exactly what Dom wanted. He hinted he'd killed me in a fight and he had the battered face and bruised body to back up his claim.

He ordered me to stay hidden until he could convince a few of his cousins to keep their distance from Great-Uncle Tonino. You know he's ready to give over control of the family business, right? Well, Dom wants to be chosen as his successor. He figures he can get ahead by intimidating the competition. I told him he's nuts, Tonino will make his own choice and he's a shrewd old man."

"So you let Dad and Leo, Giorgio, Gino, and all our cousins think you'd either just walked away from us all or died. Fuck Marco."

"I know, I know it sucks and I'm a piece of shit but I don't know how to come back from this!"

I'm shouting but I can't stop, I'm afraid if I do I'll start crying. At that point the door suddenly opens and Serafina stands on the threshold.

In a sleepy voice she asks: "Remo, what's going on?" then sees me and after looking back and forth at us one-two-three times she lets out a piercing scream.

Antony

Lying in bed, my mind replaying the evening's events, has kept me awake. That's unusual, normally I have no trouble falling asleep and sleeping soundly, but tonight wasn't normal. Hearing Serafina scream I know the night is only going to get stranger.

It only takes me a moment to step into my slippers and belt my dressing-gown around my waist before I'm out in the hallway.

Giorgio was asleep, based on his stunned expression, and now he's sticking his head out his door. I'd forgotten that he's almost completely bald until seeing him like this without his toupee.

"What's going on?"

"I'm on my way to find out, that was Serafina screaming."

He's still asking questions which I obviously can't answer so I ignore him and hustle up the stairs. The light is on in the hallway and outside Marco's room Remo and Serafina are huddled in the doorway, looking in. Leo's slept through it all.

Just then Gino comes pounding down the stairs with his sons crowding behind him. Before I can open my mouth to ask what's wrong Remo and Serafina pull apart and I can see past them to where Marco is standing.

Marco, found! Marco, alive! That's all I remember before my eyes roll back in my head and I feel my legs collapsing to the sound of frantic voices calling *Dad!* And *Antony!*

I must have been out for several minutes because when I come to I'm tucked into my own bed, propped up by pillows, and with all three – three! – of my sons at my bedside. I look up to see my brothers standing by the door but they move away when Serafina comes in carrying a tray.

"Hot tea with plenty of sugar for the shock," she announces, handing the tray to Remo while she holds the mug to my lips. I take a sip and feel the warmth flood through me. Then another couple of sips before laying my head back.

"His color is getting better," says Marco with relief in his voice. I turn to him but don't speak yet – there's too much to say and I don't know where to begin.

"Dad, I'm sorry, I'm so sorry. Can you forgive me?"

"No," I snap. "But I do still love you."

"Antony, maybe you shouldn't have a stressful conversation right now? Maybe just sip on your tea while relaxing enough to fall asleep."

"Fina's right, Dad," adds Remo opening an aspirin bottle and handing me a tablet. "Everything will look better in the morning and we'll all have plenty of time to talk then."

"But I want to know–" I begin before Marco leans in to kiss my cheek and hug me gently.

"I'm home now and that's all that matters, right?"

And he is right. There might be new things to worry about but if so tomorrow is soon enough to discover them. Right now I do feel sleepy and the biggest worry of my life, my fear for Marco's safety, is settled even if it's just temporary.

My weakness has embarrassed me. Right now the best thing I can do is sleep so I'm refreshed and strong enough to tackle whatever bad news the morning will bring.

Serafina

Taking hold of my tray and carrying it like a shield I slip through the men and back towards the kitchen, the upstairs kitchen since I was in a hurry when I made Antony's tea. After a bad shock and then a scare I need something myself but I don't know what... not tea, not coffee, maybe brandy? I've never had any but I know there's some left in the living-room and people drink it medicinally. I decide to give it a try and run into Remo on the way. But is it Remo?

"Which one are you?" I practically snarl at him.

"Fina it's me, Remo. Oh sweetheart I'm so sorry you got such a bad shock, I was planning to tell you–"

"Really? When?"

"Tomorrow, well later today I guess. I already told Marco that he needed to sit down with everyone and explain everything."

"Marco, that's his name, right? and he's your twin? I never even knew you had another brother never mind a twin brother."

"Yeah, twins run in our family well you know that because of Luciano and Lorenzo. So yes, Marco is my twin."

As he says those words Marco also appears in the hall. I look from one identical man to the other before turning my back and heading into the living-room, searching for the brandy I saw there earlier.

My hands are shaking too much to pour myself a glass so Remo – or Marco – takes hold of the decanter and pours me a small amount.

"Knock that back," he says and I still can't tell which twin is speaking to me.

"Which one are you?" I repeat again.

"Remo. Look, Marco's removed his tie and undone the top buttons of his shirt. I haven't gone to my room yet so I didn't start getting undressed."

"Was it you with me in the bathroom?"

Remo looks puzzled until Marco answers confirming it was him.

I close my eyes in embarrassment while hearing an angry exchange between the brothers. *No wonder I thought he got outside quickly* I recall to myself.

"Forget it, forget that," I insist, "I don't want to hear anything from either of you right now. I'm going to bed."

Again I turn my back to them as I walk away but one, presumably Remo, grabs me from behind. I spin round and seeing his neat bow-tie know that yes, it is Remo. I feel for him, seeing the anxiety in his eyes and knowing how worried he is about his father and even about me but right now I'm exhausted.

It's been a long day stoked-up with excitement and anxiety for the success of the party and now all these emotions swirling around inside me... A million thoughts are racing round in my head and I just want to shut everything down. A slight wooziness tells me the brandy is doing its job.

I plead, "Please let me go I-—Wait! Stay still for a moment," Remo tries to say something but I put my hand up in the universal *stop* gesture.

I step up close to really study his face, his features, from the exact color of his eyes to the angle of his jaw, his mouth... yup, I must be feeling the effects of the brandy to actually be doing this. After a couple of minutes I step back and give a satisfied nod.

Without explanation I say: "Goodnight, Remo. I just want to go to my bed." And this time Remo does let me walk away, and by time I reach the stairs I'm running.

Remo

I'm not sure what that was all about with Fina but... I don't argue. I'll save that for Marco. I head back to his room determined to have a few things out with him.

"You don't knock?" he complains when I barge in.

"Fuck off, Marco. I'm here for some answers. Starting with Fina - what was that about who was in the bathroom? Have you been pretending to be me with her? with anyone?"

"It was just a joke—-"

"I'll fucking kill you, asshole."

"It was nothing, a kiss, and then she pushed me away and ran off. I can't accuse her of being a tease but she is a scared little virgin. I don't know why you're wasting your time when Shelby—-"

"Oh give it a rest about Shelby. I already told you I'm not interested in what you two want. Why the hell would you ever think I would want that?"

"Hey, as the saying goes *don't knock it 'til you try it*. The three of us could have a blast. We did when it was Dom who was with us."

"What? Oh God, when did that happen?"

"A while back. I took Shelby to Malavita to see one of the shows and I don't know if it was the stripper or the drinks or maybe both? but she got really horny and was practically jacking me off at the table.

Anyhow, Dom came over to say hi and when he saw what she was doing suggested we take the party back to his room for some privacy. Next thing I know the three of us are on his bed fucking our brains out with Shelby taking us both at the same time, switching between cunt, mouth, and ass.

Remo it was a mindblowing experience. Seriously bro, it was so hot, we've got to do it, you'll love it."

I just look at him shaking my head. He's old enough now to know that *mindblowing experiences* are best when there's a strong emotional - loving - connection.

"You don't need me if you've got Dom to partner the two of you."

"No, Shelby won't go with him anymore. He got a bit rough and left bruises and uh, um red marks—"

I interrupt to clarify: "You mean bite marks, right?"

"Yeah okay bites but it wasn't a big deal at the time. The problem happened on her next modeling gig when the photographer saw and went mental. There was a big fuss and they had to use body make-up and it ended up that they cut $2,000 off Shelby's fee. Man was she pissed, you know she's pretty money-hungry, right?

I was with Dom when she came storming into his office demanding he pay her back the money she lost."

Marco starts laughing at the memory so I ask: "Did he pay her?"

"Yeah but he made her work for it. Ha, ha he can be such a prick. He said to her *Sure, I'll scatter these bills across the floor and you crawl along picking them up. If you do that you get to keep the money plus I'll give you the chance to earn another two grand.*

Now the floor of his office is filthy from spilled drinks and cigarette butts and even the bit of carpet is dirty but Shelby isn't paying attention to any of that, she's just watching him toss around these hundred dollar bills.

Sure enough she hikes her dress up to her hips and gets down to start crawling after the money. I'm standing behind her so I get a nice view of her ass as she wiggles along. Dom's walking ahead and he can see her tits swinging where the front of her dress dips down showing she isn't wearing a bra.

Dom stops when he reaches his chair and I walk over there so I can see her better. Remo, she is so turned on by this little performance. She's got a handful of Franklins and she's licking her lips and I swear she's going to lick the money but instead she tucks the wad into the string of her thong, you know how the strippers do?

Now Dom is waving another stack of bills like a fan and he tells her if she fucks me cowgirl style while sucking his dick the money is all hers.

Shelby's always had an unhealthy attraction to wealth but I think the real reason she agreed is because she was so horny. I'd barely sat down on the couch before she'd shifted her thong aside and slid her wet cunt onto my dick. She was so hot and ready. Dom came over with his cock in hand and shoved it in her mouth. She orgasmed first but I wasn't far behind.

I don't know if Dom came, he doesn't always. Anyhow, he zipped himself up and taking her hand kissed the palm of it before saying *I don't kiss whores on the mouth*. Then he slapped the wad of bills down.

Shelby straightened her clothes, folded up the cash in her hand, and ordered me to take her home *right now!* Dom laughed at her and she clenched her fists like she had to hold herself back from hitting him. When I dropped her off at home she said she was done with Dom, so no more threesomes."

I'm not sure which part of the story was more disturbing or disgusting. Leaving the room I call back over my shoulder: "Jesus Christ, Marco. The three of you deserve each other."

Nineteen

Marco

I surprised myself by falling into a deep sleep as soon as I climbed into bed last night, or rather early this morning. I guess it's relief at the truth coming out?

Also, it means a lot to me that Remo and I are back on track. Not completely, in fact maybe not even halfway, but we're getting there.

He's hurt that I sided with Dom against him in what he calls a sexual assault but it wasn't, I mean his asshole is still virgin, so far as I know! But I do know he didn't want Dom touching him and, well, having Dom blow him wasn't good. He said flat out that he'll never forgive either of us for that but, he'll get over it.

What really pissed him off was finding out I'd spent some time necking with Fina. He's pretty protective about her and he didn't like her thinking I was him. No, he really didn't like that and he only knows about that one time. Is he just being *Alpha Male* or does he actually have a thing for her?

I mean, I can see it but like my cousins I'm more inclined towards the model types: tall, blonde, and slender with legs up to here.

Fina has a really pretty face, and that's important, but her body is... well she obviously doesn't miss too many meals. I guess she'd be a luscious handful to warm your bed at night with that plump ass and tits out to here, yeah I see the appeal. But all those fantastic desserts she makes? Well, she must lick the icing and batter from a lot of bowls and those curves will turn obese before too many more years. When that happens she can marry Dad!

I'm glad Fina won't be at our family council this morning. I'm not sure if Gino will join us but his boys definitely won't because it involves Ferragamo family business and the less they have to do with that the better.

Giorgio won't miss the opportunity to criticize and complain. I wish Dad had never offered him a home here when Nonna passed. Giorgio picks on Dad all the time and if I wasn't in the dog-house myself I'd say something about it. Maybe Remo will.

Entering the study I spot Giorgio looking between Dad and Fina with a sour expression. Without a word she puts another muffin or cupcake or whatever she's serving onto his plate.

"You've got the right idea there, Serafina," says Dad with a laugh. "He needs sweetening up!"

She does have a pretty blush and a sweet smile that just makes you want to smile back.

"You're the one with a sweet tooth, Antony, and you had it before I ever came here to bake for you. As a matter of fact with your appetite for desserts you're practically a *mangiacake [cake eater]!*" and that makes us all laugh.

She turns when she hears me and gives me a wary look. When I say *Marco* she just shakes her head and hurries by without a word.

In addition to Dad and Giorgio's full plates of goodies there are a couple of carafes of coffee with all the fixings laid out. I help myself to a black coffee and the biggest muffin I've ever seen. It's got raisins and chocolate chips in a super-light texture that's absolutely scrumptious. The best muffin I've ever eaten.

There's only one other plate left on the tray and it must be for Remo.

"Leo, Gino and his sons won't be joining us?" I ask.

"No, they're packing up and then heading right out for their ski trip. They invited Leo to join them but it's a holiday party with Lee's family so he said he'd rather stay home with us. The twins loudly said they wish they could stay home too but Gino told them they don't get a choice."

"Gino's going on a ski trip with his ex? will her new husband be there?"

"Gino's not going with them, he's dropping off the boys and heading to a different resort for a vacation on his own. I imagine he'll try to meet a snow bunny or two."

"He's gonna come home with another unsuitable wife one of these day," grumbles Giorgio.

Dad pauses for a moment in thought before shaking his head saying: "No, I don't think so. Gino was deeply in love with Lee and her betrayal, and the end of their marriage, ruined him from ever having another serious relationship. Although he never fought her over the divorce I don't think he'll ever get that close to anyone else again."

"A one-woman man, just like you Dad."

He gives me that smile that looks like he's enjoying a secret and adds: "That's the very best thing I can hope for, for you, Remo, and Leo. To find and marry your own one-and-only."

Giorgio, the misogynistic bachelor, just snorts his contempt.

I wonder if I told Fina that I was Remo would she have been friendlier? By now I should be used to the fact that no one can tell us apart, well except for Dad, it's weird but we've never been able to fool him. While hiding out here I've had to be really careful not to run into him. Even Leo, our brother, can't tell us apart but that might be because with the gap in our ages we didn't spend much time with him. I wouldn't put it past him to invent some wearable device that will let him figure out which of us is which. Hmm, I better not give him any ideas!

Remo

As I walk into the room I hear: "I was just saying *we're all here except Remo* and here you are. Good. Grab a coffee and a snack and we can get down to business."

For some reason when Dad's behind his desk he acquires a real corporate boss attitude and it isn't put on, it's perfectly natural. Same as when he's the bumbling Papa fussing over whether his boys are eating enough at the dinner table. All these different personas are strange. I suspect there's another aspect to him when he's dealing with Great-Uncle Tonino, too.

I decide to drink a coffee before trying any of the baked goods. Everything looks delicious but my stomach's in knots. I'm worried about how Dad's going to react to Marco's story. I can already guess what Uncle Giorgio will think, Uncle Gino? I'm not so sure. I overheard Dad say Gino won't be here so maybe by time he hears the story it won't matter so much anyhow.

Marco's words replayed through my head in an unending loop for most of the night. The rest of the time I was thinking about Fina and wondering just exactly what Marco got up to with her. It certainly explains some of the puzzled looks she's given me... she must think I'm running hot and cold and playing games with her. Fucking Marco.

I still haven't forgiven him for that bullshit with Dom in my bedroom, either. I'm pretty sure I'll never be able to forgive that. Fuck, I hope he doesn't mention anything about it to Dad.

Looking at my brother I can't help but marvel at how calm and relaxed he is, drinking his coffee and munching on a muffin like he isn't about to bring Dad's whole world crashing down. Now he's picking crumbs off his plate and licking his fingers. He's so inconsiderate and self-satisfied and he even looks like he had a good night's sleep. I'm ready to fly across the room and strangle him.

Antony

"Marco why is your twin staring at you like you're poisonous? Obviously he knows some, if not all the story, so I guess you'd better tell us everything. No matter what you've done Marco you're still our son, nephew, and brother. We'll hear you out."

I lean back in my chair to study my second child. Second, by only minutes but that time counts. Marco has always resented Remo being born first, yet I never saw Remo take advantage of that or lord it over his brother in any way.

I don't understand why no one can tell these two apart. When people ask me where I see the difference I'm like *seriously? It's their eyes, and ears, and the shape of their mouths...* it's so obvious.

Personality-wise they're very different. I wonder if the distinction of being the older or the younger has shaped them? I should ask Luciano and Lorenzo what they think.

Both these boys of mine are smart, popular, athletic, healthy and good-looking. But Marco plays the fool while Remo doesn't play nearly enough.

"I guess I need to ask first if you know anything about a relationship dynamic called *Age Play*."

I shake my head just as Giorgio says *of course.*

So Marco gives us a longwinded explanation that has me side-eyeing my older brother.

He cuts over Marco saying: "Grown women pretend to be little girls who are babied and pampered by their Daddies, usually involves sex."

The three of us just stare at him, not just for knowing about this kinky stuff but for sounding so matter-of-fact and decisive. This is a side to Giorgio I haven't seen in years.

"Marco, I'm guessing the girl was underage and you were set-up. Any fear of the police being brought in? No? then what about blackmail?"

"Only by Dom."

"Didn't he participate?"

"Yeah, he did, and he doesn't care if you find out but.. I do care about it. Look if she'd really been twenty-three I wouldn't even be embarrassed because the role-playing was a blast and Dom's a lot of fun. Dad, I knew you'd be mad at me for just taking off without a word but it was only until Dom could work something out with Great-Uncle Tonino. Dom wants to be chosen as his successor and he wants to intimidate everybody else in the running."

"Jesus Antony, your boy's an idiot. It's the Ferragamo side, they've never been nothing but trouble. That wife of yours..."

Both Marco and Remo interrupt hotly saying:

"Stop there Uncle Giorgio. You don't say one fucking word against my mama."

"I don't give a flying fuck what you think of her."

Giorgio making a hmmph sound and turning to me asks: "This is how your boys talk to their uncle?"

"Sure, when said uncle is out-of-line. Giorgio, your comments don't help."

"I was only going to say that Lenora had the worst family, nothing against her."

"Well none of us can help who we're related to," I say dryly. Then turning to my son continue: Marco, Dominic implied he killed you, and by disappearing you left me wondering if I should be in mourning–"

"No, Dad oh fuck, I didn't realize–"

"I get it, you aren't the brightest boy but as for Dominic, well I don't think I can forgive him. He tormented me and he enjoyed it. I'm glad he's not my blood relative. So, there will be no repercussions from the incident and the child hasn't been damaged?"

"Not really, I mean it got kind of rough but afterwards she just played games on her phone until her mother showed up to pick her up and collect the fee."

"Her mother?" I put my hand up to stop him from answering. I don't want to know. It hurts my heart that such things go on. I don't even think I'll bother asking Gino how come he's so well-informed about this degeneracy. Whatever happened to the union of a man and a woman being a wonder and an amazement? or whatever that old marriage phrase is.

"We can put this incident behind us and move forward, yes?"

"God yes, please."

I nod and wave at them all to leave asking Remo to tell Serafina I'd like to have a few minutes of her time, to have a word alone with her, when she comes to clear away.

Twenty

Marco

"Fina, this time you see me coming, right?" I love seeing her blush, all that creamy skin turning dusky rose. That's how her plump round ass will look if I put her across my knee. Dom's shared all kinds of sexy kink with me and I'd really like to try out some of that stuff myself.

Then I remember that her nipples are light brown and I get distracted thinking about teasing them to a darker color. Gently grazing her hard nipples with my teeth, smothering my face in her soft, fleshy boobs. Having her under me squirming and moaning with pleasure and desire. Mmm, heavenly.

But way too young. Not too young to fuck but too young to fuck and dump which is exactly what I would do. I don't want to be tied down playing boyfriend to just one girl but that's what a young girl would want from the man who took her virginity. So tease and flirt but walk away. Otherwise Dad will kill me. But first... a nice soul-searching kiss.

I pull her close and starting at her forehead lay kisses from there down beside her eyes, her cheeks, nose, lips but her mouth stays closed and I realize she isn't kissing me back.

"What's wrong sweetheart?"

"Are you being yourself Marco? or still impersonating Remo?"

"Wow! you can tell us apart? Or maybe just when we're this close, hmm? Does Remo hold you differently? Tell me. Does he kiss you differently than I do?"

She steps around me and continuing down the hall tosses the comment *Remo has never taken advantage* over her shoulder.

Damn.

I'm at odds with everybody in the house and I don't like feeling this way. Dad's disappointed, Remo's disgusted, and Fina's mad at me. Gino and his crew wisely found a way to stay clear of our drama and Giorgio is miserable company, I've got nothing in common with him... guess that leaves little Leo.

Actually, my little bro must be fourteen or fifteen now so he'll enjoy hearing some stories about my sexual conquests. It's all sex at that age and, still pretty much at my age, too. If not, we can at least play a video game.

When he's at home Leo spends most of his time in his bedroom which is beside Fina's. It doesn't even occur to me to knock but turns out he's locked his door. I can hear music so he's in there.

"Hey, it's Marco let me in."

"Go away, I'm busy."

Busy? he's barely a teenager, how can he be busy. I start pounding repeatedly until he gives in and flinging it open yells *What do you want???*

I shoulder him aside and step into the room. It looks like a tornado came through, so that's normal for a kid his age. His computer set-up is something else, though. He's got *three* monitors and none of them are showing porn or the latest car/crime/battle video game. Instead it looks like those TV shows where somebody's hacked into a computer system and sequences of numbers are racing up the screen.

"What's with the nerdy shit, Leo?"

"Marco just say what you want then get out. I'm busy doing stuff."

"Like what?"

"You wouldn't understand so why would I bother to tell you? What do you want? has your laptop frozen from all the viruses you download with those sketchy sites you visit? or do you need your phone unlocked?"

"That's Dad's thing not mine. And those sites aren't sketchy they're educational," I give him a nudge and grin adding: "and they're *inspirational.*"

He just rolls his eyes at me. It would be cute if he was a girl.

"I just thought you might want to hang out since you're only on holiday for a couple more days."

He squints as he evaluates that statement and I hate that this kid is making me feel uncomfortable so I punch him in the shoulder and tell him to forget it.

I'm almost out the door before he speaks saying: "You've been acting like a real shit, Marco. You really did a number on Dad with Dominic and that's all kinds of fucked up. Nobody's told me what happened but I know Dominic was involved and even I know he's bad news. What were you thinking?"

"Oh grow up, Leo. You don't know everything."

I slam the door shut behind me and stomp next door to my room. They're all pissed off at me because of Dom but right now he feels like my only friend. I lie back on my bed and give him a call.

Serafina

Remo's been grouchy all morning and I think it's something to do with whatever happened between him and Dom last night. Or it might be Marco because I overheard angry words exchanged up by our bedrooms. They stopped when they saw me so I just nodded a greeting then hurried on by.

Marco. Wow, what a thing. I would never in a million years have guessed, have known, that Remo had a twin. And the two of them are identical, too! Well, practically.

Now I'm trying to figure out if it was Marco or Remo who trapped me in the bathroom when I was delivering clean towels. I *think* it was Marco... and not long after I saw Remo outside which makes that seem likely. But I'd like to know for sure.

I'm so deep in my own thoughts when Remo comes into the kitchen it's like I've summoned him. Startled, I blurt out my question: "Was it you, that day in the bathroom, when you um.. when uh–" I hate blushing, it makes me feel like a kid, but I can feel the heat flooding my cheeks.

Remo's brows draw together in a massive frown. I should have known better then to question him when he's already grumpy but I can't take the words back now.

"What happened in the bathroom? When? It was Marco, not me. What did he do?"

"He um, kinda made a pass but I thought it was you!" I quickly add when his eyes flare with rage. "But he stopped as soon as I said *stop*."

His mouth works but no words come out, he's obviously struggling to hold back. *I've made things worse*, I think miserably and it must show on my face because Remo pulls me into a gentle hug.

"I'm sorry he assaulted you, Fina." When he lowers his voice it's a lovely deep rumble. I feel myself melt into his embrace. "I only asked because I just told him that you've always been a gentleman with me."

"And then you started to wonder if that was true?" I can hear that he's smiling. "Were you hoping it was me?"

Stepping free of his arms I tell him not to make fun of me. Ignoring that he draws me close again but stops when our faces are only inches apart so he can look into my eyes. We stare at each other for awhile and I don't realize I'm holding my breath until his lips meet mine in a tender kiss. A soft, warm kiss with his tongue lightly touching mine. It's the best kiss I've ever had and then it gets even better.

I feel Remo's fingers comb through my curls as he holds the back of my head to hold me steady while his kiss intensifies and his mouth claims mine with passion. From warm to hot, soft to hard, lightness to pressure. He's tasting me, controlling me, owning me. Everything around me dissolves forgotten as I focus on this heated moment. I've never.. I can't... I want... I want him.

My arms have wrapped around Remo's neck and he's clasped me so tight my breasts are squashed against his hard chest. Our kiss goes on and on and the phrase *time stood still* is a real thing.

I shift my weight to my hip and my pelvis comes in contact with his groin so I feel the hard length of him. That's because of me! he's grown erect because of me and I gasp in surprise.

Remo groans from his very depths as he pulls back, leaving at least of foot of space between us. He bends his forehead to rest against mine as he murmurs *Fina, Fina, sweet girl*. Standing upright with his hands on my shoulders, holding me in place, he gives me a rueful grin and a tingle in my lady parts is so insistent I squish my thighs together.

"Dad wants to have a word with you in his study." He gives me one more panty-flaming smile and then he's gone.

Antony

There's something's up with Serafina and, happily, it's something good if her distracted smile is anything to go by. She always shows a sunny disposition but this smile is more like a private memory. Hmm, I hope it has something to do with Remo.

Remo is a handsome, successful man who meets plenty of suitable women through his business but instead of a particular girlfriend he seems to have several. All of the ones I've met at our family social gatherings have been beautiful and pleasant young women. He seemed to be spending a lot of time with Shelby but she hasn't been around for a while now.

Why am I so sure Serafina can capture and keep his heart? The girl is completely innocent and artless, nothing at all like the career girls he dates but I just feel... ah well, I can't interfere so to the matter at hand:

"Serafina I want to apologize for the mix-up about my boys, you must be awfully confused and wondering what's going on. You see... it's not something we talked about because none of us knew exactly what was going on. I have to backtrack a bit to tell you the whole story but let me start by saying you discovered there's a great deal of antipathy between Dominic Ferragamo and myself, right?"

I have her attention now and she nods wide-eyed, not wanting to interrupt.

"Well, the reason for that is I knew, in my heart, that Dominic was responsible for Marco's mysterious disappearance. There was even a suspicion that Dominic had actually *killed* Marco but Uncle Tonino got involved and said he would look into things which basically meant *hands off* and I was prepared to ignore that but Remo convinced me not to call in the police. He told me he was certain Marco wasn't dead because of some kind of twin thing he felt, and I agreed to give Tonino time to investigate.

Marco and Remo are quite different in character. Where Remo is more grounded, serious about growing his business, working towards a goal, Marco is still trying to find his way. He's a dabbler, trying this thing then that one and, so far, not finding his passion. He will, there's no one-size-fits-all time limit on growing up, and I'm confident Marco will achieve his milestones at his own pace.

Unfortunately this causes quite a bit of friction between the two of them. Remo gets impatient which makes Marco act childish and then Remo gets even angrier.

So Marco suddenly vanishing on a whim didn't ring any alarm bells but I heard gossip about a fight, a physical fight not just a quarrel, between him and Dominic and I got the strangest sense of doom. I know that sounds terribly dramatic but it truly was a feeling of dread. That's when I took my worries to Tonino who, as I said, announced he would take over the inquiry.

The thing is Dominic *acted* like he had harmed Marco, he refused to comment, just smirked at me saying *I can neither confirm nor deny* like he was a politician! Remo told me he'd try to get the truth from Dominic and then you came into our lives as a very welcome distraction for me.

I didn't want to burden you with our concerns but I'm sorry I didn't clue you in sooner, I can only imagine what you thought when you saw the twins together last night."

"It was a shock but I'm the one who should be apologizing for overreacting. I mean, I didn't need to scream–"

"That wasn't much of a scream, I would have shouted my head off!" That makes her laugh and the tension leftover from my story is gone.

"Now, to finish up. It turns out Dominic was involved but Marco's subsequent disappearance was voluntary. The two of them had some scheme going and the details of that are best forgotten. So, my dear, you have an extra housemate, Marco, but with Gino and his boys away for the next week things will be quieter than usual."

"Well thank you for explaining all of this, Antony, you didn't have to but I appreciate that you did."

"I'm very much invested in your happiness, Serafina. Ever since you got here my stomach thinks it's died and gone to Heaven. Which reminds me, that Victoria Sponge you made was light as air and I hope it's not too tricky a dish because I'd like to see it become a regular on our menu."

"Oh it's not tricky at all, sponge is easy-peasy."

"Lemon-squeezy."

"Oh!" she laughs with delight, "I've never heard that part before."

Twenty-One

Serafina

I'm bored with my own company today so I head to the family room hoping someone's around or might come by. I hear a couple of voices and I hurry into the room eager to see who it is, but just as I step through the door I hear a woman's laughter.

She's gorgeous. Blonde and slim, with a cover-model's face. She's perched on the arm of Remo's chair while Marco stands with his arm slung across her shoulders. She shoots me a glance but doesn't pause in her conversation continuing, still with a laugh in her voice:

"Remo don't be like that. You know I love you madly, you're marriage material, but I also love Marco because he's so much fun. It's ridiculous to think I could only love one of you, I mean you're absolutely identical in every way."

In a husky tone she adds: "In every inch, too."

I'm still standing in the doorway where I came to an abrupt halt, stunned to be hearing that this is Remo's girlfriend? or Marco's? I'm confused and I guess it shows on my face.

The woman asks in an impatient tone of voice: "Yes? Do you want something?"

Remo turns his head and notices me. He moves to get up but the woman presses one hand on his chest and the other wraps around the back of his neck.

"Serafina, come in! This is Shelby, my... our, friend."

"Shelby? What kind of a name is that?"

"Huh," the woman huffs in response, "Says the girl called *Good Night*."

I have to think for a moment before I understand what she means and explain that Serafina is taken from Seraphim – Angels. Then I ask again what her name means.

"Well, it doesn't mean anything. I'm named after a famous car, the Shelby, a Mustang from the sixties."

"High-performance and sporty," quips Marco.

"High-maintenance and expensive," retorts an unsmiling Remo.

Shelby pouts at him and tries to climb in his lap but Remo stands up and moves over to the window. Pulling back the curtain the expression on his face shows he wishes he was out there, not in here.

"C'mon Remo," she whines, "I'm still your girl."

"Our girl," Marco clarifies.

"That's right, I'm yours and yours," she answers looking from one twin to the other.

Realization hits me because this is exactly like one of my steamy romance novels with hot twins and I feel the blush creeping up from my neck to my cheeks. Probably my forehead is shining red too. I'm so embarrassed, I'm such an idiot!

"Excuse me I've.. I'm sorry, I didn't mean to interrupt, I'm, I'll.. I'll just go now," then I turn and flee.

I hear Remo's voice calling *Fina, wait!* but the door closes on Marco's voice saying *you can't leave yet Remo, we need to talk this over and figure it out.*

Why does every encounter with Remo leave me feeling like such a fool? I guess because I am a fool, and I keep getting fooled. No! I keep *letting* myself get fooled. Shame on me, as the saying goes.

I need some fresh air and head through the upstairs kitchen to the patio-deck in the backyard. I walk out onto the lawn. I spy a red ball a ways out, under a tree, and wonder if it was left behind by a visiting child or if the Cirellis ever had a dog.

As I draw closer I see it's actually a bocce ball, and there's a low-walled court marked in the grass. I pick up the ball and fight back the urge to hurl it as far and as hard as I can. Preferably through the window Remo is standing at. Hopefully knocking down him, Marco, and *Shelby* like a row of bowling pins.

Behind the trees I see a shed and wander over to it. The door isn't locked and sure enough inside is a rack of bocce balls as well as croquet mallets and hoops, a child-sized badminton net strung between two stands, lawn darts *hmm, bet that's dangerous in a house full of boys,* and assorted balls for different games: soccer, football, baseball, and frisbees.

I slot the bocce ball into its proper place but instead of coming back out of the shed I sit down in a spectator's chair. It's pretty flimsy but seems to hold my weight okay. Shelby sure is slender with long, long legs.

I sort of want to cry but why? nobody's betrayed me, there's been no relationship to betray. I thought that Remo showed interest, although he seemed to run hot and cold, but once I discovered Marco's existence well, that explained that.

Marco enjoys flirting – nothing more – and it wasn't Remo kissing me in the bathroom or in the hall. Shelby's right in saying the twins are identical so I guess kissing Marco is like kissing Remo but it's not the same. Good kissers always do a good job but it's the feeling, the emotion, the lust, happiness, and joy that adds the thrill.

Shelby's comment about *every inch* means she's had sex with both of them but based on what I heard that's didn't actually happen at the same time. But it sounds like she wants both of them? and Marco's in full agreement.

What would it be like to be in bed with both men? What would it be like even with just one of them? I shake my head at myself. There's definitely no point thinking about seeing and touching their penises. *Dicks*, Fina, surely you can say *dicks* in your own head. And *fucking*, too. There's no point thinking about either of the twin's dicks, even if they are identical, fucking my pussy. They aren't interested. Face facts and move on.

I love my job baking treats for Antony and the rest of the family, and I love living here in the comfort of this beautiful home. I am not going to lose it or give it up because I'm mooning over a man. To heck with men, with everybody. I'm sick and tired of being used. It seems like my whole life has been a me performing one duty after another and it isn't fair.

I loved Marta with all my heart but she shouldn't have put me in the position of go-between with her and Peter after Dietrich threw him out of the house. I was just a kid and it was wrong to make me lie and cover up. It certainly changed the way I acted and reacted to Dietrich.

Then, when Marta got sick, it was wrong of her to suggest I quit school to stay home as her nurse and companion. I'm grateful for all the cooking lessons she gave me, but most of our time together was spent watching TV or talking – activities that could have happened in the evening and on weekends. I shouldn't have been allowed to drop out - I should have been allowed to live a normal teenager's life.

Once it was certain that nothing would make Marta well again I understood and agreed with her not wanting to end her days in a hospital. She wanted to die at home. But the Stutts have plenty of money and could easily have hired a nurse, two nurses, instead of relying on teenage me to do an adult's job.

Even after all this time I feel guilty thinking these thoughts but... I suffered emotionally through all the set-backs too but nobody helped me. I had to put on a brave face and stay cheerful. It really was too much to ask.

I suffered emotionally through all the set-backs too but I had to put on a brave face and stay cheerful.

Peter, well, I can't even blame him for pretending to be my boyfriend because that romance was all in my head. Marta encouraged it and made me promise to watch over him and help him, even though he's four years older.

Peter never hesitated to sponge off me – there! I've finally admitted it to myself. Peter always played on my sense of obligation, just like both his parents did. All he ever wanted was to take everything I had. If I opened my wallet to give him twenty dollars he'd take the remaining five dollar bill as well, leaving me with nothing. He didn't care, he never cared for me or about me.

These are some ugly truths I'm digging up but it's best to get it all out.

Peter wants me to agree to a date with Dominic which is really weird because Dom's a big boy and can ask me out himself. But Peter said something about repaying Dom for something, owing him a favor, so it won't be a real date like dinner and a show.

Instead it's supposed to be *a long staying-in date* which has to mean sex, right? What else could Dom and I do for hours? I mean, we can't even have sex for that long. At least... I don't think so.

I figure he'll want to continue with that bondage thing he started, and play around for a bit, then introduce me to sex – no doubt Peter has told him I'm a virgin – and then napping, have some food and maybe watch TV, then sex again.

That's a hell of a favor Peter's asking me for.

For the first time I can think of I actually said *no* to Peter. I mean, Dom is super-sexy and so good-looking with a handsome face, muscled body, tons of tattoos that I'd love to explore... but I don't want my first time to be planned out like this... I want romance and wooing and... Remo.

Dammit Fina, wise up! nothing's gonna happen with Remo. Maybe I should take Dom up on his offer. I don't want to lose my virginity to some fumbling boy or a smooth-talking man who will leave me feeling tricked.

I guess me still being a virgin is an outdated, old-fashioned thing. Really, it's a burden. I should just think of it as a *rite of passage* like they have in all those coming-of-age movies. A few drops of blood, maybe, and a few moment's pain, probably, but then I'll be normal. No more drama or expectations.

That makes me think of Antony's story about his Ella. What a thing... and she didn't care what anybody thought. I wish I could be like that! He really loved her, too. Lots of people gossiped about her and she didn't care and neither did he. They just believed in each other and that was more than enough for them. After she died he never remarried. Theirs was a once-in-a-lifetime love affair. So sweet.

I don't think I'll ever find someone to love me that way, after all I'm a nobody. I have no family or friends. Luckily, I do have a kind-hearted employer and I'm so thankful that I ended up here. When I think of what could have been? A naive girl with little money and no where to go out on the streets? I have good reason to be very grateful to Antony Cirelli.

None of what Antony told me actually explains why he thought Dom had *killed* Marco. Marco definitely was missing – in hiding, I guess – but you don't automatically suspect murder when an adult disappears. And why would he even imagine Dom could do something like that? No, there's got to be a lot more to that story.

Maybe the trouble was between Marco and Dom so Antony blamed Dom when Marco left? It's all a bit of a mystery and really none of my business. Except that I'll do anything I can to help Antony in any way because he really saved my life.

I wish I could just go back to being bored instead of having all these thoughts swirling in my head. Feeling used, taken advantage of, then feeling sad and lonely, angry at myself for having such a foolish imagination, concern for my boss.

Oh well, I can't be worrying and wondering about all this stuff now because I've got to prepare Antony's afternoon tea. I have two new treats for him to try which I'm sure he'll adore.

Entering the house the same way I left I come out of the upstairs kitchen into the hallway. I'm about to head downstairs but Remo is at those stairs, waiting.

When he sees me asks: "Were you outside?"

I immediately reach up a hand to tame my hair, figuring it must have been blowing all over and is messy. I feel that my cheek is cold and realize I was out long enough for the cool wind to color my cheeks. Remo's looking at me with real interest but how can that be? It can't, it's just me attributing the storylines from the romance books I read into real life. It's all just make-believe on my part.

Remo

I didn't look outside because I never imagined Fina would be out in the yard in this cold. I always associate her with indoor things yet her cheeks are rosy and her hair is curling wildly around her face. She looks beautiful and healthy although it doesn't look like she's been crying I can tell she's unhappy. Probably because of Shelby.

I've hardly seen anything of Shelby lately and didn't even notice. Her career keeps her on the go traveling all over the place, and I never made an effort to track her down. I haven't even missed her.

Just as well since Marco's been dipping his toes in that pool and apparently with Dominic as well. I can't understand why any couple would want a third to join in. A threesome? With me? Do they even know who I am?

What is it with Marco lately? Why is he going out of his way to piss me off? I'm not really angry about Shelby, she's a gold-digger who sleeps around and he can have her - without me - but what's with all this sneaking behind my back? He might not have pretended with Shelby but he sure impersonated me with Fina.

It's funny but now that she knows about the two of us she can tell us apart, just like Dad can. Not at first, though. I think she was so upset at discovering there were two of us she was too angry to look closely. She doesn't realize how unusual it is for anyone to know us individually, and that means she's a perceptive girl.

"I didn't even think to look for you there. I thought you were in your room refusing to answer when I knocked on the door."

"Why wouldn't I answer?"

"I thought you were mad at me. I mean, about Shelby and all..."

Her expression settles into a perfect *resting bitch face*, a look I've never seen on her before. She actually raises one eyebrow and drills me with a cold stare asking: "Why would I care?"

"Oh! um, well, because Shelby was rude to you. She didn't mean to be, she's a complete narcissist and never thinks about how her words impact others."

"Sounds like a real catch," murmurs Fina and I can't help but explode with a bark of laughter.

"Okay who are you and what have you done with Fina?"

She cracks the tiniest of smiles at my joke and suddenly it feels like everything between us is good again. Just then I hear my father calling out a greeting to Shelby. Turning, I see she's been standing further down the hall listening to us for God knows how long.

"It's ages since I've seen you my dear," booms Dad. With his arms open wide he drags Shelby into an embrace then hooking her elbow with his leads her to us. He attaches me with his other arm and happily beams from one of us to the other. "I'm sorry Remo couldn't bring you to my little soiree but it was a boys-only event. No lovely ladies at all, so dull!"

"Except I guess your new maid was there, working."

Dad looks puzzled a moment before his eyes light on Fina. "Oh you mean Serafina? Ah, she's not a maid, Shelby. Serafina is a heavenly pastry chef – such talent, such skill – I'm so lucky to have her."

"Oh so she's *yours*, is she?" My eyes narrow at the implication behind Shelby's words but Dad just brushes it off.

"She is, that's true, because although Serafina bakes for everyone I seem to be the only person in this house who isn't worried about their waistline! I lap up every bite because everything is always delicious. In fact, my dear, you look like you could do with a few desserts yourself before you fade away to nothing."

"Desserts? Ugh," Shelby fakes a shiver as if the very thought is gruesome. "I guess they're okay for people who don't care how they look," she casts a sideways glance at Fina with her windblown locks, "but of course I'm always in front of a camera or on a runway so I don't have that luxury."

"Oh that's such a shame but you've *got to make hay while the sun shines* or however that saying goes because in a job like yours your face does have a *best before date,* doesn't it? So unfair, but the public is very fickle and there's always an appetite for someone new and younger. Tch, tch, tch."

I study my wily parent and detect a wicked glint of humor evident in his eyes although his face remains the picture of innocence. So he did clue into Shelby's little digs at Fina. I should have realized he would do so. I turn to share a secret smirk with Fina but she's gone.

Since we're blocking the hallway her only exit is down the stairs to her kitchen so I know wheres he went. I don't follow her. If I do my so-called girlfriend will come after me and I don't want Shelby invading Fina's space.

Sighing, I turn back to Shelby suggesting we go for a drive. She's up for it but won't be so pleased when she hears what I've got to say. Shelby ended our relationship the moment she got involved with Marco, but I guess my lack of interest means it was already over. I'm not even surprised at how little I care.

Serafina

About an hour later I'm delivering my tray laden with goodies to Antony's study. He exclaims in delight as he tastes every offering and makes guesses, usually correct, about the ingredients.

"But this chocolate icing Serafina, it's got a bite that I love, my tastebuds are on fire and craving more, but I don't... no, it's not cinnamon, I can't figure it out?"

"Just a smidge of chili powder."

"No! What ever made you think of that?"

"I caught an episode on one of those shows where people try to convince rich entrepreneurs to invest in their invention or product and when this person mentioned adding spices to chocolate bars I had a lightbulb moment and decided to give it a try. You like it?"

"I do, I really do. Who would have thought? Of course there was that fun movie from years back called *Chocolate* or no, I think it was *Chocolat* and the woman kept adding secret ingredients that made people fall in love or something. This is exquisite – you are brilliant, my dear Serafina."

Obviously I have one of those praise kinks I've read about in my stories because Antony's compliments send a tingle of warmth right through me. Not to my lady parts, but deep inside nevertheless. I'm still enjoying the glow when Giorgio comes in. He's always able to scent out a trayful of sweet treats although he never raves over the results.

"Good afternoon Antony, Serafina. I saw Remo putting that girl Shelby into his car and driving away, it's been a long time since she was here, but she looks as lovely as ever. I'm sorry I missed saying hello." He turns to me and I find his hooded gaze cold like a reptile, specifically a snake.

I get the impression he wants me to know Remo and Shelby have gone out together. He's watching me closely and I hope none of my inner turmoil shows as I return his look with mild interest. Such a nasty man.

I return to my kitchen, my refuge! and pull out my phone. It's odd that my Contacts don't include Peter, who was supposed to be my boyfriend, but he did phone me once so his number is in my call history. I text him now asking him to pass on the message that I'm willing to have this date with Dom. Why not? Why the hell not?

Kind of a roundabout way to do things, I guess, but Peter's not my boyfriend. I'm over that misapprehension now.

Peter

I don't get many texts so I'm always a bit surprised and suspicious when a notification comes in. It's from Fina and, oh thank Christ, she's willing to see Dom. I've been keeping a low profile, trying to stay out of his way, but now I can tell him the good news. He's in his office. I've avoided him because he keeps threatening me but he won't any more.

I head down the hallway and stop outside door to knock and wait for permission before entering. After a pause he calls out *come in if you dare* which isn't encouraging but he'll be happy to hear this.

Dom looks intimidating in his big office chair behind his desk. There's a woman I've never seen before sitting on one of the loveseats. She's looks like a Goth with her dyed black hair and heavy make-up. Like Christine. Is that style making a comeback? She's not like the girls he usually bullies, in fact she looks a *mean girl* herself.

Dom's leaning back in his chair with his arms folded behind his head and a satisfied smirk on his face. I see why when Trix, the stripper with the huge fake boobs, squirms her way out from under the desk wiping her mouth just as Dom zips up his jeans.

"Was that okay, Dom? Can I go now? I want to get something to eat before my first show and–"

"Yeah I'm good, Trix, but you can't leave until you take of Monique, that'll give you something to eat," he says with a smirk. If he sees his dancer's shoulders slump he ignores it and turns to me with a cold look on his face. "What do you want Peter?"

"It's Fina, she messaged that she wants to see you so what should I text back?"

"Serafina? Oh that's excellent news, Petey! Have a seat and we'll watch these two while I think up a response."

I sit down opposite Monique who hikes up her leather skirt showing that she's naked underneath. Trix shuffles in front of her and Monique places each of her feet on Trix's shoulders. I have to slide to the edge of my loveseat so Trix's head doesn't block my view. She doesn't seem too sure what to do and leaning in starts slowly kissing the other woman's slit until Dom says:

"If you make Monique cum in the next five, no we'll say ten minutes, then it'll count for double a blowjob against what you owe me. Is that good enough incentive, Trix?"

The girl nods then gets to work with enthusiasm. Going down on a chick doesn't do anything for me but I like watching this.

Trix is sticking her finger in Monique's hole while she's licking and nipping Monique's clit. Then she slides another finger inside and starts pumping her hand back and forth. With her other hand she's exposing Monique's clit and we can see it get red and shiny.

Monique's face has no expression at all until suddenly she arches her back while her thighs hold Trix's face tight against her cunt and she lets out a stuttering grunt. Her hips buck a couple of times and then she kicks Trix away.

"Trix your chin is wet with Monique's slime, no don't wipe it off, come here, yeah just like that, and sit on my knee."

The girl gets up to obey Dom's command although her hands clench and it's obvious she wants to clean herself up.

Getting Trix settled in his lap Dom unhooks her bra and pulling it off plays a bit with her big tits. Finally he wipes the cum off her face and smears it across her nipples. Lifting her boob to his mouth he sucks the nipple hard. Trix's face shows discomfort, maybe even pain, but I can't tell if that's from arousal or if he's hurting her. Maybe both. Dom now moves to the other nipple and the one he abandoned looks bruised and swollen. Yeah, he sucked hard enough to hurt her.

Finished, he lifts the girl off his lap and tells her if she puts on a good performance tonight he'll let her cum after her show but not to dare masturbate without his permission or he'll add it back to her debt. Trix pouts but nods in agreement. I'm pretty sure Dom is the only one in this room who thinks these little activities have actually turned her on.

He smacks Trix hard on her ass and sends her on her way. Meanwhile Monique has pulled her skirt back down and sits with her eyes on Dom, waiting.

"Petey here doesn't really like fucking girls but he'll do you if I tell him to. What do you say?"

"I'm good," Monique replies without even looking in my direction.

Dom nods, smiling to himself as if he's heard the answer he expected, then says "Okay then. Come back around midnight, we'll be ready to sell some product then."

Without a word Monique gets up and leaves us alone in the office. Dom's bored look is gone as he asks me to read out Fina's message to him. When I do so he tells me to text back that we'll pick her up at 9:00 and to let Antony know she's coming Club Malavita to see the floor show and yes, we'll bring her home but it'll be late.

I ask him a couple of times to repeat what he said before he slaps me upside the head, takes my phone out of my hands, and thumbs the message himself.

Since he's in a good mood I ask him why Trix owes him blowjobs.

"Well, to begin with she was just paying me back half of the money her boob job cost. We worked out a price list for sexual favors and she keeps a running tally. She still owes me a few grand. But then I caught her blowing Big Tony and explained if she's going to service one bouncer she has to suck off all of them and say it's a little gift from me, and I reimburse her."

"But Big Tony is her boyfriend, isn't he?" I ask, confused.

"Yeah, so? She still has to blow me and anyone else I say. You want one from her? No? No, you'd rather be taking her place under this desk, wouldn't you?" Unlike most people nowadays Dom still wears a watch and he glances at it before telling me *okay, come here, we've got time.*

Twenty-Two

Serafina

Dom and I are sitting together in the back-seat of the car while Peter drives us like he's a chauffeur. Dom takes my hand and bringing it to his lips kisses my fingers. I guess that's his signature move or something. It tickles and I like it.

"I'd pull you close to cuddle but then I won't be able to see your beautiful face," he tells me. My eyes widen and I smile at the compliment.

I spent extra time preparing. I shaved my armpits and legs, tweezered my eyebrows, added a leave-in conditioner after washing my hair... I even used waterproof mascara so I don't get smudgy raccoon eyes. I did wonder if I should do something about my pubic hair but decided to leave well enough alone. I don't want ugly little red bumps, or prickly hair from trimming the length. Besides, it's not too bad and it is silky soft. *No need to condition that hair,* I giggle to myself.

This is all just so unbelievable. Here I am holding hands with the most amazing guy. I'm giving my v-card, as my novels call it, to an incredibly handsome man with a hot body and a sexy deep voice. And he's giving all his attention to me! He's staring and smiling and complimenting me.

My heart is pounding and I can't seem to catch my breath properly. He's noticed because his eyes are now focused on my heaving chest. My nipples are poking at the lacy fabric of my bustier. They ache to feel his touch, his mouth...

Suddenly he pulls me close in the tightest embrace with his mouth crashing down on mine unleashing a mad passion. He's devouring my lips and his deep murmur awakens strange new desires deep in my core.

I forget about Peter driving, I forget about Remo and his girlfriend Shelby, I forget about Marco making a fool out of me, and I even forget Antony's antipathy towards Dominic, because in this moment all I can think of is Dom's hot mouth claiming mine. His tongue invades and explores, his hands pull me deeper into his embrace. This kiss is everything and I am lost in it.

All too soon the car stops and Dom pulls away from me. I'm reclined against the seat with my eyes half-lidded, my lips loose and puffy and a heat flushing from my cheeks right down across my chest.

"Bella Fina, la piu bella ragazza, mia Fina," he whispers, his eyes racing over my face and body then back up again to meet my eyes. I just want to stay in this moment forever. I know I'm not beautiful but I yearn to hear him say it again and again. I understand enough Italian to know he's saying I'm *the most beautiful girl* like he believes it.

Peter opens the back door and the spell is broken. Dom draws me out of the car and tucking my arm in his leads me into Club Malavita. The party is in full swing with exotic dancers working the poles and topless waitresses working the crowd. Other than that quick glimpse of Gigi in the store-room I've never actually seen another woman's naked breasts.

All heads turn towards Dom as he guides me through the press of happy, excited people. I feel their eyes following us.

The lights strobe, synchronized with the pounding beat of the techno club music. I'm caught up in the atmosphere of night-time revels of the young, the wealthy, the beautiful... and I'm with the leader of them all. I should probably play it cool but I can't keep the grin off my face.

We stop at a raised area cordoned off with thick ropes on heavy stanchions, and guarded by muscular men whose faces are expressionless.

Dom is ushered in and we sink down on plush seats with a good view of the whole scene. There are several bottles of champagne chilling in a tub of ice. Dom motions to Peter who pours us both a glass. The noise of the crowd and the music makes it too loud for conversation but I can hear Dom's deep purr of contentment as he nuzzles my neck and whispers endearments. Feeling his mouth planting kisses on my throat is so exciting and I'm beyond happy just to be here, to be with him.

Lots of people, both men and women, look up to where we're sitting. I can see their upturned faces and sense the envy and longing. *Don't worry,* I tell them in my head, *I'm wondering why me? too.*

Peter flops down in a couch across from us and starts playing with is phone. Every now and then he darts a glance at Dom and then at me but when I catch his eye he quickly looks away.

Something is niggling at the back of my mind but I can't concentrate with Dom's long fingers slowly stroking up and down my arms. I let my head fall back against his shoulder and hear him chuckle. He urges me to drink more champagne. It's not as tasty as I thought it would be but the bubbles do tickle my nose and that makes me giggle.

When I finish a third glass he says *good girl* and standing helps me to my feet. It's hard getting out of the soft furniture but Dom's strong arm pulls me up.

Once again he directs me through the throng of people, a much more boisterous crowd now, until we leave the main floor and go into the relative quiet of a hallway. This leads to another room with a bar but no music. There are some people scattered around the edges and I realize this is where we came when Dom did that thing to my arms with the rope. I'm hoping he'll do some more of that but maybe not here with all these people watching.

"Now Fina," he says, looking right into my eyes. I can see that his are sparkling and he's smiling with anticipation. "Tonight is a very special night for you and for me and for Peter, too."

It's good he's holding me by my upper arms because when I swing round to find Peter the room sways with me. "Peter?" He's looking at Dom, not me, and I can't read his expression.

"Yes, Peter. I'm afraid Peter's been a bad boy. I caught him skimming some of the product he was supposed to be selling for me."

"Product?"

"Drugs, Serafina. Selling drugs is how I make my money. Those people drinking and dancing out there are my best customers. Peter isn't a customer, he's a pusher who works for me but now he's turned into an addict. You knew Peter was a user, right? Well, he betrayed my trust and that kind of behavior can't go unpunished now, can it?"

I'm having trouble paying attention to his actual words but I follow the cadence of his voice and comply by shaking my head *no*.

"That's right. So I've been doling out a few physical punishments but it isn't enough. Peter needs to pay with a really severe punishment because I let him get close to me and now I have to make an example out of him. Otherwise people will think I'm playing favorites, they'll think I've grown weak, they'll think they can get away with disrespecting me. I can't let that happen, can I Fina?"

Again, I shake my head.

"But Peter is scared, and he should be, so he's made me a counter-offer instead. Do you want to know what that offer is?"

I start shaking my head but when his hand cups my chin and turns my gesture into a nod I keep it up, continuing to nod a few times, saying: "Yes Dom, I want to know."

His grin is huge as he answers: "He's offered me you!"

I just stare blankly, eager to share the joke but not getting it.

"Fina, he's offered up you, your body, for me to do whatever I like with for the rest of the evening. I wanted longer but you living in my uncle's home complicates things. However, we'll manage with the time we have and you will be mine, completely and utterly mine. I will do whatever I want with you and this will release Peter from his debt to me."

Part of me is all tingly at the thought of submitting to whatever fun sexy games Dom wants to play but in my muddled brain is a growing concern that it can't be all pleasure if it's Peter's punishment. And why should I take it anyhow?

"But what does Peter's debt have to do with me?" I manage to ask.

"Peter tells me you owe him, Serafina. His family took you in and you took all their love and time and attention – even his inheritance – away from him. He was kicked out of the house and you got to keep his parents all to yourself–"

"No! it wasn't like that," I interrupt, but Dom just goes on.

"Just like a little cuckoo bird, you invaded the nest and pushed all the fledglings out of their rightful place."

"No! No, I never did that."

"Was Peter thrown out?"

"Well yes, but that–"

"And you got to stay for years afterwards, right?"

"Yeah, but I–"

"Sounds to me like you do owe Peter, Serafina. You do have an obligation to him."

Dom leans back and gazes at me with one eyebrow lifted in an inquiring look. My glance darts from him to Peter, who is biting his lip and looking concerned, then back to Dom who waits patiently.

"You've twisted everything and now you're putting me on the spot. It's not nice, Dom, it's... it's mean and... it's cruel."

"Oh little girl, I am mean and cruel. I'm not nice at all and I want you, I crave you. If you love Peter, Peter who has been a big brother to you for so long, then you will pay his debt. Even if you do think it's a mean and cruel obligation."

My head is spinning. There's something wrong with all this but Dom's persuasive voice and Peter's needy looks are convincing me that their argument is sound. "What do I have to do?"

"Just submit to me, Serafina. That's all. I will take care of the rest."

"But what is the rest? What are you going to do?"

Still holding my arms Dom pulls me closer and leaning down to ensure he has my complete attention his voice drops to a sexy whisper that sends chills down my spine.

"I will strip you, I will punish you, I will pleasure you, I will make you beg and you will give me the most wonderful, delightful, exotic-erotic night ever!"

I don't realize I've sucked in my bottom lip until I feel his eyes following my movements. His words have thrilled me – despite my misgivings – and I find myself nodding.

"Use your words, Serafina. I need to hear you give your consent."

Time stands still for one long breath which I exhale on the word *Yes.*

Dominic

She's agreed, at last.

Of course I don't need her consent because now that I've got her here I'll just take what I want. No, getting her consent is something I'll throw in her face later when I remind her she wanted it and agreed to it when she said *yes.*

I've waited way too long for this moment. My hungry demons are rising, ready to come out and play with the delectable innocent Serafina.

Already Peter's relief has morphed into concern. He's reaching for me, trying to extract a promise of what? restraint? compassion? Ha! Peter has delivered this charming girl but he better stay well away from me. I'm accepting Serafina as payment for now... but if Peter keeps hanging around he'll soon incur another debt and that one he'll have to settle himself.

I don't want him to watch me with Fina, or to know what's going on. I don't want any of them to see us so I holler at everyone to get out. There's some grumbling among the shuffling sounds of departure so I draw my gun and fire off a shot. No one screams in pain so my bullet didn't find a target but at least they're hustling out the door now.

Peter has remained. I turn a cold look on him.

"Dom," he pleads, "You won't hurt her—"

"I will," I answer.

"But not really, I mean it will just be like sexy punishment, right? Fun spanking time with just a little pain to make the pleasure more…"

I just keep staring at him until his voice dwindles away. Fina is shaky on her feet and I'll need to get her lying down soon. I simply point to the door and Peter, head drooping, leaves.

"Peter?" her voice says his name like a question and he pauses but keeps going without turning around.

I turn back to my girl, my captive, and tell her it's time to get naked. She gives me a look full of consternation and I chuckle as she frowns. I'm still holding her close so I take hold of her shirt at the collar and with one mighty jerk I rip it open sending buttons popping. I know it's too much to imagine she'll do a striptease but I'm quite happy to strip her myself.

Spinning her around I pull her ass into me as I bend her torso forward. She staggers a bit but keeps her balance.

"You told me how you get this top off so go ahead," I instruct. As I feel her open the bustier I pull down her leggings and panties and slide them off her feet. Now she's totally bare and I feast my eyes on all her creamy skin. She's a little dizzy from the champagne and she rocks a bit as she stands before my hungry eyes.

Serafina is a curvy, voluptuous young woman – truly delicious! and with wavy pubic hair, when's the last time I saw that? All the women who work here at the club are waxed bare. I wonder if I have time to wax Serafina? No, I want to play with her curls which I'll tug hard enough to make her cry.

Her long hair drapes across her shoulders and I grab a handful of it and twist tight, pulling it from her scalp, while pushing her down on her knees. She stumbles but ends up exactly where I want her. Kneeling, looking up at me with frightened eyes, her mouth forming a tantalizing O.

Serafina

I'm naked and already overwhelmed with shame although Dominic hasn't touched me yet. Instead he's having a leisurely look at me from head to toe while enjoying the blush on my cheeks and the brightness of unshed tears in my eyes before he yanks on my hair and forces me to the ground.

He takes off his shirt and I'm distracted from my own worries by the glorious art covering his upper body. Skulls and snakes circle and showcase his biceps, forearms, and abs. Following the line of his torso my eyes move down until I see his erection clearly outlined against his jeans.

He pulls my face into his groin and rubs himself against me through the thick denim. I'm confused about what he wants me to do but he steps back and sits on the edge of the bed and beckons me closer. I'm not sure if I'm allowed to get up so I play it safe and shuffle towards him on my knees. I can see he likes that.

"I'm going to start your lesson with a full and proper spanking. But it won't be the *fun spanking* Peter spoke of. Well, it will be fun for me. So what exactly can you expect? Hmm, let's see... I'll start with these gorgeous tits. Now, sit on my lap, straddling my legs and facing me, then lace your fingers on top of your head."

I do so gingerly because of my weight, but he firmly presses me down. I can feel the muscular width of his thighs supporting me. Maybe it's because he wears eye make-up but I seem to forget that Dom is a very big, strong man.

When I raise up my arms as instructed my breasts lift and sway, my nipples already growing hard under his close scrutiny.

"I like the color of these little nubs, Fina."

He fills both hands with my breasts making fists to squeeze and massage, scrunching them together then rotating apart. It feels good but also a bit impersonal and I'm just thinking how I'd prefer more of a caress when suddenly slap, slap he strikes with his right hand and then his left. Each smack isn't too hard but it's followed in quick succession by another and another and another and soon my breasts are burning and I'm leaning my body back, trying to escape.

"Stay still and behave, Serafina," he commands in his deep voice, sounding colder than I've ever heard him.

"But that hurts, Dom."

"Good, now shut up."

Using both hands simultaneously he slaps upward from the underside of my breasts. And then again and again and again. Each swat makes the flesh bounce and jiggle and looking down I can see my skin has changed to a dusky pink. My nipples are dark brown with a reddish tinge, and I'm aching from a throbbing pain. When I try lowering my hands in protection he gives my wrists a vicious twist and puts them back in place.

Still Dominic continues slapping up and sideways At one point he cups one breast to spank the mound of flesh, then repeats the process with the other. By now I'm panting, tears streaming down my cheeks, but I have to keep quiet. Besides, I refuse to beg or plead. I can take this.

After telling me *there, that's your tits done* Dom flips me face down on the bed. I'm no lightweight but he lifts me easily so he must be very, very strong. It really hurts to have my hot and achy breasts pressed into the mattress but at least he's stopped hitting them.

"I like a good old-fashioned - meaning bare bottom over-the-knee - spanking just as much as the next man, Serafina, but what you're getting isn't foreplay. No, no *sexy spanking* for you. This will be pure punishment for *my* pleasure, not yours."

I hear him move away from the bed but I'm afraid to turn my head and watch. Part of me foolishly believes if I'm obedient and quiet and still he might forget about me, or at least show some sympathy.

"I got the most marvelous early Christmas present, well to be honest I bought it myself because I couldn't resist! It's a collection of spanking implements that comes with it's very own wall-mounted hanger for easy storage and easier access. Look here, Serafina." I turn my head as instructed and see him wave at a display of various items hanging on the wall closest to the bed. He points to each group saying: "Look how many different paddles, canes, whips and floggers, and one each of a wooden wide-backed hairbrush, spanking ruler, riding crop, and a tawse.

I feel like a kid in a candy store I've got such a great selection and it's all brand-new, well except for one cane that I already used. I used it on Peter, actually. He cried like a baby."

I feel waves of fear and revulsion roll through me. Sure, I've read *Fifty Shades* and have fantasized about getting an erotic spanking but this... this is going to be something else. The thought of any of these tools in the hand of a madman like Dominic is truly frightening. I watch him take an item down and begin whirling his arm around.

"This riding crop will be perfect on your little virgin cunt," he declares, the glee evident in his voice. "And this intriguing piece is called a *tawse*. Very effective on the palms of misbehaving schoolchildren, and it's supposed to be absolutely wicked on a bare ass. Yeah, I've decided on these two. The whips and the canes welt and draw blood which I'll have an appetite for later on, but right now I want to start marking you up without bloodshed.

I'll have you kicking your legs, twisting and turning, sobbing and begging for my mercy that well, obviously, is something you're not going to get!" He finishes with an eerie giggle then begins spanking me with the leather tawse.

With his left hand Dominic holds my wrists together above my head while using his right to smack me painfully over and over and over again and to my everlasting shame I *am* squirming in a futile effort to escape, *and* squealing from the sting. Before long I'm shouting and shrieking. I'm suffering from a burning pain all over my bum and the top of my thighs.

When he finally stops and flips me onto my back I'm crying so hard I can't see out of my tear-filled eyes. He quickly secures my wrists and ankles to the bed's built-in restraints which spread me wide and helpless.

Stepping back to study the picture I present Dominic gives his head a shake and uncuffing my ankles produces something he calls a *sling restraint*. He clips a cuff around one ankle, runs the strap around the back of my neck then attaches the other end to my other ankle. He adjusts a bit of padding to prevent the edge of the sturdy leather from digging into my neck. Then he grabs the loose ends from the ankle straps and yanks hard to tighten them. As he does so my legs pull up until they're bent at the knee.

"Yes, this is better for a woman with your type of build. If you had long thin legs I could tuck your ankles behind your head but this works quite well and, frankly, I prefer your meaty flesh over a scrawny, bony body. I like a bigger canvas, so to speak.

Now let's see if we can't lift everything up a bit further." He pulls on the straps asking: "Does that hurt?" and when I cry out from the pain he again replies *Good*.

So now my arms are restrained, my legs are spread wide and bent unnaturally, and my lower body is raised up so my vagina is fully exposed. Dominic runs his finger from clit to anus so yes, that's on display as well.

"That's tits and ass done so now it's time for your pussy spanking."

Dominic returns the tawse to its proper place and comes back smacking the riding crop against his thigh. He combs his fingers through my soft pubic hair which offers no protection to the tender skin underneath. It really hurt when Dominic hit my breasts and bum but neither compare to having my vagina spanked.

The thwap-thwap sound of the riding crop repeatedly, horribly striking from my mound right down to my anus plays against my grunting *unghh* sounds of agony. My flesh is on fire and it's excruciating. Only my hands have ever touched down there and the skin is so tender.

Just when I thought it couldn't get any worse of course it did. The friction made my clit swell and that ultra-sensitive bundle of nerves really suffered from each slap, throbbing tortuously between strokes.

"I need a photo of this!" Dominic declares and I groan to think of my humiliation being digitally preserved. He gets out his phone and takes several long shots as well as close-ups. I'm sure I'm a sorry sight but he can't keep the grin off his face.

Finishing with the pictures – for the time being at least – Dominic once again rummages in the carry-all and comes up with a device that, strangely enough looks like a microphone. He explains it's his *magic wand* and when he turns it on and I hear the buzz I panic. I'm fully exposed and already suffering from the thrashing. When he touches the head to my clit I can't hold back my scream, it's extremely painful.

Keeping in camera range he films himself amping up the speed on the hand-held control. If his video has sound my hoarse screeching will testify to the power of the wand in the hands of a sadist. After an eternity he switches the device off and I'm wailing in tormented anguish from my overstimulated nerve endings.

I don't answer when he says: "You're my first virgin, Serafina, and I will enjoying teaching your body how best to please me."

Without warning he pokes his index finger straight into my anus. The sharp pain makes me holler at the intrusion but that doesn't stop him.

"You can start pleasing me by answering *yes, Dom or Sir or Master.*"

He pulls his finger out out then goes in again and adding a second begins He pulls out then goes in again, sawing back and forth. It really hurts. I beg him to stop, saying *it's disgusting there.*

"What, here? Why? because there's shit in that passage?" he laughs when I screw up my face. "Oh dear girl you are SO innocent. I'm going to stick my fingers up your ass in order to stretch it for my cock. I'm going to stick my tongue up there, too. But, if it makes you feel better I can clean you out first. Yeah, sure, let's give you an enema."

"WHAT? No! No, don't do that–" I cry out in a panic.

"Oh you know what an enema is, do you? How?"

"Sometimes I had to give one to Marta, Peter's invalid mother, when her medication constipated her so bad and, you know..." I trail off in embarrassment.

"So you were an unpaid nurse doing all the nasty stuff, hmm? Well good, that means you'll know what to expect. Although... I imagine you used a gentle Castille soap mixed into warm water and inserted the nozzle slowly... hmm? Hah! that ain't gonna happen here, sweetheart."

"Dom, please-please-please don't do this, don't!"

"Oh I'm definitely going to give you an enema, Fina, but later. It will be messy so I'll have to do it in the bathroom but right now, while I've got you all nicely trussed up, I want to use your dirty asshole just as it is."

I can't bear this, I'm utterly wrung out and every inch of me hurts. My body sags in misery, already resigned to the next assault, because I can tell Dom has just gotten started.

Twenty-Three

Remo

After making it very clear to Shelby that our relationship is over I dropped her off and came back home to learn Fina has gone out with Dom. Of all people why would she let a monster like Dominic get within fifty feet of her? Christ I hate him.

I'm surprised Dad let her go with Dom but there's no point asking *why?* he'll just say *where were you?*

I'm worried about Fina. And I can't help but think her finding out about Shelby had something to do with this. I go looking for Marco figuring he's the most likely one to have answers.

I knock as I enter his room finding him asleep, fully dressed, on his bed.

"Get up," I order and he calls out *what? what?* before coming fully awake. He rubs his face and runs a hand through his hair. Looking at him is exactly the same for me as looking in a mirror.

In one of those moments of twin ESP he says to me: "Fina can tell us apart."

"When we're in the same room?"

"No, not only then. I saw her in the hallway and she knew it was me." He screws up his mouth as if the memory isn't pleasant. I narrow my eyes and ask him what he did to her.

"Nothing! I swear. Well, I tried, but she blew me off. Called me by name and said she can tell who's who because you never try to take advantage of her. Something like that."

He tilts his head to give me a speculative look. "You like-like her, don't you?"

I don't say anything and he continues: "But you know, she's got nothing on Shelby. I mean, Shelby's a successful model. She's got the face, the body, and those legs..."

"Fina has a beautiful face and a full curvy figure but more important she's a sweet girl with a kind nature. Shelby's a bitch who played both of us. You can keep her, I already made it clear that I'm done."

"What makes you think I want your leftovers?"

"Umm, let's see, how about past history? Marco you always chased after every girl, and then as we grew older all the women, that I ever showed any interest in. I don't know why, we don't really have the same taste yet over and over you've got them cheating on me. And none of it matters because once I know you've fucked them I lose interest, and then you don't want them anymore either. You know for being my twin you act like you're my worst enemy."

"Fuck Remo that's not true... okay I did get together with Shelby because she's so hot and when I found out she was up for a threesome – yeah, it was her idea by the way – I was all for it. But I might have guessed you'd be totally uptight. Just like you are with Dom."

Marco's reminded me that I want to know what going on with Dominic so I let that comment slide. He's leaning back against the headboard of his bed, relaxed. Now's a good time to get some answers.

"Yeah what's up with him and Fina?"

"What do you mean?"

"I mean she's out with him right now."

"Really? He asked me about her but I didn't think he was interested, not really."

"When you say he asked about her–"

"Just what did I think of her, doesn't she have beautiful skin – I said she's sure got lots of it and he laughed and said she was perfect – then he asked if Antony lets her go out at night. I told him I have no idea, but Dad's not a tyrant."

"Well Dad just told me that Dom and Peter, the guy she grew up with? just picked her up and Dad wasn't happy about it but he couldn't say no, she's an adult."

"Does Dad have a thing for her?"

"Jesus, no! You sound like Uncle Giorgio. Dad thinks the world of her but only in a father-daughter way. And not your kind of twisted Daddy and Little Girl crap."

Marco can't resist shooting me a stupid smirk that just makes my fist clench with the urge to punch his mouth when he says: "Hey, don't knock it until you try it."

"Seriously Marco? after all the trouble you got into over– you know what? forget it. Just tell me if you know where Dom has taken Fina."

"I don't. I mean there's Malavita but he's at the club every day so it wouldn't exactly be a date, would it? Of course if that guy Peter is with them then it won't be much of a date. Peter's gay and he's involved with Dom."

"What about you?"

"Aww, not really. He's into some kinky shit and some interests me, some doesn't, but I wouldn't say we're involved. Not really."

"Hmm, well if you hear anything let me know. Fina's an innocent and Dom can't be trusted. I still haven't forgiven you two, you know."

I leave his room and head back downstairs. There's no point hanging out in my room by myself, I won't be able to control my bad thoughts about whatever it is Fina and Dom are doing. I'm just at the head of the stairs when Leo flings his door open and seeing me calls out:

"Remo? Marco? come here, you've got to see this."

Leo looks pretty worked up but I really can't get excited about seeing his high score in some *shoot 'em up* video game. I'm just about to make an excuse when he darts out of his room and grabs my arm to drag me back with him.

"Hey!"

"You've got to do something about this, I can't. I don't know how. Look, LOOK!"

He's dragged me into his room now and is pointing at the middle monitor in his work station. When my stunned mind is finally able to make sense of what my eyes are seeing I plop down into the chair, gripping the short arm-rests.

"What am I seeing? How did you get this? Is this in real-time? Can you trace it? I know I'm asking a lot of questions, Leo, and we'll talk about the hows and whys later but for now just answer, okay?"

"Okay Remo, uh this is video being shot from Dominic's phone which I'm getting because I cloned his phone at Dad's party. I think this is happening right now but because the camera is steady I can't be sure if it's filming or replaying previously filmed. And yes, I have the GPS co-ordinates, the video is being played in Dominic's club Malavita."

"Right, good, I'm going. We'll talk about this cloning shit when I get back."

"I'm coming with you, I want—"

"No, Leo—"

"I'm coming!" he insists.

I free up my arm that he's clutching and explain: "Leo, come on, you know you can't even legally enter the building."

"But I want to help Fina."

"You already have, Leo, what you've just done here is big, so big, and I need you to keep monitoring and copying. We'll destroy it all later but in the meantime we might need a record.

Also, tell Dad. You might think he can't handle seeing these images but he's a tough guy and you'll be surprised. You get Dad and I'll get Marco. I'm putting my phone on silent but we'll stay in touch."

I give him a quick hug, damn I'm proud of this kid, then hurry to get Marco. He's already in the hallway asking what all the noise is about but I don't waste words. I just grab his shoulder and propel him ahead of me down the stairs. I don't have time to stay and talk to Dad, we need to get to Fina right now. As I hustle Marco down the stairs I explain:

"Dom's got Fina and he's torturing her. We have to get to her, she needs our help."

"Wh- what? Dom wouldn't do that to Fina, you're wrong."

"I just saw a live feed. Well, I might have seen a video of a live event but for sure the video is being played at his club so we're going there now and we'll–"

"No! wait. What if you've got it all wrong? What if this is a scene they're playing? I don't want to get on Dom's bad side."

"Dom only has a bad side, Jesus Marco can you hear yourself? We're talking about Fina, the girl who couldn't say shit if her mouth was full of it. Now come on."

"Remo, wait, what exactly are you planning to do?"

"One: rescue Fina. Two: kill Dom if necessary. Are we clear?"

"I'm not sure if I..."

We're outside now and even though the light is dim I can see his features clearly enough to spot that Marco looks confused, hesitant, even scared. He's no use to me if he's going to side with Dom when we get there. I need to know.

"Are you with me, your brother and twin, or are you choosing Dominic? I need your answer right now."

He just stares back at me with indecision all over his face, his mouth is working but no words are coming out. I've always known there is a weakness in Marco born from jealousy, resentment, spite... his ambivalence now is telling me everything I need to know, no matter how much I hate it.

Turning quickly I run to our parking area at the back thankful I didn't garage my car and can save a precious minute or so. I back out with the engine roaring and am just about to throw it into gear when the door is yanked open and Marco tumbles into the passenger seat.

"I'm not doing this for you, asshole, but for Fina."

"Buckle up, we're laying rubber."

Leo

I make Dad sit on my chair because his face has gone gray. I've heard people say that but I've never seen it before and it's scary. All the color just drained away when he realized what he was looking at. He looks worse then when he collapsed at the reappearance of Marco.

I can't stop talking, babbling I guess, but it seems to help. I've explained to Dad how I came to have the video and then everything Remo said and what he and Marco are doing now.

"He said I have to keep watching in case we find something, some clue, or something we can use later. I'm not exactly sure why. Watching is really tough, Dad, and I don't know if I can keep–"

"We have to, Leo." He reaches up and pulls me into his side with his arm wrapped tight around my waist. "If Serafina can bear to live through this then the least we can do is be her witnesses. I'd say you don't have to look, that I'll watch instead, but I might miss a crucial clue, Leo. Your young eyes might spot something I don't catch. I'm sorry son, it's a helluva thing to ask but.."

"I'll do it for Fina, Dad. I'll do anything I can to help her. I just... I guess it's just uh... I feel bad for seeing her like this, like... no clothes on and being a victim."

"Being victimized, Leo. Serafina has done nothing wrong–"

"Oh, I know that!" I interrupt but he continues saying:

"Unfortunately it's what Serafina thinks about herself that will matter. If she fears we're disgusted by her or pitying her or repulsed, well... what's happening to her is repulsive but she's an innocent angel being abused. She's utterly blameless. Your cousin Dominic on the other hand..."

"How can he do this? Dad, he's enjoying it." I can feel my face screw up in confusion and anger.

"Well, since he's doing it we can assume that's the case but–"

"No, he is. I can see it on his face." Dad leans closer to the monitor then turns to give me a questioning look.

"Leo, how can you see Dominic's face?"

"In the mirror, right there," I point to the screen and when Dad still doesn't see what I'm talking about I draw a selection around the area and enlarge it. There are mirrors in the headboard and on the wall above the bed. Maybe even on the ceiling but we don't have that angle.

"See? That's Dominic and look how he's grinning. It's so creepy and sick. Jeez, Dad I can't believe he's actually having fun." I spit out the last word like it's poisonous but Dad isn't listening to me, he's deeply in thought.

"Leo, can you take a photo or a still picture or something of this image, this close-up and also a screenshot or whatever you call it of the whole screen just to show the close-up in context?"

"Sure, can I just slide your chair back for a minute?" Dad moves out of the way and I do what he's asked, taking several stills focusing on my maniac cousin's evil smile. I save the images and move them over to one of the other monitors so they're within reach but not blocking the main video.

"Excellent, excellent, Leo. We can use these photos for sure."

"But Dad, what if... well. I'm not sure how to say this but what if Fina doesn't want to do anything about the attack? I've heard lots of rapists go free because their victims are too frightened or too ashamed or something to go to court."

"I understand what you're saying, Leo. Unfortunately the nature of our adversarial court system means the victim is on trial just as much as the perpetrator."

Typical Dad, but this time he's gone into his lecturing mode as a means of distancing himself from the horror on the screen.

"However, if Serafina wants to press charges we will be with her all the way. I suspect though, that she won't. She isn't confrontational by nature and I'm pretty sure she'll try to sweep it all under the carpet. I will, naturally, insist on providing her with counseling to aid her recovery from this ordeal. We will all do everything in our power to help her.

No, I'll be giving this proof to Uncle Tonino. I don't have to convince anyone that Dominic Ferragamo is a sadistic psycho – he's done that to himself right here. And this proves he's unfit to be Tonino's designee. He can be an enforcer or a torturer in the *famiglia* but he certainly can't be in charge. I mean, that stunt with Marco. No, I only have to convince Tonino and this will do the trick.

Thank you Leo, you've done a really good job. First, in alerting Remo to the problem, second, initiating and facilitating the rescue, and thirdly, producing definitive proof. Excellent work, son."

I throw my arms around Dad's neck just like I'm a little kid again but his pride in me just makes me want to bawl. What a baby I am.

Twenty-Four

Dominic

I give Fina a break telling her to rest up for *part two*. She immediately drifts off, using sleep as an escape. Serafina's mother is dead and so is her adopted mother and I think that accounts for some of her innocence. She grew up without a woman who could warn her about men. Especially about men like me.

My mother ran off, or is missing, it depends who you ask because there are several different stories. She wasn't seeing anyone in particular when she disappeared which makes the running off theory unlikely. But as she got older the quality of her men dropped and since they were no longer wealthy there was no reason - no disgruntled heirs - to make her go missing.

It's a mystery to everyone – except me. I know she worked her way through plenty of boyfriends because I was her first but in the end she didn't want me to be her last so I killed her.

As a boy I'd lived for Mother's kisses and hugs. She always smelled so good and was so soft, and I slept so soundly when I was cuddled in her warm bed at night.

I hated when I was put in my own room because a man was staying over. I resented giving up my place beside her but I was just a kid, easily slapped around, if I fought or complained. But during those times when there was no one else I was the favorite and Mother taught me how to be her *very best boyfriend*.

Did she corrupt me? I've asked myself that question numerous times and always end up deciding the answer is no. What she did was call out the darkness that already lived inside me. I've read a lot of Nietzche and his words usually resonate except for the misquote of his line about *staring into the abyss*. What's wrong with being a monster? Why fight my nature, why not just be?

Mother liked educating me in the ways of sex but once the student's knowledge – and strength – surpassed the teacher's well, she didn't want to play anymore. Especially the new lessons I wanted to teach her. Too bad, she'd given me a taste for pain and humiliation, blood and force, depravity and debauchery. I hope the orgasm she had when I strangled her to death fulfilled her heart's desire. It was definitely the best I ever had.

I'm not going to kill Serafina, but she is going to get a few lessons in pain. Once she's broken I'll introduce her to some pleasure and then we can begin the whole cycle all over again.

She's stirring now which is good because I'm impatient to start up again. I don't have any smelling salts and I don't want to give her poppers, those will only relax her muscles. I prefer her terrified and tense, her nerve endings will be more receptive.

I've replaced the padded sling with a rough-fiber rope. Just pulling it tight hurts my hands so I know her soft skin will suffer abrasions. Pulling hard I force her legs up much higher so her knees are near her shoulders and I have good access to both holes below as well as her mouth. She's conscious now, though still a bit groggy, and complaining that she's uncomfortable in this position and sore all over.

"Oh sweetheart, I haven't started yet. This is just preparation. Now let's see, you've been spanked enough to color up your tits, ass, and cunt, and now I've got you tied open for easy access. You are a virgin, right?"

"Well, yes but–"

"All your holes?"

"All? What do you mean? I've only got one!"

Oh her naivety is delightful! "I mean here, here, and here." I say as I poke her cunt, asshole, and mouth for emphasis.

"Of course I've never, no one, no one does anything *there*. I know you said you were going to but you didn't really mean it."

"You're joking, right? You don't think people fuck in the ass?"

"No, it only happens in books and that's not real."

"Anal sex definitely *is* a thing, Serafina."

"No it isn't, no one well... homosexual men uh, make love there, but women don't, we don't have a prostrate gland so–"

"Oh, you think you need a prostrate to enjoy it? Fina, Fina, Fina, you have to much to learn. Plenty of women enjoy ass fucking. You won't, because your virgin asshole is about to be raped without any prep or lube so yeah, it's gonna hurt. You'll probably bleed a lot. You'll definitely scream, I'm gonna make sure of that.

Then I'll fuck your pure little cunt, more bleeding, and then I'll stick my messy cock in your mouth and fuck the back of your untouched throat. That's why I'm not giving you an enema this time 'cause if I do my cock isn't going to be covered in shit, just cum and blood. But we'll definitely do the enema another time - for shits and giggles ha-ha. Something to look forward to!" I add with a grin.

She's squirming against her bindings even though every move plainly hurts. Her frown of concentration is so cute... as if she can actually figure a way out of this.

"All three of your holes are going to party hearty and I'm going to cum in you and on you. Obviously I won't be using a condom. Since you're a virgin you're clean but it's really unlikely that I am, yeah, probably not... oh well, that's your problem.

Oh! and you're not on birth control, are you? Well, well, well won't *that* be interesting. With all the bareback fucking we going to do there's a really good chance I'll knock you up, hmm."

Her face takes on a look of utter horror at the thought of being impregnated with my child.

"After all the fucking I'll be primed and ready to administer a good beating. I haven't decided yet which instrument to use. I'm thinking flogger but I do enjoy wielding the rattan cane. Swoosh, whoosh. And then there's my knives... mmm-mmm. Oh that's right baby, you go right ahead and cry. Cry hard, you'll be shrieking and sobbing before we're done."

"Dominic, Dom, why are you doing this to me? When you made the deal using me in order to erase Peter's debt to you, I knew you would expect sex but this isn't anything like what I imagined."

Oh, this is just too delicious! I curl up on the bed beside her and gently push her hair back off her forehead. In a soft, friendly voice I ask for an explanation. "Did you expect we'd have a romantic date?"

"No, I mean not here where you work and, I guess live since you have a bed, a big bed, so no I knew it was going to be a sex-date, not a date-date."

"And you hoped I'd introduce you to the delights of carnal knowledge in a gentle yet exciting way? That your deflowering would leave you with a treasured memory to cherish?"

Adding first one thumb then the other I pry her open enough to press in with the head. I'm just throbbing with eagerness. Still stretching with my fingers I manage to push in the whole head and once I've ripped through that first tight ring I'm able to plunge deep. The small, narrow passage fits so snugly that I feel constricted. I love it!

I'm sure the wetness I feel is blood but I'm disappointed when I pull back to look and there's nothing to see. I thrust in again and again even harder and rougher. There will definitely be blood by time I'm done.

I pound her repeatedly loving the feeling of that hot tight hole clenching and spasming around me.

"Fuck! I meant to use that condom with the ginger lube on it. Oh Serafina, that one will just destroy you! The more you fight me the more it will burn. Okay, I'll remember to use it after your enema, you'll be more sensitive then anyhow."

With enthusiasm I renew the anal assault and her cries have turned into hoarse shouts of extreme pain. I have to pull out and give my cock a hard squeeze to keep from cumming. Such a strong urge to completely let go with hands and teeth and cock to fight and ravish her. Squeezing and biting and pounding. Ugh, it's so hard to resist, to hold back, but the longer I can control myself the more pleasure I'll get.

"Now that I'm sunk deep in your asshole I can free my hands to molest your tits some more. They're red and showing bruises from my fingertips but I want to mark them up a lot more. Bite marks too.

First I've got to rub that clit raw. I wonder if it can bleed? I think there must be blood vessels because it gets engorged. Here, can you feel my nails? Does it really hurt or have you gone numb?"

She doesn't answer, I can see her drifting into her own headspace but I won't allow that. I grab and squeeze all of the gorgeous flesh of her tender tits and both of her eyelids fly open in shock.

I know I've got some nipple clamps somewhere and I'll put them on her, as tight as I can screw them, when I fuck her virgin cunt. For now I'll just bite down and, oh yes, listen to the music of her high-pitched keening.

Serafina

My head is woozy, like I'm going to faint, but I know I won't find any relief that way. The pain is too sharp, too intense, too demanding for me to escape into oblivion. It feels like I've been stuffed so full that my flesh is splitting apart with knife-like sharpness. My body is fighting hard to repel the invader and I'm sure tensing up isn't helping but I can't relax. I'm in agony. I can barely breathe.

Other than the pain the only thing penetrating my consciousness is Dom's overwhelming presence. The smell of his sweat and arousal, the sound of his dirty words and raspy breathing, and the feel of his hot skin sticking to mine. My eyes are screwed shut because I'm so afraid of what I'll see in his if I open them, as he keeps urging me to do.

The way he's got me trussed up allows him easy access to everything so while he's sodomizing me he can still bite down on my nipple and all over my breasts. And he does, hard.

"Open your eyes and look at me, Serafina," he commands, biting again and again until I obey. This new aching in my breast helps distract from the ongoing torment in my anus.

I look into Dom's eyes and am chilled by the empty depths, I can see that there's absolutely nothing there. He's become non-human, a devil, a soulless demon. And then I see what frightens me the most: his malicious evil grin, lips skinned back over bloodstained teeth. My blood. My fear feeds his depraved appetite.

My terror opens an escape route to a safe space in my brain. As a child I once fell out of tree hurting my wrist and although it was only a sprain I suffered a continuous throbbing soreness. They dosed me with something that acknowledged the pain's existence, but I could no longer feel the extreme hurt it caused. Thankfully, retreating into my mind has let me reach that stage.

Now if I could only turn off my thoughts. Thoughts about how foolish and irresponsible I've been, how let down I've been by my own unreasonable and undeserved expectations. How I'm in this dire predicament through nobody's fault but my own. Well, obviously Peter and Dom contributed to this horror but... I put myself in harm's way.

Acting like a child in a snit I turned away from Remo and fled into the arms of Dominic. Why did I think he'd treat my gift of virginity with gratitude? Why did I ever consider it a gift to begin with?

Eventually this physical pain I'm experiencing will heal. It will lessen to discomfort and then fade to memory, but I'm afraid this disappointment in myself, my regret and shame over my own actions, will never go away.

Dom slaps my face openhanded, backhands me, then slaps again. He's furious at seeing me slip away.

"Oh no, Serafina. You stay with me, no passing out, you need to feel everything."

He squeezes my breasts really hard and my eyes gush forth with more tears. By now my face is streaked wet from crying and a runny nose.

Dom licks up everything: tears and blood and snot and sweat and spit.

I try to turn my head away but he stops me saying: "I want to taste all of your flavors, Serafina. I know my time with you is limited, and I need to experience it all. I'm gonna fuck your mouth now and you can lick your own shit and blood off my cock."

My stomach heaves but settles at the overall relief from him pulling out of my butthole. The inner membranes are still hurting but at least my muscles can stop palpating and start to relax.

Dom is looking at his dick and muttering something about *expecting to see more* and I'm momentarily satisfied at having denied him something.

That feeling is short-lived when he tells me: "I need to get harder and I can't do that without hearing you scream soooooo... oh yes, that'll work," with a snide laugh he says: "Don't go anywhere, I'll be right back."

I hear him rummaging around for something. Finally he turns asking me if I've heard of a *Wartenberg Wheel.* I think his question is rhetorical so I don't answer but he shrieks out the question again while landing two hard punches to my stomach. I scream out *NO! Sorry but no.*

My obedience soothes his rage and he continues in a matter-of-fact tone: "Well then it won't make sense if I say this is similar. No matter. This is a weapon worn over the hand like this," he demonstrates showing me a metal shield fitted over the back of his hand and extending like talons. "It's meant to claw the skin of the enemy but the length of these razors can be adjusted and, for you my kitten, I think little kitty scratches will do... for now."

I cry out *no! No!* but he doesn't hesitate to draw first one armored hand and then the other down the underside of my breast across my belly. It's a sharp, stinging pain that makes me shriek. Like a paper cut it throbs as blood wells in the shallow slice.

"This won't scar you, Serafina, although that's something we might like to investigate next time–"

"There won't be a next time, not ever, Dominic!"

He starts to laugh but is cut short when the door bangs open and with wholehearted relief I hear footsteps come racing towards us.

Twenty-Five

Remo

I explain about the video Leo found when Marco asks why I think Fina's in trouble but otherwise we don't speak during the drive. I'm too busy concentrating on avoiding potholes and wildlife as I race down the dark country range road. There's never much traffic and that's a blessing right now. Squealing into the Club Malavita parking lot I fling open my door and dash out of the car, leaving Marco to find a place to park.

I know I won't get past the bouncers at the front so I race around to the warehouse and say a *thanks God* prayer when I find one of the side doors is open.

Bursting into the room I'm immediately drawn to Fina, my poor girl is hurting and crying, but then I catch sight of Dominic. His red cock is shiny with cum and his face is split wide with a manic, wild-eyed grin. I detour to drive my fist into his stupid face. He snarls at me and tries to fight back but I'm in the zone and just keep hitting him again and again.

He collapses then but smirks at me saying: "You must be Remo because Marco wants to pound me in a different kind of way, don't you Marky?"

Over my shoulder I see Marco enter and hesitate a moment when he sees me fighting Dominic. Before I can bark out an order he goes to help Fina.

I've broken Dominic's nose and the blood is gushing down his chin and chest.

"What a mess you're making of my pretty face Remo, and I can't even wipe it away because see?" He holds up hands with metal sheaths over his fingers and long sharp... Christ, they're claws! If he'd slapped my face with those he'd have shredded my skin. That's when I see they're blood-tipped - Fina's blood! - and I totally lose it, smashing into his body and punching all over.

He's still grinning and the urge to wipe that satisfied look off his face is overpowering until I hear Fina cry out so I drop Dominic in a heap and rush to her side.

I forgot my jacket when I hurried out of the house so I peel off my sweater to cover her. The vee-neck isn't big enough but it's better than nothing. I just want to bundle her in my arms to shield and protect her. First, I've got to free her from this horrible contorted position Dominic's tied her into.

Flicking open my knife I saw at the hairy rope around her knees and see first one, then the other drop to the bed. Marco is working on her wrists so I start massaging where the skin has rubbed raw, trying to get her circulation going again. Fina is crying weakly, she's probably feeling all pins and needles, pain and complete exhaustion.

Her breasts are streaked with thin lines of blood, her belly and groin are striped in red welts, her anus is bleeding, and she has bite marks from her shoulders right down her body... and I take all that in from only a quick look.

"I'm going to fucking kill you," I warn Dominic.

"Don't threaten me, Remo. You have no idea just how powerful I've become while you've been busy being a *Square John*."

"It's not a threat, asshole, it's a promise." I want to say more but I have no time for him, Fina needs me now.

"Sweethcart? do you want to go to the hospital?"

She buries her face against my chest, giving her head a furious shake.

"You'll need to have tests done is you're going to prosecute him—" I begin but she shouts me down yelling *No! No!* I don't blame her, not the way rape victims get brutalized all over again on the witness stand, and if we don't involve the police it will be easier for me to deal with Dominic myself.

Marco

"No! No!" sobs Fina, twisting her tear-streaked face away from me, "I'm ruined, I'm disgusting, I don't want you to see me this way."

Remo's punching out Dom but he stops and comes straight to her. Wrapping both hands around her face and forcing her to look him in the eye he answers:

"I want to look at you for the rest of my life. You aren't ruined, you've been assaulted, abused, and hurt and we will all do our best to care for you and comfort you. Me, Marco, Dad, Leo, everyone will."

I knew he liked her but I sure didn't see that coming. His words and voice are so... heartfelt. I envy him the strength of his emotion and take another look at the girl, trying to see her through his eyes, but there's no spark for me. Sure a pretty face is important and she's got that but, let's face it, the girl can easily lose forty pounds. She doesn't compare to Shelby, not in my opinion. Oh well, to each his own as they say.

Dominic is quiet now, sitting in a chair, but I don't trust him. I've found a knife and am cutting the ropes at Fina's wrists while keeping one eye on him.

He strips some metal gauntlets or something off his hands and then lets his head flop back. Dom's naked and unarmed but he owns guns so I look around to see if there are any weapons near by.

He catches me looking at him and grins. He knows my eyes are on his body, admiring the ink just as much as the rippling muscles of his lean physique, right down to his pierced cock.

He looks from me to Remo saying: "I've ruined your property."

Remo tells him that Serafina isn't property. He's right and Dom is wrong but... I can't help but look at him with lust in my eyes. Of course he sees it and his interest is piqued. Stroking his semi-hard dick he asks:

"Do you want a taste of me, Marco? I'm still coated in the mess from Fina's ass but I think it's just her blood and my cum. I don't care if you don't."

I close my eyes to hide my thoughts from him and return to helping Remo free up this girl. His girl.

"Don't ignore me Marco, Listen, I didn't get a chance to fuck her cunt or her mouth yet which means Peter's debt isn't paid off yet, Fina," he calls over to her and laughs when she jerks in fear.

"Marco you and me can get together, have some fun huh? maybe get some of the guys and really do a number on her, okay? I was thinking–"

But he gets no further before Remo's got his hands tight around Dom's throat and has shut him up by strangling him.

Dom's face quickly turns red and he's struggling to pry Remo's fingers away but he can't, he's suffocating. They thrash about and end up on the floor and I'm sure Remo is going to kill him.

The repercussions if he does kill Dom, a made man, are unimaginable so I hook my forearm around Remo's throat and fight hard to drag him off. I almost don't make it but hearing Fina scream brings Remo back down to earth.

He flings Dom away but not before I see Dom gasping for air, his neck red with Remo's fingermarks, and his cock hard with arousal from the near-asphyxiation. When he catches my eye he sticks out his tongue and waggles it at me. This time bile rises in my throat.

Dom staggers out of the room. He'll be going for a gun or his bouncers so turning back to Remo and Fina I yell *we have to get out now!*

Twenty-Six

Serafina

Remo and Marco have freed my arms and legs but I feel like rubber, my muscles have no strength. I'm so weak and in such pain. The pins-and-needles feeling stings me all over.

Remo is rubbing my limbs to get the circulation going but I can't bring myself to help. I just want to curl into a ball and die. Of shame, of pain, and regret.

When Remo talked about evidence for court I totally panicked. No way am I going into a courtroom. How can I explain? Sure, I was brutally assaulted against my will but I was the one who initiated contact, I agreed to be here, I agreed to a date with Dominic.

Even though none of that gave him the right to brutalize me in the minds of everyone – myself included – I asked for it. I mean I didn't, I had no idea what he was planning, but I put myself in this position. My fault, my regrets, my private business.

While thinking these thoughts I have drawn my legs up and now Remo is rubbing my back coaxing me to stand so we can leave. Yes, God yes I want to get out of here but I certainly can't walk through the nightclub naked!

"My clothes are gone, they're all ripped up, I need something to wear."

Remo's face showed compassion a moment ago but now he's back to looking angry.

I cower under that look and he's immediately contrite and comforting saying: "Shush, shush. I'm not mad at you sweetheart. You just need to try to relax while we figure something out."

Then calling over his shoulder to Marco he tells him to check the bathroom for big towels. Meanwhile he pulls his sweater over my arms and down my head until I'm at least covered to the waist. His sweater is soft, probably cashmere, and it smells like his citrusy scent. I wrap my arms tight around my body and hunch up my legs until I can rest my chin on my knees.

"I found this, it's better than a towel," says Marco holding out a man-sized terry-towel bathrobe. Between the two of them they hold me up to help me into the robe. It comes down to my ankles and is wide enough to wrap right around me.

"Fina, did you bring a purse with you?"

"Oh no, I didn't. Just my phone but..." I look around helplessly but it's Marco who spots the flashy pink case and brings it to me, slipping it into the pocket of the robe.

"What's the best way out of here?" asks Remo and Marco points to the door beside the bathroom.

"Through there, I'll bring the car up right now."

Being held between the two men, looking from one face to the other, I'm struck at how identical they truly are. Oh, I see some differences but I guess they're slight enough for most people to miss.

For me it's easy to see how Remo's nose is a little thinner at the bridge, and both his eyes are exactly the same size, and there's the faintest dimple on the right side of his mouth when he smiles. He hugs me tight when Marco leaves and for the first time in what feels like hours I've stopped being frightened enough to draw a breath that doesn't feel tight and constricted.

We're so close I wonder if Remo can hear or feel my pounding heartbeat. He shifts his grip to hold me more securely while we stand in silence, waiting for the car to pull up. I stagger a bit under a wave of exhaustion and Remo scoops me up into his arms to carry.

Marco blocked the door open when he left and he holds it now so Remo can get through with his burden. I'm no lightweight but he's carrying me with ease.

Marco lets the door slam shut then opens the car's back door for Remo to maneuver me inside. The backseat is small in this sportscar but he keeps me on his lap and Marco pulls up the passenger seat in the front so Remo can stretch his legs out a bit more.

"You're strong," I comment and he smiles, telling me he plays Rugby to keep fit.

"Bruised, but fit."

"I thought that was an English game?"

"It is, but it's really popular here too. You'll have to come and watch me play some time."

"Oh! I'd like that," I say, but then I realize where I am and why, and something so commonplace as attending a sports event is just impossible to imagine.

I start to cry again and he pulls my face against his chest while he rocks me as best he can in the small space. We don't speak again and I sob for the rest of the drive.

Marco

I am so relieved when we pull up to the front door to see Dad standing there waiting to help. He'll know what to do for Fina. For all of our lives Dad has always been steady and calm, able to deal with the big and small emergencies growing boys encounter and ready to help in every way. He used to joke with us that the scariest phrase he ever heard was *Daaaadddd, call 9-1-1* and he heard it a lot!

He looks pale in the light from the hallway. I guess he's been feeling the strain ever since Leo told him what was going on and guiltily I realize my recent behavior hasn't helped.

I stop the car and jump out to open the back door. It's a squeeze but Remo manages to get himself and Fina out in one piece.

"Take Serafina straight up to her room, son. Marco, can you lock up after you put the car away?" He doesn't wait for an answer, just trots up the stairs after them.

It only takes me a few minutes to drive the car round to the garage then come back inside. In that time Fina's been put to bed, still wearing the dressing-gown and Remo's sweater, and propped up with pillows. She's cradling a mug of hot chocolate and I can see the tremble in her hands from the doorway.

"Drink up, Serafina. The caffeine in your cocoa will speed up that sleeping pill I gave you. I know you'd rather shower and get into your own nightclothes but no, you need to fall asleep as quickly as possible. Sleep is the most important thing right now. You sleep and in the morning you'll feel stronger. Maybe even a little bit better. I'll be here to watch over you so you have nothing to fear, not now that you're safe at home with us."

Her eyes seem impossibly huge as they lock onto Dad's face searching for reassurance. She sees something there that settles her and she obediently finishes her hot drink.

Antony

The boys are hovering. I see that Remo's shivering, both from reaction and being in the cold air without a jacket so I pack him off to have a hot shower.

"Serafina is safe in my care so I want you to shower and then go straight to bed yourself. I don't want her kept awake talking, remembering, none of that."

Remo casts a longing glance at Serafina but I gently steer him away adding: "You did real good, son. You've brought her home to us and now we're going to help her heal."

He doesn't say anything but gives me a hug before leaving the room.

Since I'm already standing I go over to the little writing desk and switch on the lamp there so we have some light before heading back to the night-stand to turn that one off. Serafina's face is now in shadow and she'll be able to sleep more comfortably.

Drawing Marco out of the room I stop in the doorway and speak to him in a low voice: "Marco, you must break off this friendship you have with Dominic. It's bad enough what he did to you but what he's done to Serafina is unconscionable. If you don't end things with him you'll end up tainted too. Dominic is toxic and poison spreads insidiously."

I've half-expected an argument but instead Marco nods at my words telling me: "Dom's parting shot was..." he shudders and can't continue. I don't press him, I don't need to know his cousin's vile words.

"I'm going to sit with Serafina tonight and I don't want to leave her even for a moment so do you mind getting my book and reading glasses? they're beside my chair down in the study."

Marco hurries to fetch those items and when he returns I pop into Serafina's bathroom to quickly relieve myself before beginning my vigil.

Watching over her is an honor, not a chore.

Giorgio

It's about 3:00 am so either very late or very early, depending on how you look at it. But it's not unusual for an old man to wake up in the wee hours. After shuffling into the bathroom to urinate I now find I'm too tired to get up but too awake to go back to sleep. This happens to me a lot.

Something terrible happened to Serafina tonight. As usual nobody shares any details with me but Antony is worried sick. I heard them come home and immediately move upstairs but I didn't want to get in the way so I stayed in my room. Now that I'm awake and all is quiet I decide to go check.

There's a light showing under Serafina's door so I tap very quietly and a moment later Antony opens it but blocks the doorway. I look over to the bed and I know he thinks I'm trying to spot evidence that he's been lying in it with her but I'm not. I'm only concerned about her well-being and recovery.

Serafina is very pale, lying on her back with her body so still she doesn't seem to be breathing. I hear myself stumbling over the words as I ask *is she's doing okay?* in a low voice.

Antony steps into the hallway pulling the door almost shut. There are only nightlights burning in intervals along the corridor but we can see each other clearly enough and he knows my concern is genuine.

"She will be, Giorgio," he says, taking hold of my hand. I didn't realize it was cold until I felt the warmth of his palm clasping my fingers.

"Look, I realize you think I'm always thinking the worse–" I begin but he interrupts to tell me that's exactly what I do and it's okay because he came to terms with that many years ago.

"Years ago?"

"Yes. I remember when you fell for that girl Christine Higgins and our parents refused to meet her and forbade you to have anything to do with this non-Catholic girl. You honored their wishes so I figured you didn't really love her after all. But then I saw how you changed, how you turned inwards, and became an unhappy man with festering bitterness.

They were wrong to interfere, Giorgio, and you were wrong to listen to them, but I also remember that things were very different back then. The wishes of the Church, and those of our parents, were paramount.

But when my time came to fall in love only to face the same backlash against my choice, although for a different reason, I was able to rebel because I had the example of you. You were like *The Ghost of Christmas Future* showing me what would happen if I didn't follow my heart.

I have always been grateful to you for that, and sorry for not standing up to our parents with you."

Christine, just hearing her name brings back memories both wonderful and terrible. I can't believe that I'm hearing this from Antony and before I even think about it the words escape me: "So *that's* why you've put up with my miserable self all these years!"

He laughs and nods as he agrees saying: "Oh yeah, that's the only reason why."

"Our parents said terrible things about Elenora, and I might have done so too back then, but I saw that you and your Ella loved each other deeply. She was definitely the right woman, the best choice, for you."

"She was indeed," he replies and I see that his eyes have grown shiny with unshed tears even after all these years.

"I'm sorry about making snide remarks and giving you funny looks about Serafina, Antony. I know your intentions towards her have always been completely honorable. Serafina is the daughter of our household."

He brightens when I say that and adds: "I hoped that someday she would be our daughter-in-law but after tonight..." his voice trails off and he shakes his head.

Although we're whispering his voice drops even lower when he says: "She's been so badly abused. I blame myself–"

"For what?" I interrupt. "From what I've heard the blame for this lies squarely with Dominic Ferragamo!"

"But I should have warned her about him, I blame myself for not speaking up."

"Then we're all guilty, because we all kept silent," I say, surprising myself with a yawn.

I think I can fall back asleep now so I give my younger brother's hand a squeeze, glance in for a last look at the sleeping Serafina, then head downstairs to my own bed. I feel... well, I don't exactly know how I feel but I think things will be well.

Antony

I'm glad Giorgio and I had that chat. Really, it was long overdue. Serafina has brought us closer together.

Returning to my chair I catch sight of a photo in a silver frame so before I sit back down I go over to take a look. I can see from the familiar features in the faces of the man and woman that they're Serafina's parents. What a handsome and happy threesome they make!

I feel badly when I realize Serafina is Catholic and I've never offered to take her to Mass. I know she doesn't drive and there's no church within walking distance of us here.

The Roman Catholic Church and I parted company after the way my Ella was treated. That's why we had a civil ceremony. I've attended other people's weddings, christenings, and funerals but I don't participate in the rituals. Any time I'm in a church I just act like I'm a Protestant, a visiting guest.

Ella never changed her mind about our religion either so none of our boys are baptized in the Church. That's also why I chose a crematorium for the brief service when she died. There were mutterings and complaints in the family but I was suffering the loss of my soulmate - why would I care about anything else?

But maybe Serafina will want to speak to a priest after what she's just gone through. She certainly should have some kind of counseling but... I suspect she'll want to put it all behind her.

I have no advice to give and I can't tell her what to do, especially since what happened to her is so far beyond my comprehension. I cannot believe she had to endure such a thing. I really do feel so guilty about it.

Twenty-Seven

Antony

A week has passed since that unforgettable night and I'm ready to meet with Uncle Tonino to discuss the matter.

I never go to his home. Well, home isn't accurate since it's really a fortified estate. I visited once with my Ella early in our married life and once was enough. I was afraid to catch anyone's eye, and didn't know where to look in case I saw or heard something I shouldn't. It's really scary to be in that environment when you're not a protected member of it.

So I invited Tonino here and said Remo would fetch him. I refuse to let Dominic cross my doorstep. I don't want to see him, and I'm afraid his presence would crush Serafina, to say nothing of Remo being charged with murder if Dominic comes within arms-length.

So we have the old man settled comfortably in my chair behind my desk so he can look at my computer screen and I've ensured we'll have privacy.

Fina is still leery about leaving the house so instead of suggesting going out to a matinee I've tasked Leo and Marco with keeping her occupied watching a movie in our entertainment room. Uh-oh, I should have made sure they don't pick a horror flick.

When I walked down the hall earlier I could hear them all arguing the merits of mixing candy in with their popcorn and I'm sure that's Serafina's idea. I still remember that delicious hint of chili in the chocolate icing.

I close and lock my study door, I don't need Giorgio poking his nose in here either, no matter how good his intentions might be.

"So Uncle, I know you're a tough man who has lived through a lot but I'm still going to give you a heads-up, a warning if you will, that this video clip I'm about to play is really nasty. Even more so because you'll recognize that it's Serafina who is being tortured and, I'm sorry to say, your nephew Dominic is her abuser."

Tonino squints at me asking about the circumstances so I explain that Dominic took Serafina to his club, Malavita, willingly I'm sure, but no way did the girl give her consent for what happened. And the source is Dominic's own phone since he's the one who videoed the activity. Luckily Tonino hasn't asked how we got the clip off of Dominic's phone. I'd already queued it up so now I just have to hit the play button.

Dominic started his movie after he's beaten Serafina all over and had her bound in some sort of leather strapping that bent her legs and pulled them wide apart. Very graphic, very explicit, and of a high resolution that clearly shows her red skin and her tears. There's audio and Tonino signals for me to turn it up. I'd rather not, the sound of Serafina screaming and begging for mercy already haunts my dreams, but the Capo's hearing isn't what it was.

The video stops when Serafina falls back either asleep or unconscious. When it starts up again she's been wrapped up in a coarse rope that's forced her legs up much higher. All of the girl's genital area is fully exposed and Dominic's conversation makes his intentions clear.

Serafina's shrieks of pain when he rapes her anally are agonizing to listen to. Equally bad is Dominic's cruel yet delighted laugh. That sound will haunt me for a long time.

The video portion ends when Remo and Marco explode into the room but the audio memorializes their attack on their cousin.

Turning away from the screen but not meeting my eyes Tonino asks: "What does the girl want?"

"To pretend it never happened, and to never see Dominic Ferragamo again. She doesn't *want* anything except to forget. I'm the one with a demand for justice."

At that he does look up at my face. My expression is stern and unforgiving when I add: "While performing this abomination Dominic's face was caught in the mirrors around the bed."

A couple of clicks of the mouse and I have several stills of Dominic's gloating visage. His eyes are alight with excitement, his grin stretches his mouth wide, he's salivating, and his color is high. There is no mistaking the sadistic delight he's experiencing as he torments Serafina.

I see Tonino's eyes move from one photo to the next when finally, and I'm sorry it's taken this long, I see him wince. The stoicism he showed throughout the video only flickered momentarily.

"And what does *justice* look like to you, Antony?"

"That your great-nephew Dominic never inherits your empire. You can see his warped desire has driven him insane. If you put him in charge your legacy will end quickly and with bloody destruction. No actually it will die in ashes because he'll burn it all to the ground."

Tonino ponders for only a minute, taking another look at the still photos, before nodding in agreement. "The nightclub has been a bad influence on him. It puts too much temptation in his way."

Personally I think Tonino is being wilfully obtuse but I don't want to argue with the old man. I'm only interested in one outcome.

"I thought that when Loretta married Dominic Riccolini she brought tainted blood into the *famiglia*. That's why I let her annul their marriage and return to her maiden name but things I subsequently learned, from both Riccolini and Dominic Jr, made me realize that she was the problem all along. I was blinded by pride in my bloodline for too long.

Well Antony, I give you my word Dominic will never be allowed to rule this *famiglia*. He's shown that he cannot be trusted with that much power. I'll take him out of the nightclub and I'll keep him close by me as a bodyguard. I'll make sure he understands I know I have to keep an eye on him - and why.

I can't thank you for showing me this but I understand that you had to do so. Despite everything I've seen in my long life, good and bad, I can still be... let's say *taken aback* by human nature.

Now, as for Serafina, I like that girl and I'm very sorry to know this happened to her. I will settle some monies on her–"

"That's not necessary, Great-Uncle. Serafina will soon come into an inheritance. We're all going to look after her," says Remo, speaking for the first time.

I notice his eyes are wet even though he stood well away from the computer during the playback but he narrows them now and his gaze is cold.

Tonino studies him a moment before agreeing: "Some secrets are best kept secret. Now, can I trouble one of you to take me home?"

Standing I help him out of the chair saying I'll accompany him on the ride. I haven't offered any hospitality and that will deliver our message stronger than words.

Still, the old man can't resist a parting shot which underlines the vicious nature that propelled him to the top of his *famiglia*. Turning to extend his hand to Remo he comments that while a leader needs to control his impulses those same base desires are excellent qualities in an enforcer.

"Plus, I can make good use of Dominic if I give him free rein as an interrogator," he adds, with a twisted smile.

My boy's lips have turned white from the effort of clenching his jaw tightly but he says nothing and simply returns Tonino's gaze.

I'm positive we all share the thought that Dominic Ferragamo won't live a long life, but I can't help wondering if he won't outlast his great-uncle. Dominic is certainly not a man I would want to keep close by me!

It's very likely I'll never meet Tonino Ferragamo again. I especially hope to cut all ties between him and my sons.

Remo

Great-Uncle Tonino didn't have much to say to me when I brought him to meet with Dad and I was glad. Beyond asking about his health or discussing the weather I find it difficult to have a conversation with him.

Dad was great. He laid out all the facts and backed what he was saying with the videos. Those stills of Dominic's sick pleasure were the clincher, Leo did a great job. Despite me wanting to say something Dad had it handled so I kept quiet.

The three of us left the study and I walked to the front door to say goodbye. No matter what I think of Great-Uncle Tonino he is an old man and family, even though I'm not part of his *famiglia*. Thank God.

Dad told me *the kids* were watching TV so I headed to the den. Marco must have left already because I only saw Fina huddled in a comforter on the loveseat while Leo sprawled on the floor in front of her. They had a selection of snacks and drinks on the coffee table and were both dipping into a big bowl of popcorn balanced on the sofa cushion.

Using the popcorn as an excuse to draw close I help myself to a handful and nudge Leo with my foot. The screen is showing one of the Die Hard movies which I know he's seen several times. He makes a production of yawning and stretching before saying he's going to turn in. Since it's only mid-afternoon Fina just smiles at his antics.

Steadying the bowl with one hand I settle down beside her just as I pop a handful in my mouth only to spit back in my hand saying *What the...*

"Fina, I almost broke a tooth! why are there Smarties or M & Ms or whatever the hell these are in the popcorn?"

"They go great together, Remo."

"No they... well, okay it's maybe not bad. Just unexpected." I chew a bit more and help myself to another handful before putting the bowl on the table. Reaching my arm across her shoulders I draw her in to snuggle. I'm munching happily and she gives a contented sigh but once I finish eating I give a deep, heartfelt sigh and she pulls back to look at my face.

"This is going to be the hardest conversation," I begin, looking into her beautiful chocolate-brown eyes. "I'm in love with you, Fina."

"And that's hard to say?" she gives me a teasing smirk but I can see the uncertainty in her eyes.

"No, it isn't hard but it is wrong. You've been through a terrible ordeal and you need time to recover and sort out your thoughts and feelings. You don't need to be adding my emotions to the mix, even if I do love you."

She shakes her head at me answering: "You don't, you know. You just feel sorry for me and maybe a bit of a knight-in-shining-armor? since you rescued me, I mean."

"You're wrong. I loved you way before Dominic got his hands on you. Don't you remember when we first met? You offered your hand and I held it in both of mine, not willing to let go until Dad made me. I think I knew then."

A little frown appears between her eyebrows. "Well, you never said–"

"No of course not, you were quick to tell me you had a boyfriend."

"But you didn't seem to take that seriously, I mean I had to tell you more than once–"

"What? No, that's not right. You told me and after that I was careful to keep my distance when... oh that bastard Marco. How many time did he come on to you as me? Often enough that you had to *remind me* about your boyfriend?"

She bites her lip, looking worried, and I'm almost overwhelmed by the urge to take that lip into my mouth and soothe it with licks from my tongue. Being so close to her, in such an intimate setting, is harder than I thought it would be.

"Oh Remo. It's embarrassing to think of that now, how easily I was fooled but I never knew there were two of you! Nobody ever said anything and when Antony referred to his sons I thought he meant you and Leo. I didn't know Marco even existed."

"Yeah, none of us talked about him so I don't know why I'd assume you did know. But I guess if anyone ever mentioned twins you only thought of Lorenzo and Luciano. It's weird how things can get confused and mixed up."

"And I'm a good example of that! I mean, I thought I did, you know, have a boyfriend. And I remember regretting it, too. But let's forget all that, it's over. I'm glad you've told me how you feel. Just hearing the words makes me all warm inside but it's also kind of scary, too. See..." she takes my hand and looks searchingly into my face saying, "I'm not ready to–"

"Sweetheart, shush!" I interrupt. "You don't owe me an explanation and that's something you need to learn Fina. You make your own choices and your reasoning is yours, you never owe anyone an explanation for your behavior.

Honey, I know you're not ready for a relationship with me or anyone else just now. No, what I'm trying to do is, oh hell, I shouldn't have said anything about how I feel. Listen, I'm not going to hang around pressuring you into making a decision. That isn't fair. I'm going to give you space and the freedom to meet other people, to discover what you like and don't like, to have opportunities–"

"You mean you don't want me." She speaks the words in dry, flat voice but I see the shine of tears in her eyes. I grasp her hands tightly, I have to make her understand.

"Hey, I want you more than anything, *anything!* but Fina you've never even gone to a high-school dance. How many men have you even met in your life? Fina, you've never given yourself a chance. You haven't had a loving relationship, you've never had sex—-"

"I have, he.. he did it to me."

"Oh honey Dominic sodomized you and it was rape."

She gasps and stammers: "How do you know what he did?"

Puzzled, I answer without thinking: "Because of the video we saw." When she just shakes her head questioningly I add: "You know, the video from Dominic's phone that Leo hacked—-"

"Leo? LEO SAW?! Oh no-no-no," she cries out before burying her face in her hands. I'm worried she'll start hyperventilating so I draw her close to calm her but she pushes me away.

"Who else saw?"

"It doesn't matter—-"

"It DOES matter, it MATTERS to ME," she's upset and angry and embarrassed.

"Leo saw what was happening to you and immediately came to get me to ask what we could do to help. I told him I would find you right away. He insisted he wanted to come too," She lets out a groan so I hurry on: "But I convinced him he had to stay and keep monitoring." Taking a deep breath I add: "And I told him to get Dad."

"Antony saw it too," she says in a dull voice.

"Honey, Leo needed Dad's comfort, and Dad loves you, he had to see what was going on. You understand that, right?"

Still pathetically subdued Fina nods her agreement.

"But no one else saw it, Leo wouldn't let Marco look although he tried. Oh Fina, my family is just no good. Both of my brothers have groped you, I lust after you, Giorgio makes suggestive comments – the only one of us who's any good is Dad. But we all care for you, sweetheart. I know you feel ashamed but you did nothing wrong. You were victimized."

"I was but... I have to accept some of the blame. I'm the one who went to Dominic," she shudders when she says his name out loud for the first time since the assault.

"Again, that's because you've led a pretty sheltered life up until now. I'm not saying it's been an easy life, I know it hasn't been—"

She interrupts me saying: "No it was good, actually. I loved Marta, despite understanding now that she took advantage of me emotionally, but I was very happy at the time. I think it's because of my parents.

I was seven when they died and sure that's young but not too young to remember. I have so many wonderful memories and pictures of the three of us in my head. They loved me so much and that love gave me a... a foundation, I guess. I will always have them in my heart."

I'm really touched by her words. I think it goes a long way to explaining her sweet nature. "That's wonderful to hear, Fina. I'm so glad you had that strong love in your life. But it doesn't change the fact that you haven't had a chance to get to know any men.

Fina, I want to give you your freedom but I hope someday you do choose me. But only because you want me, not because I'm the first man to ever say *I love you*."

"But if you love me, and I love you, why would... oh. Oh, I see, I get it. Because you know what Dominic actually did to me... that video... you're disgusted with me. I'm damaged goods." Despite widening her eyes the tears spill again but she holds her head up high.

"Don't you dare put yourself down like that! You are anything but damaged, Serafina. You're strong and resilient and so, so lovable. But I have to do right by you and let you test your wings. Really, Fina, ask Dad, ask Mrs Finch, ask your friend from the coffee-shop, they'll all agree that I'm doing the right thing."

"Then why does it hurt so much?"

"Oh baby I know it hurts, I'm hurting too."

Now her voice does crack with a sob. "No, you're rejecting me."

"Fina I'm not, truly, I won't be seeing anyone else. I don't need to, I already know who I want. But there might be someone else for you to find, someone you want more than me, and I have to at least give you your chance, your space, to find out."

She shoves her hands against my chest and her tears flow freely as she gasps for breath shouting: "I deserve better than this Remo, and I hate you, hate you." Before stumbling off the couch and kicking her feet free of the comforter to run from the room.

I close my eyes, utterly dejected at how poorly I must have handled things considering how they turned out.

"Hmm, that went well."

I look up to see my twin has come back and is leaning against the door frame smirking at me after listening in.

"Fuck off, Marco. I don't need your bullshit right now–" I start saying but he cuts me off.

"Get off the moral high ground Remo and just act human for a change. Fina doesn't need you being some saint of a martyr she needs a man holding her tight and promising to keep the demons at bay."

"What?"

"What what? You're not the only one who has *feelings* you know."

Angry that he's getting me riled I turn on him: "How many times did you come on to her, pretending to be me?"

"A few times. Not recently but sure, I did make a pass but not as you. I didn't know she didn't know about me. I never did know what all the secrecy and drama was about."

"You're the one who caused it!"

"No, that was for Dominic but forget that, it's over, we're done with him. I just want to tell you that you're being all kinds of stupid right now."

"Thanks for that, Marco. Thanks for dropping by."

I turn away and moodily eat another handful of popcorn. I hear him leave the room but I don't look up when he's back a moment later.

"Remo."

It's not Marco, it's Dad. I'm sure I've got a scowl on my face so I try to smooth away that expression. He doesn't come in the room, just stands in the doorway like Marco did, and folding his arms over his chest gives me a disappointed look.

"What? You too?"

He strides over to me and perches on the arm of the sofa, reaching out to give me a shake. "Your motives are good, thoughtful, selfless, and pure, okay? but for once your brother is right. Serafina needs the reassurance of your love and she needs it now, not in a month or a year from now."

"But after her ordeal—"

"After what she's been through it's more important than ever that she be given tender, loving affection. Serafina is never going to go out to mingle with strangers, think about it! First of all she'd be terrified and secondly she has no self-confidence."

"But she should—"

Again he interrupts me saying: "No, you don't get to say what she should think or feel or do. Your job is to be here in a supportive loving role.

When she recovers if she decides to leave and breaks your heart in the process well too damn bad. Too bad for all of us but we all put her into the hands of that evil man and if there's a price to pay for that then we'll pay it. What matters most is her well-being."

"But Dad, I am putting her first. I want her to have her chance."

"I get it son, I do. I respect what you're saying because I know it isn't easy but, geez Remo use your head. Serafina isn't going to go find her freedom, no, she's going to curl up inside her shell and maybe never have the courage to venture out."

"Oh that would be the worst thing to happen."

"You're right, it would. You know from what we've learned of Serafina's upbringing she didn't have a lot of choices, she was emotionally blackmailed in my opinion, and in some ways her development was stunted.

But even without that I don't think Serafina ever dreamt of spreading her wings and taking the world by storm. I think that girl's happiness is found in heart and home. And I'm sure you can make her happy. We've already seen that you can make her unhappy, right? I mean she did run out of this room in tears and you need to fix that."

I'm thinking over his words and realize I'm embarrassed at myself, trying to play the hero by being all noble about giving Fina her space. Looking up at Dad I see Uncle Giorgio has come into the room too.

"Is everybody going to get in my personal business?" I complain but he ignores me, determined to speak his mind.

"Your business, huh! We're all affected by what's going on here even if some of us are kept out of the loop," he casts a baleful eye at Dad who merely returns his stare.

"I haven't been told the whole story but if Dominic Ferragamo was involved then it's nasty and it's bad. From the scraps I've pieced together I understand that terrible things were done to our girl and she needs to be taken care of. Remo, go be the man she needs."

That's a surprising statement coming from Uncle Giorgio. He's never liked women... not that he's attracted to men, at least I don't think he is. I don't he think likes people period. So for him to say something like that to me well... it has impact.

I get up and pushing past them say: "Excuse me, Dad, Uncle Giorgio, but I've got to go find my girl."

Epilogue

3 months later

Serafina

It was hard to keep Remo at arms-length but both Antony and surprisingly, Giorgio, encouraged me to *teach him a lesson*.

And it worked really well except... when the time came for me to finally forgive him I couldn't overcome my fear and repulsion of intimacy.

Our plan backfired.

Remo is so attentive and sweet and loving, and I really, really want to make love with him but I just can't. I start to shake and I can't get enough air and I get so scared.

Apparently it's a panic attack and Remo thinks it means I should have got counseling to help me get over the events of that awful night.

He says that even now it's not too late to get professional help telling me: "I'll take you to every appointment sweetheart, and I'll even come in the office with you if that's you want. I'm here for you, Fina."

But I hate to have him think I'm weak. Instead I'm trying my own brand of therapy which is to force myself to come to his bedroom at night and lie in his arms.

Remo

She's trying so hard to please me but she can't relax. Her eyes are moist with unshed tears of fear and frustration so I kiss them closed.

"Rest, and we'll just cuddle for a bit, sweetheart," I say.

"But I know you need more—-"

"Stop," I interrupt her. "I'm 100 percent certain we'll get there and I don't mind how long it takes. Just holding you makes me happy, Fina."

She sniffs then complains that we've been kissing and caressing for an hour and she isn't any closer to letting go. "I'm going to lose you, Remo. I know I am. Why would you bother with someone like me? You can have any girl, any beautiful sexy girl like Shelby—-"

"I've had Shelby and I choose you over her a thousand times."

Now the tears do fall as she cries out: "But why?"

"Because I love you, that's why. I love you with my heart, my soul, my mind, and someday we'll love each other with our bodies."

"Oh Remo, it just doesn't feel like I'll ever be able to love you the way I should. The way you need."

"Baby look what I'm doing here. I'm gently squeezing your breast and see that? Your nipple goes a darker color as it grows hard. If I rub it with my thumb like this the whole aureole puckers and it gets even harder. That's your breast and your nipple responding to my touch.

Now notice how you've lifted your chest, pushing your other breast towards my hand because it wants some attention too. No, don't blush, honey, it's a wonderful thing. There's nothing wrong with your body, Fina. It's healed and it's reacting exactly as it should.

The barrier is in your mind. Not that that makes it any less real! No, we both know the ordeal you've been through was utterly devastating. But see, even though your breasts were slapped hard, punched till they bruised, and roughly squeezed and cut until you screamed, they can still feel erotic pleasure when they're lovingly caressed.

You stiffen up and clench your muscles when you remember the pain you experienced but, in time, you and I will overwrite those terrible flashbacks with fantastic new memories. I know we will."

I prop myself up on one elbow to lean over her. She's so lovely lying in my bed with her thin silk nightgown pushed down to her waist, practically naked. All pink and blushing and biddable but her eyes are worried.

I want to make her laugh so in an over-the-top evil Eastern European accent I say: "One of these days everyone will call me *Dr Frankenstein* because I've created a monster – a sex monster - called Serafina Liriani. She will want sex all the time here, there, and everywhere. She will be demanding orgasms left, right and center!"

I'm rewarded with a giggle and when I tickle her she laughs louder.

"But until then I fucking love holding your pillowy ass in my hands," I straddle her so I can reach down and grab hold of her luscious ass, "and rub my face in your pillowy tits," I suit the action to my words, "And I'm just crazy about how soft and warm and sexy you are. I'm looking forward to the day when I get to bury my face between your pillowy thighs and lick you like an ice cream cone!"

Fina's breathing has quickened but there's more fear than lust in her expression so I hurry to reassure saying: "Holding you naked in my arms, your cuddly body pressed up against me, is pure heaven."

I can't resist teasing her by adding: "Pillowy heaven." She smiles at that silly remark and lightly punches my arm.

"Oh Fina, one of these nights we'll be making out and your thighs will just naturally part and you'll reach for me - without either of us even thinking about it, it will just happen - and then we'll both know that you're ready.

I love you so much, Serafina. No matter how long it takes I will wait."

Don't miss out!

Visit the website below and you can sign up to receive emails whenever Lori Laidlaw publishes a new book. There's no charge and no obligation.

https://books2read.com/r/B-A-RDEBB-NOIYC

BOOKS 2 READ

Connecting independent readers to independent writers.

Also by Lori Laidlaw

Alpha + Omega Wolf-Shifters
Dominant + Violent + Hot = An Alpha Male
Her Claiming Bite = True Love

Standalone
Lockdown + 3 Alphas = Heat: An Omega's Thrilling Dark
Romantic Adventure
Girlie: Undeniable Attraction Enemies to Lovers Steamy
Standalone
Cruel Obligation
Jane's Special Adventure
Captive's Deception
Finn and Marbeth
"Princess Weds Killer" = Fake News

Watch for more at https://lorilaidlaw.com.

About the Author

Lori says:

I love the fun and excitement in the Adult Romance genre and all of its sub-categories. It's such fun to write!

I'm half in love with all of my characters... and their moods range from playful to dangerous and everything in between!

The men are unfeeling and cruel until the innocent heroine melts the ice from their hearts and turns them into OTT possessive touch-her-and-die alphas.

My stories are multiple POV expressing mature themes and passionate encounters with enough steam to stimulate your imagination.

It's all about the love.

Email: AuthorLoriLaidlaw@gmail.com

Website: https://lorilaidlaw.com

Bluesky: https://bsky.app/profile/lorilaidlaw.bsky.social

Facebook: https://www.facebook.com/people/Author-Lori-Laidlaw/61555470454210/

Goodreads: https://www.goodreads.com/author/show/29566696.Lori_Laidlaw

Read more at https://lorilaidlaw.com.